THIS FALLEN WORLD

BOOK ONE OF
THE FALLEN WORLD

Christopher Woods

Blood Moon Press
Virginia Beach, VA

Copyright © 2018 by Christopher Woods.

All rights reserved. No part of this publication may be reproduced, distributed or transmitted in any form or by any means, including photocopying, recording, or other electronic or mechanical methods, without the prior written permission of the publisher, except in the case of brief quotations embodied in critical reviews and certain other noncommercial uses permitted by copyright law. For permission requests, write to the publisher, addressed "Attention: Permissions Coordinator," at the address below.

Chris Kennedy/Blood Moon Press
2052 Bierce Dr.
Virginia Beach, VA 23454
http://chriskennedypublishing.com/

Publisher's Note: This is a work of fiction. Names, characters, places, and incidents are a product of the author's imagination. Locales and public names are sometimes used for atmospheric purposes. Any resemblance to actual people, living or dead, or to businesses, companies, events, institutions, or locales is completely coincidental.

Ordering Information:
Quantity sales. Special discounts are available on quantity purchases by corporations, associations, and others. For details, contact the "Special Sales Department" at the address above.

Cover design by Ivan Cakic.

This Fallen World/Christopher Woods -- 1st ed.
ISBN: 978-1948485708

To Wendy, the love of my life.

* * * * *

This Fallen World

Chapter One

I walked down the dreary street. Smoke hung in the air from the fires burning in the alleys that led back into dark corners filled with the many people less fortunate than those who resided in the buildings alongside.

Before the Fall, those in the street would have been rounded up and hauled away in vehicles to be incarcerated. Now, twenty years later, you'd find a better grade of people living in the alleys than the ones inside the buildings. Hell, maybe it wasn't so different, then.

Those that had inhabited the city twenty years ago were pretty despicable. I know this because I was one of the bastards. How things change.

"Fresh fruit, Mister?" a voice asked from my right.

I glanced toward the young girl with an apron full of apples. Then pulled one of the apples from her apron. As I polished the apple on the lapel of my long coat, I listened for the tell-tale buzz from my rad marker. There was no buzz so I handed the girl a coin.

"Wow," she said, "is that an Old World coin?"

"They called 'em quarters," I answered. "Worth twenty scripts. Take that and hide it well. There's a grocery store over on K Street. He'll change it for you. He's good people."

She pulled a bag from her pocket and dropped the rest of the apples into it. She handed it to me.

"Mister, that's ten times the worth of the whole bunch," she said. "Thank you."

She slipped the quarter into a pocket and disappeared into the crowd.

I continued my trek down J Street. I couldn't spread too many of the coins I had found around too quickly. I had many more where that one had come from, but if word got out I was spending a lot of Old World coins, one of the Warlords would surely come down on me.

It didn't hurt to help the people around me when I could, though. Most of the good will I had around the city had come from similar acts. Those on the street didn't have much, and when I helped them, they remembered. There will be a time I'll need help, and there are quite a few people who will remember.

J Street crossed Third Avenue ahead of me, and my destination wasn't far down Third. There was a bar called the Strike Zone there. My contact had said he had a man who wanted to meet with me about a job. I tended to use the Strike Zone as a meeting place for potential customers.

I had helped the owner find his kidnapped wife eight years ago, and he kept a booth unoccupied for me to use at any time. Good will is a priceless commodity in a fallen world.

I came within view of the bar and there were crowds of people waiting to enter. Some things never change. People search for escape from reality in any world, Fallen or not.

The doorman nodded as I strode past the line of waiting patrons, some of which yelled in anger.

"Kade," he said as I reached him, "welcome, as always. You're booth is clear, and there is a guest awaiting your arrival."

"Thanks Sam," I said and walked into the noisy, smoke-filled room.

I made my way across the large room full of dancing men and women. The music pounded some sort of digital created music from the Old World. I had found a stash several years back of several kinds of Old World music discs. I traded most of the discs to Jared McKnight, the owner of the Strike Zone. I had kept a small collection of a style of music called Blues. I liked the Old World Blues music. Most of the rest had been dance music of some sort or another. Some digital, some of what they had called Country, R&B, and Hip-Hop. I didn't care for most of those.

The Old World music had brought crowds of people into the Strike Zone, and Jared had been making money hand over fist. Then the local Warlord had stepped in and began taxing Jared to keep his bar open. Now Jared made enough to get by but not much more.

"Kade!" Jared's voice boomed across the room.

I looked to my right to see Jared waving at me. He was pushing through the crowd toward me.

"Mathew Kade," he said with a huge smile. "A sight for sore eyes!"

"How are ya, Jared?" I asked.

"Could be better, but I'm still here."

"How's Jenny?"

"Pregnant."

"Really?" I asked with a smile. "Congratulations, my friend!"

"Thanks, Kade," he said. "It never woulda happened without you."

"I'm pretty sure I didn't have anything to do with that."

His laugh boomed across the room again.

"True enough," he said. "But you found her for me, Kade. I can never thank you enough for that. And now I'm about to be a father."

"You deserve it, man," I said. "Take good care of 'em."

"Will do," he said. "I'll be by your table in a few. Had a little episode we have to deal with. Someone didn't like my reservation policy."

"I'll talk to ya then," I said and made my way to the booth in the back that was conspicuously empty.

As I slid into the booth, I could see two people with an interest in me. One was an older gentleman in an old suit. The other was a young man who had a perpetual snarl on his face.

I motioned to the older gentleman, and he made his way toward my booth.

"Mathew Kade," I said with my hand outstretched. "I understand you have a job for me?"

"Yes I do," he said. "My name is Cedric Hale. I need you to find my daughter for me. She disappeared three days ago, and I haven't been able to find a single clue as to where she has gone."

I motioned for him to have a seat

"What made you search me out for this job?"

"I worked for a company called Obsidian," he said.

My eyes narrowed.

"I'm not here to let your secret out, Mr. Kade," he said. "I know what you were. I know what happened to you. It's amazing that you were able to rebuild your psyche into something more than a drooling vegetable. Yet you did. You have the skills to find my daughter, no matter where she is."

"You know a lot about me, Hale," I said, "and I'm not very comfortable with that."

"When the end came, I know you were still in the imprinter, and it scrambled your brain," he said. "I also know, you spent three years inside the Obsidian building, under treatment for serious mental illness. No one even knows how you did it, Mr. Kade. Treatment did nothing and then one day you just stood up and became Mathew Kade.

"I'm not here to blackmail you or any such nonsense," he continued. "I just know what you were capable of before the Fall. If you have a fraction of that capability, you can find my daughter."

A commotion on the floor caught my eye, and a bottle was hurled across the room. I was on my feet and caught the bottle in my left hand.

For just a second, I was someone else. The young man with the perpetual snarl was staring into the cold dead eyes of someone entirely different from the man who had been sitting at the table. His eyes widened in fear, and he ran into the crowd.

In a moment I sat back down.

Hale was smiling, "A fraction."

I stared at him in silence.

He placed a coin in front of me. I looked at it in surprise. It was a solid gold coin from the Old World. Probably worth ten thousand scripts now.

"This is a down payment," Hale said. "You find her, you get another. Return her to me unharmed, you get three."

"I'll see what I can do."

"Thank you, Agent," he said softly.

I nodded.

He passed me a folder, and I opened it to see a picture of a pretty young red-haired woman. She appeared to be late teens or early twenties and that could be bad. This fallen world is hard on young beautiful people.

Warlords could swoop in with their troops and steal people at will. They were Warlords because the held the weapons or tech that gave them control over those around them.

There had been incidents for years. I had a great disdain for the term, Warlord. They were the ones who had found some advantage and abused it, for the most part.

There were a few good men, such as Wilderman, who held the reigns of fourteen city blocks. He provided protection to those who lived in his domain. He taxed his people but he also provided true protection.

Miles to the East, there was Joanna Kathrop. She held sixteen blocks and ruled with an iron fist. She had found a cache of weapons and provisions in her area several decades back. Her cadre of loyal soldiers backed her and she established her rule of that area.

There were others, both good and bad. The majority of them were bad. They ran single and double blocks. The Warlord that controlled the area where the Strike Zone was located wasn't the worst, but he was far from the best.

I turned the page and found the sector that Hale and his daughter had lived.

"You were under Yamato?" I asked.

"Yes," he said, "he took down the Bishop a decade ago."

"Yamato's always been fair," I said. "Did you take this to him?"

"He couldn't help me," he said. "She was traveling across the city."

"What the hell was she doin' travelin'?" I asked. "Was she in a caravan?"

The Caravans were the only semi-safe way to travel the city. You paid for your ticket, and the Caravans paid their tax to run through the Zones.

"She was going to the new College, set up by Kathrop, in a small Caravan run by a man named Drekk. He claims she never showed up for the last leg of the trip."

"Drekk," I spat the word out. "I've heard of Drekk. If you want to travel anywhere, you have to use the Accredited Caravans. You can't use people like Drekk."

His face fell. "We didn't know about this until it was too late. We aren't rich people, Mister Kade."

I looked down at the coin still in my hand, and looked back to him with one eyebrow raised.

"The life savings of both my family and the family of Seran Yoto, her fiancée."

"Poor would not be what I would call this, Hale," I said. "There are people right in this room who won't see this much wealth in ten lifetimes. You dwell inside the Scraper. You have running water and electricity. Don't ever try to pass yourself off as the poor. It's insulting."

He nodded.

"Who set up the Caravan?"

"I set it up through a man in the Scraper. His name is Denton. He owns a supply store on the bottom floor."

"Ok," I said. "That's where I'll need to start. I'll be there first thing in the morning."

"But the Caravans don't run at night..."

"Some people, it's safer to leave alone, Hale. When you get back to the Scraper, tomorrow, I'll have some answers for you."

"How will you cross three zones tonight?"

"I'll walk, Hale," I said. "Corporate Agents can take care of themselves."

"You haven't been an Agent for twenty years."

"You're right, there." I said, "I'm something else, now. I'll see you tomorrow night at your Scraper."

I stood and walked away from the booth. Jared was beside the bar, talking to several suits.

"Yo, Jared," I said. "I'm on a job for a few days. Ya can fill the table if ya need to."

"Be careful, Matt," he said. "Last time Jenny took a week to get you patched up."

"I'll try, buddy."

I had a feeling about this one. Things looked bad for Maddy Hale. Drekk wasn't known to be trustworthy.

Life can be dangerous in this Fallen World.

* * * * *

Chapter Two

I started walking back up the Avenue toward J Street. There I turned toward the West. I took a pack of Nic-Stiks from my pocket and lit one up. They had outlawed cigarettes nearly fifty years ago, but they had made a comeback after the Fall. I wasn't even sure why I knew that.

As I passed a group huddled around a trash can of burning refuse, I took the bag of apples I was still carrying and handed one to each of the people. I took the others over to several huddled against the wall.

"Rad-free," I said and pulled my rad marker from my pocket and held it up.

They all began eating probably the first fruit they had eaten in months. I nodded to them and continued west. I could travel that direction through one Zone, but I would have to bypass the next one by heading north. Anyone who set foot in Derris' Zone would wind up eaten. A South bypass was also out of the question. I imagined Blechley was still pissed at me after I had broken his collarbone and killed three of his lieutenants last year.

My eyes roved across the street as I continued. Shadows darted along the left side of the street. They thought I was an easy mark. My whole body was set on a hair trigger as I waited for the rush from behind. The shadows were the diversion, the true danger was from the rear.

I heard a slight scrape, and I was on the ground, three feet to the right, crouched. They hadn't adjusted, and they plowed through the spot I had been.

"You get one warning," I said. I flipped my wrist and the straight razor flipped open in my right hand. "Walk away or die."

My voice was calm, and I waited for a second. Then I stepped forward, toward the two men in the street. They turned and fled. Nine out of ten fights are avoided by the lack of fear they sensed in their former prey. The straight razor was for the tenth.

A familiar voice came from the darkness. "One of these days, they're not gonna run, Kade."

"True enough, Wilson," I said. "What are you doin' out here?"

"The Boss sent me to back you up."

"And why would Teresa do something like that?"

"She heard you were on the job and remembered the last time. She kinda likes you for some odd reason."

I chuckled. "It's my charming personalities."

"Probably," Wilson Poe answered. "Either way, I'm here to back you up. I can go with you or follow along behind, but I'm coming."

"May as well come with me," I said. "Keep me from talkin' to myselves."

Wilson walked out of the dark. He was six feet tall and built like a tank. I didn't foresee anyone wanting to tangle with Wilson. He didn't stand out at night because he wore black pants and a black sweater, and his skin was almost as dark as his clothes.

"You could try to blend in with the night a little better," he said. "Who the hell wears a tan trench coat and walks the streets at night?"

"Not many people," I said. "This way people know what they're about to get into."

"With one of the local Warlords pissed at you," he said, "maybe you should try *not* to stick out."

"What makes ya think Simon would still be pissed at me?"

"You did break his collarbone."

"He's still alive."

"You made the man beg, Kade."

"No," I said. "He chose to beg. I didn't plan to kill him. He begged on his own."

"Somehow, I don't think he sees it that way, Kade."

"His boys shot me three times," I said. "I killed a lieutenant for each bullet. Now why would I do that if I didn't plan on him living to learn from the lesson? He can't blame me for the begging."

Wilson just chuckled, "I guess he should have studied a little Kade logic before he shot you."

"Exactly."

"You see the guy on the right?"

"Yep."

I flipped the straight razor out and started cleaning my nails with it as I passed under the street light. The form slid back into the shadows, silently.

"I really need to get me one of those," Wilson said.

"Very handy tool."

"No doubt," he said.

He tapped the sword across his back. It was close to five feet long, including the hilt.

"This tends to make them think before starting a ruckus."

"Not as useful in close quarters," I said.

"If they get in close quarters with me, they deserve what they get."

"Ya gotta point," I said. I had seen Wilson lift the side of a car before. If they got close with the man, he would break them in two... or three.

We were nearing the border of Derris' Zone.

"Gotta head north on Twelfth," I said, "Don't feel like takin on Derris' bunch."

"One of these days, someone is going to have to do something about that place."

"True," I said. "I don't think I wanna take that on tonight, though."

"I don't want to either," he said. "When you decide to, make sure to let me know so I can go on a vacation. Somewhere far away."

"Shit no." I said, "That's at least a two-man operation."

"I would hesitate with two thousand men."

"Where's your sense of adventure?"

He just shook his head. "I can't believe she likes you this much."

"She's always trying to help the 'special' ones. She's got too big of a heart. She loves puppies."

"We talking about the same woman?"

"I think so," I said. "Teresa Manora...beautiful...blonde...great big..."

He looked at me with that look he gives those that may be broken in half soon.

"Heart...I was gonna say heart. Where's your mind at, Wilson?"

"Sure you were," he said. "Teresa Manora, Matron of the Society of the Sword. She has iron in her blood, steel in her bones. The Warlords tread lightly around her."

"Yeah, that's the one," I said, "and she loves puppies."

"How are you not dead?"

"Just lucky, I guess."

"You would have to be."

We made the turn up Twelfth Street. This would bring us into the Zone of Zane Palmer. He wasn't the nicest guy, but there were far worse. His guys were a bunch of punks, but most of them were held in check by Zane. One of his standing rules was, if one of his guys picks a fight and loses, he wasn't worth the money he was earning. He didn't tell them not to pick fights, just not to pick a fight they would lose.

The only problem with such a rule was the fact that a lot of punks had an overinflated opinion of themselves. If we were lucky, there wouldn't be any incidents.

"Think we can get by Zane's guys without one of 'em being stupid?" Wilson asked.

"I doubt it," I said. "Ya know how they travel. In packs. Their stupidity feeds off each other."

"A guy can hope," he said.

"Always expect the worst," I said. "You'll never be disappointed."

"That's a pretty crappy outlook on life, Kade."

"Rarely am I disappointed." I said, "Just look to your three o'clock."

"Yeah, I see 'em," he said. "I was hoping for the best."

"Now you're disappointed."

"Shut up."

"I'm not disappointed."

"Shut up."

We spread apart to give ourselves room to move. There's a time to try to talk your way out of a fight, and there's a time to just prepare and let things run their course. The one rule we had to follow was simple. They attack, we kill them. If we attack, the whole Zone becomes hostile.

There were only ten. I decided I wouldn't need to call up any reinforcements. I just waited patiently as the crowd of punks swaggered across the open ground between us.

"Mathew Kade," the one in the lead stopped about ten feet from me.

"You know who I am," I said and looked past him, "and you only brought nine others?"

"I won't need no help for the likes of you, Kade."

"You really want to try by yourself?"

"I want that bounty all to myself," he said.

"Your funeral," I said. "Wilson, hold back unless anyone else decides to join in. I would hate for this idiot to have to share his bounty."

"You got it, Kade." He drew that huge sword from his back and stepped to the side.

"Go for it, boy," I said with my razor resting lightly in my right hand.

He lunged forward with a gleaming blade in his hand. I stepped by him in a flash, and he continued his lunge to land, face-first on the cracked cement. He tried to push himself to his hands and knees, and there was an audible wet splash as his intestines hit the concrete under him. There was a whimper, not from the dying punk, but one of the others facing me as I stood there with my head cocked to the side, as if I was listening to someone.

"Who would like to try to earn that bounty, next?" I asked. "Or would you like to try to earn a nine way split...well...more like a four way. I'll definitely get five of you. Of course, my friend will get the rest. So it's really a lose-lose situation for you boys."

They turned and fled, leaving their erstwhile companion lying in his own intestines.

She's a cold bitch, this Fallen World.

* * * * *

Chapter Three

"You didn't even get anything on your coat," Wilson said.

"I try not to," I said. "These are expensive. Hard to find."

"No doubt," he said. "No one else wears anything so useless. It has to get in the way with all the floppin' around your legs."

I just stared at him.

"Sorry," he said. "That must be one of those rules of yours. Kade's Rule, Number Twelve. Don't insult the useless coat that will probably get Kade killed at some point."

"I see how you wanna be," I said. "You're just jealous. You can't have one. They don't make 'em big enough to make a circus tent."

Wilson got very quiet.

"Pre-Fall nonsense," I said, "Sorry, I find I have random knowledge of the world before the Fall. Nobody wants to think about The Circus."

"There was a Circus before the Fall?"

"There were a lot of 'em," I said. "Not like this perverted version we have now. It was a place where people had a fun time, watching others do tricks and things. Did you know that clowns were even funny things back then?"

"My God," Wilson said.

We lost a lot when the Old World fell. Many of the things I had random memories of simply didn't exist anymore.

"You're young, Wilson," I said. "What? Twenty?"

"Twenty-three," he said. "I don't remember any of the world before the Fall. I was a baby when the Corporate Wars hit their final climax. The nukes took out so much of the world."

"There aren't many of the cities left," I said. "We got lucky, here. There's the Rad Zone to the north. Fifty miles south and there wouldn't be anything left here."

"Sometimes I think it was for the best," I said. "The Corporate War had consumed everything in its path. I'm not even sure they knew what they were fightin' for anymore."

"How the hell do you know all this shit?" Wilson shook his head, "You're not that old."

"You'd be surprised how old I am," I said.

Wilson looked off to our left, "You see 'em?"

"Yeah," I said. "Only two of 'em."

"Some people are just better off left alone," a voice came from the pair of shadows.

"Come on out," Wilson said, "and we'll talk about it."

"I'll keep my distance for a moment, yet," the voice returned. "It has come to my attention that Kade is traveling tonight. I felt it would just be easier to escort you through my territory rather than lose as many men as it would cost to collect a certain bounty."

"You must be Palmer," I said.

"Zane, if you please."

"Ok, Zane," I said. "I'm just passin' through. There's really no need for violence. You're boy back there was determined."

There was a sigh, and Zane stepped out into the light. "I hoped I would get here before any of my idiots."

"You sound disappointed," I said.

"Not this again," Wilson said.

Zane looked at us with one eyebrow raised.

"It's one of his stupid rules," Wilson said. "Expect the worst, and you'll never be disappointed."

Zane chuckled. "That is a sad outlook on life, Mister Kade."

"That's what I've been saying," Wilson said.

"Who, here, is disappointed?" I asked. "Not me."

Wilson sighed.

"You're welcome to join us, Zane," I said. "You can come along, down to Yamato's if you want."

"I'll have to pass on that," Zane said. "Yamato is a little upset with me at the moment. Something of a romantic nature has occurred between my son and his daughter. Those sort of things tend to cause a little bad blood."

"Hopefully, you can work it out," Wilson said.

"Expect a full scale war," I said. "You won't be disappointed by whatever ends you may reach."

"You travel with him, willingly?" Zane asked Wilson.

"My boss ordered me to."

"That would explain it."

I shrugged and continued walking.

There was some activity around the Scraper as we came nearer to the center of Zane's Zone. It wasn't any of his men; it was merchants setting up stalls all along the foot of the Scraper.

"Farmers comin' in tomorrow?" I asked.

"That they are," Zane said. "Should be a prosperous day for me. We've done well this month, and I should be able to buy extra stores this time."

For those in the scraper I was sure. Those on the street had to do the best they could. But the Farmers were a boon to the street dwellers, too. They sold to all and were protected by all.

If the Farmers quit coming, the city would starve. They kept their own Militia and guarded their caravans quite well. There was, occasionally, an idiot who would try a run at a Farmer caravan. The roads would be littered with their dead, and the Farmers would roll on through. Whatever Zone they were in when attacked would not be visited that month and the neighboring Zones would be rationed to barely enough to get by.

It was in everybody's interest to leave the Farmers be. Anyone caught messing with the Farmers would be dealt with, severely.

Eight years past, one of the Farmer's daughters had been kidnapped from the Caravan. The Caravan had stopped and sent word home. Half a day later, five hundred seasoned Farmer warriors descended on the Zone. The search that ensued ended after they found her raped and murdered.

This was the only time I had ever worked for the Farmers. They sent a representative to me and hired me to find out who had done the deed. After an investigation, I found a pearl that had belonged to her where it had rolled into a crack in the floor of the head of the Warlord's Guard.

The Farmers left with two heads on pikes. The head of the Guard and the Warlord's son. The Warlord was told that he would be left alive to prevent any other transgressions against the Farmers. If he failed to prevent even a minor transgression, his head and the heads of every member of his family would join the son's.

No one messes with the Farmers.

The days when the Farmers are in a Zone are usually the most peaceful days a Zone ever sees.

"It's a good day when the Farmers come to the Zone," I said. "I think they're scheduled to come to our Zone next week."

"True," Wilson said. "Sure to be a very good week."

Truer than he might think. The Farmers were the only place I could take a large amount of Old World coins and sell them. They, as a rule, kept every transaction a secret.

We continued onward to the west. We were nearing the boundary of Zane's territory.

"Can I ask a question?" he asked.

"You can ask."

He chuckled. "This bounty on your head. Is it true that you killed three of his men and broke his collarbone?"

"Fairly close to true," I said.

"That sounds like there's more."

"He was looking for a Society kid," Wilson said. "He found where they were holding him. It was a couple of Blechley's lieutenants. When he went to retrieve the kid, he was shot three times by Blechley's men."

"He took the kid and hid him. Then he went to Blechley's Scraper. He cornered Blechley, and killed three of his lieutenants, right in front of him. One for each bullet. Then he took a two foot spike, and hung Blechley from the wall of his throne room by the right shoulder, thus breaking the man's collarbone."

"Jesus, Kade," Zane said.

"Then he fetched the kid and returned him to our Zone."

"After being shot three times?"

"He's hard to kill."

"It would be easier if people would just do the right thing," I said.

"You'd have a better chance of Dynamo granting you free power to your Zone."

"That would be something for the record books," Wilson said.

"True," I said. "Nothin' is free from Dynamo."

Dynamo was the guy who had gotten control of the old electric plants in the center of the city. His Zone supplied a great deal of the power for the whole city. There were some Scrapers with windmills and solar cells but they couldn't supply enough power to run a Scraper in comfort. So every Warlord paid their tax to Dynamo. You could get by without his supplied power, but no one in the Scrapers wanted to give up the comforts of running water or climate control in the Scrapers that still had that comfort.

We reached the edge of Palmer's Zone. He turned to me. "Good luck, Kade. Watch your back; that bounty is a hundred k."

"He really wants me dead," I said.

"You should have killed him."

"If I'd killed him, he wouldn't learn anything."

"Seems he didn't learn the right lesson from his last encounter with you," Zane said.

"He may need another lesson."

Zane shook his head and held his hand out. "Good meeting you, Kade."

I grasped his hand. "Same here, Zane. Take good care of your people, and you'll do well."

He nodded and strode into the darkness. Several shadows that had been tailing us converged on the track he had gone.

"I must be slipping," Wilson said, "I only saw two. There were four."

"Five," I said, "and they were good. Probably some of his lieutenants."

"Damn, I really am slipping."

"I barely caught on to the fifth one," I said. "She's slick."

"She?"

"Yeah," I said. "She smelled like roses."

"Damn it, man."

We headed back to the south on Seventeenth Avenue. From there we would pick up J Street, once more. J Street led straight to Yamato's Scraper.

"A hundred k is pretty high, Kade," Wilson said. "I wouldn't be surprised if we ran into a lot of trouble over the next few days."

"You plan on workin' this whole case with me?"

"I wasn't until I heard about this bounty," he said. "I don't think the Boss would appreciate it if I left, and you got all killed and shit."

"I can take care of myself," I said. "But don't think for a second I don't appreciate the help. It certainly helps to have someone I trust at my back. The problem is, I don't know where this is goin' before it's over."

"Guess we'll just have to wait and see."

"We'll run into another bounty hunter before we reach the Scraper," I said.

"Plan for the worst?"

I scowled as a group of them strode into the lighted street from the shadows ahead of us.

"Not disappointed."

"Shut up."

"Do we have to wait for them to attack?" Wilson asked.

"Hell no," I said. "That's Corso and his pack."

Corso was a well-known figure. He made a business of hunting those with bounties on their heads. He usually stayed out of the more respected Zones, but a hundred k must have been more temptation than he could stand. A pity.

"Good," Wilson said and pulled that massive sword from his back. "I was getting bored."

I thought about reinforcements, but chose to handle this one myself. Who needed reinforcements when you had Wilson? I glided toward the group with my razor in my right hand.

I think they had planned to have some sort of threat session or something, because there were a lot of surprised faces as a six foot tall tank slammed into their midst with four and a half feet of sharpened steel, covering a six and a half foot arc in front of him.

They tried to scatter and Wilson pulled his blade through an equally devastating backswing. Several tried to get behind him and I glided by them. The first tripped as his hamstrings were severed. The other didn't have time to react before I was behind him and my left hand snaked around his neck to pull his chin backward. The right made a lightning slice across his windpipe.

Properly slitting a throat is a learned skill. You cut too deep, your blade hits bone and dulls. Too shallow and your victim isn't dead. I like to slide that little extra distance around the side and catch the carotid as well. My own version of the double tap.

I slipped away from my victim and ducked down to slide my razor along the left side of the one I had hamstrung, just deep enough to slice about halfway through his kidney.

His screams told me he was out of this one.

Corso, himself carried a pistol. It was an older weapon called a revolver. He was taking aim at me, so I moved. The shot went wide to my left, as I had gone right. I dove forward and down as the second bullet screamed over my head. I rolled and launched myself left this time, and his next shot was wide again. I felt the next one tug at the bottom of my coat just as I reached him. My blade sliced from his straddle, straight up to his sternum as another shot whistled past my ear.

I snatched the gun as I passed him on his right side with my left hand and his insides tumbled into the street. With a deft move of my left hand, I flipped the gun into a firing position, and shot Corso's second-in-command right between her beautiful blue eyes.

Make your choices wisely. Consequences are deadly in this Fallen World.

* * * * *

Chapter Four

I dusted my coat off and looked, sadly, at the single hole near the hem along the bottom.

"You still don't have any blood on your coat," Wilson said.

"Yeah, but look at this," I said with my finger poking through the hole.

"I think you'll be fine," he said. "You can hardly see it."

I sighed. "Maybe I should start a tab for Simon to pay when I go visit."

Wilson chuckled. "You are kidding, right?"

I stared at him.

He shook his head, and we resumed our trek. The screams of Corso's pack had become whimpers and moans by then. Soon enough we had walked out of earshot of even those.

"I got blood all over me," Wilson said.

"Good thing you wear black," I said. "It takes a certain finesse to wear light colors. I'm pretty sure that thing wouldn't ever be able to be wielded with anywhere near the finesse it would take. Stick to black."

"Four people and not a drop of blood on the coat," he said with a shake of his head.

"If it wasn't for the rollin' on the ground, I'd get a white one."

"I don't even doubt that."

"Looks like we made it to Yamato's," I said.

The huge Scraper we were nearing was bigger than any in our own Zone. "The Old World used to call them skyscrapers. Just another of those useless facts floating around in my noggin."

"I could see that," he said. "They are so tall they scrape the sky."

"I think that was the idea," I said. "They even date back before the Corporate Wars. They used to house businesses in the old days. Then, later, they became the seats of power for the Corporations. Now, as it was then, the wealthy reside in the Scrapers. The poor do the best they can."

"How do you know all this shit?"

"Too many imprints, each with its small piece of knowledge," I muttered.

"Imprints?"

"Maybe I'll tell ya about it someday," I said. "There's some work needin' done here first."

"How 'bout you tell me what this case is?" he asked. "I seem to have been volunteered for a mission I have no idea about."

"Kidnapped girl, stolen from a Caravan. There's a shopkeeper here who set her up with Drekk."

"Drekk!" he spat the word out.

"I had pretty much the same reaction," I said. "First I'm gonna find out if this shopkeeper is just stupid, or if he set up Hale to lose a daughter."

"Hold!" the guard just outside the main entrance to the Scraper said. "It's a little late for visitors."

I slipped a ten script into his hand as I shook hands with the man.

"Just a little business to conduct," I said, "then we'll be on our way."

He nodded and motioned for us to proceed. This part was easy if you had a few scripts. Without it, I would have had to bring some form of proof I was working for Cedric Hale. Easier to just bribe your way in.

I held up a five script, "Can ya point me in the direction of a shop owned by a guy named Denton?"

"Sure thing," he said and the script disappeared. "Straight to the back, last shop on the left. He's closed up this late, but he lives in the shop. He may open up if you wake him."

"He'll open," I said. "Later, Guardsman."

"Keep out of trouble."

"You just spent a day's wages in the tunnels," Wilson said as we entered the Scraper. "Must be getting paid well for this one."

"I'm thinkin' Denton is gonna be more than happy to reimburse me," I said.

"Already convinced he's dirty?"

"Fairly certain," I said. "We both know how Drekk works."

"True enough," he said. "He usually stays away from the wealthier ones."

"Maybe he's trying to move up in the world," I said. "If so, he's just started swimming with the sharks. I don't think he even knows what he's gettin' into."

"Probably true," he said. "What's a shark?"

"Top of the food chain in the ocean."

"Never seen an ocean," Wilson said. "Could you imagine travelin' that far at a time?"

"There are people outside the city that do that kind of travelin'," I said. "Maybe someone can get the city under control enough for someone to do that sort of thing again."

"No one could afford to bribe their way through that many Zones."

"What would ya think of a city that a person didn't have to use a Caravan and bribes to cross?"

"Good luck with that, Kade."

"Everybody's gotta have a goal, Wilson."

"Try to focus on one that you might be able to reach," he said. "I can name three reasons within a three mile radius that would hurt that goal. And that's just the 'Big Three' reasons. There are hundreds of slightly lesser reasons after those."

"Yeah, I can think of a few, too."

"Derris."

I nodded.

"Blechley."

"Not as big of a worry as some would put on him," I said.

"Whatever," Wilson said, "but then there's The Circus."

"Yeah, that could be troublesome."

"Those are just the local 'Big Three' reasons," he said. "Shall I go on?"

"Nope," I said. "I know you love to hear yourself speak, but we're here."

"I have no idea what you're talking about."

The shop we were standing in front of looked to be a General Goods store. I could see containers through the metal fence that undoubtedly held food supplies like flour or rice. There were various sorts of clothing, cooking utensils, and jars of spices. Overall, it appeared to be a fairly successful store. The shops inside the Scrapers were much different than the shanties and open shops around the outside.

I rattled the fence, loudly.

I heard grumbling from the back of the store, and a man came stumbling from the dark fumbling with a set of keys.

"It's late," he said.

I held a ten script where he could see it.

"We're leaving early tomorrow and we need provisions," I said.

"Come in," he said, eying the script.

He opened the lock on the side of the sliding metal gate, and pushed it to the side far enough to let us in. It truly was a good thing Wilson wore black so the bloodstains on his clothing were hidden.

We stepped inside and followed Denton toward his counter.

"So, how many provisions do you need? Will this be a long trip and are you the only two traveling?"

I listened to the questions he asked. They could be innocent questions or they could be questions meant to fish for enough information to set someone up for some sort of ambush. So far, they were possibly innocent.

"We're traveling to the east. We need enough for two into Kathrop's Zone."

"Dangerous traveling to the east, my friend," he said. He pulled a map from under the desk and placed it on the counter. His finger pointed to the spot where Yamato's Zone was marked. "If you were to take this route, you could bypass several of the more dangerous zones."

He traced a route east, then north around several zones. Still there was a possibility of innocence.

"Are you familiar with these zones, my friend?" he asked as his finger followed a trail east.

"Can't say I've ever traveled those."

His finger backtracked just a tiny bit and turned south into Ramos Antilles' Zone. That was the clue I had been looking for. I've studied this city for nearly seventeen years, and I know the safest routes to almost anywhere. He was trying to send us right into the hands of someone I knew would almost certainly detain travelers and probably take anything of value from them.

"What can ya tell us about a possible caravan?"

"There's a caravan coming through Jaxom's Zone tomorrow about noon," he said. "If you're interested in that option, word can be sent for him to meet you at a pre-chosen point so that you can join them."

"How would you get a message to the man?"

"I have a short wave radio." he said, "Most of the shops inside the Scrapers have ways to communicate."

"What sort of cost would this caravan run?"

"His standard rate is forty script per Zone traveled. From Jaxom to Kathrop is eleven Zones. So four hundred and forty script would take you through."

His price was too cheap. A caravan wouldn't make much money at forty script per Zone. Normal rates for an accredited caravan were a hundred script per Zone.

Everything was screaming that the shopkeeper was crooked. He would get kickbacks from Antilles or kickbacks from his caravan. The next question would make or break it for me.

"So, who's the Caravan Master? Maybe one of us knows him."

He smiled. If we weren't familiar with the area, we wouldn't know Drekk. "His name is Hodipis Drekk, and not a finer Caravan Master will you find in this corner of the city."

"Is that what you told Cedric Hale when you booked the trip for his seventeen-year-old daughter from here to Kathrop?"

"What...what?"

"The most important question you'll answer this night is the next one I ask."

Wilson stepped back to the gate and slid it closed.

"Just who do you think you are, coming into my establishment and...?"

His words cut short as he saw, for an instant, the cold, dead eyes of an entirely different person staring at him.

"I've been hired to find the girl and bring her home," I said. "My name is Mathew Kade."

His face went several shades toward white when I said my name.

"Oh dear God," he whimpered. "What have I done?"

"That's exactly what we're about to find out," I said. "Tell me everything."

"He'll kill me."

I moved like lightning. His back slammed into the wall behind him, and my left hand clinched around his throat. "Worry about me."

"I-I'll t-talk," he stuttered.

"Tell me."

"It's Drekk," he sputtered. "He pays me to send people to his caravans. It's supposed to be a simple ransom."

"Kidnap and ransom?" I asked. "Then what are the demands? Hale received no demands."

"I-I don't know, Mister Kade," he sobbed. "He just sent word that the girl was gone."

"How many people have you betrayed, Denton?" I asked, my voice vibrated with anger. "How many lives destroyed? How much did he pay you to send a seventeen year old girl out into this perverted abomination of a city?"

His hands trembled as they withdrew a pouch of coins from his belt. "Take it. Please don't hurt me."

"Hurt you?" my voice rang in the room, "it won't hurt...long."

His scream never even made it out of his mouth.

* * *

Hale arrived about mid-morning the next day to find Wilson and me sitting, patiently on the steps leading up to the Scraper. He approached me warily.

"Looks like he expects the worst," Wilson said.

"He won't be disappointed."

"Have you found anything for me yet, Mister Kade?" Hale asked.

"I have some news," I said. "There was a plot to kidnap your daughter and demand a ransom for her return. Something went wrong, considering you haven't had any demands. You haven't had any, have you?"

"No," he answered in a sad tone. "Who was behind it?"

"Denton had a hand in it," I said. "The one behind it was Drekk. I'll be visiting him later today. When I have news I'll bring it to you or send it with someone else."

"Please find her, Kade," he said. "She's all I have left."

"I will."

There was a commotion from the Scraper as several of Yamato's Guards exited the front entrance. They had held people from entering half the morning.

"What is the meaning of this?" Hale asked the Guards.

"Found a shopkeeper this mornin', Mister Hale."

"He was hanged last night," the other Guard said. "Wasn't a robbery, though. There were thirty coins scattered on the floor around him."

Hale looked at me with gratitude writ across his face. Thirty coins for the betrayer. The consequences seemed proper.

Six hundred script is what he had been payed. Thirty coins from the Old World. He had sold a seventeen year old girl for seven dollars and fifty cents.

Life is cheap in this Fallen World.

* * * * *

Chapter Five

We walked toward the north. Wilson was quiet. The case had become something else after the last night. He was there, for Teresa, to help keep me from gettin' myself killed, sure. But he had looked straight into the eyes of that shopkeeper with me. We witnessed justice being served and both of us knew that justice is what we were truly after.

"Do ya think there's a chance the girl is still alive?" he asked.

"The truth is," I said, "there's not much chance of it. But we'll find her, or we'll find her body. Either way, I plan to set this right. You ok with that?"

"Damn straight, I am."

"Good," I said. "This might get ugly before we're through."

"You have no idea," he said. "I used Denton's short wave last night. Reported to Teresa. She's called out the Knights and put them on alert. We drag this out in the open, and the Knights are ready to do what is needed."

Knights of the Society of the Sword are some of the toughest bastards walking the city streets. You don't become a Knight easily. Wilson Poe is a Yeoman of the Society, and he's a walking army in his own right. There are thirty-five of the Knights. The majority of the Society are Recruits, Yeomen, and Squires. The Knights travel the city, and they hate this sort of thing. But it's a big damn city and there's a lot of this sort of thing going on.

This had just gotten much bigger than Wilson Poe guarding my back.

"Well, what say we give the Knights a target then?"

"That we will."

We headed north toward Jaxom's Zone. It was a Zone north of Zane's. At least we would eat well, with the Farmers in Zane's area today.

The streets look completely different during the day. There were still some of the bravos standing idle along the street in various places. But there were regular folks as well. Travel through the Zones was always dangerous but travel at night was unheard of for the regular inhabitant of this fallen city. I heard music from ahead of us as we neared the Farmer's wagons.

They traveled with huge box wagons made of strong wood and banded in steel. The box wagons held almost anything that could be traded in the city or in the country around the outside of it.

There were entertainers, players of music, and even a wagon that opened up into a stage for what used to be called theatre. Plays were also a common term for them, and that's what they still were called. I'd sat and watched a play in our Zone, three years earlier.

It had been a reenactment of the Fall. I left halfway through the show. I had lived the Fall and I remembered so much from before. I didn't want to relive it as they reenacted something that vaguely resembled what had truly occurred.

For a time, I had thought that, if they knew what really happened, they would try to become something better than this mockery of the civilization that had been here before. Who was I kidding? Humans are some of the vilest creatures this world had ever spawned. Then I would meet that one person that would give me hope that all, truly, hadn't been lost, and there may be a small chance that Humanity deserved to survive.

Those, like Maddy Hale, who disappear into the maw of this great creature spawned by the evil nature of Humanity, need someone to stand up for them. I saw a part of this in the Society of the Sword. Teresa didn't strive to control all of those around her. They flocked to her because she was a good leader. She cared about those who followed her. Technically, she was the Warlord of our Zone. Steiner was just the Warlord in name. What Teresa decided would be followed or Steiner would be removed rather quickly.

He charged his tax, lived in his Scraper, but he would rather roll down the street over barbed wire than to cross Teresa Manora.

I smelled something divine.

"What is that smell?" Wilson asked.

"My god," I said. "I think it's a taco."

"A taco?"

"You have to eat some," I said. "First time since the Fall I've smelled a taco."

"It smells different."

"Oh, that's because they are," I said as I saw the source of the wonderful smell.

Wilson followed me to the wagon. An old lady who had to be sixty worked over a wood-burning grill. There were shells in a rack and tortillas in another rack for burritos.

"You've made a man's dreams come true," I said to the woman as I reached the rough counter she had set up around the grill. "I haven't had tacos in decades."

"You don't look old enough to have lived long pre-Fall. Probably no more than ten years old. You had tacos?"

"Little older than I look Gran," I said. "Had tacos before the Wars really heated up."

She nodded. "Age is treating you well. What can I prepare for you?"

"I want four hard shells and whatever my large friend wants."

She turned her gaze on Wilson. "You, I would guess, have never had a taco."

"You'd be right," he said. "I'll try the same as he got."

She reached into the wagon and drew out some peppers I never thought I would ever see again.

"Jalapenos?" I asked.

"We grew our first crop this year from some seeds we traded for from the West Caravans."

The West Caravans travel the route between the eastern coast and the western coast of the continent we lived on. It was a hell of a distance and there were several Rad Zones out in the middle of what used to be a great country. The nukes had been used to destroy the part of the country that provided most of the country's food production. They had planned to cripple the Obsidian Corporation, who had gained control of that country.

The Caravans traveled far to the south to pass the Rad Zones and were the only connections we had with the other side of the fallen land.

"How would you like them topped?" she asked.

"Load 'em down," I said with my mouth watering.

"And you?" she asked Wilson.

"I really don't know," he said. "Same as his, I guess."

"Two script," she said.

I motioned Wilson back and slid another Old World coin across the counter, and she raised her eyebrows in surprise. It really wasn't common to use Old World coins. They really weren't just laying around everywhere. It was a good way to cash them in when dealing with the Farmers, though.

She started to make change and I motioned for her to stop.

"I could use a little information, Gran."

"You ask, and I'll decide if the pay is enough."

"Nothing too major." I said, "My friend and I are in a hurry to get to Jaxom's Zone so we can't stay and really look around. I need to know if Grenwas is with you folks this year."

"Yes, he is," she said. "You'll find him around the Scraper and about halfway down the street. I'm guessing you may need weapons?"

"That, we do. You keep that and good fortunes be on your day."

"That information is free, young man, but I have something that may interest you. What sort of weapons do you need?" she said. "My son was lost to us in an accident this last year. He was of the Farmer's Guard. I intended to sell his weapons while in the city this week. If you are fond of the blade, the Farmer's Guard use only the best."

"Very fond of blades," I said. "It's not often quality weapons are available. I would love to see what you have."

She went to her wagon and pulled a chest from the corner. She laid it atop the counter and opened it. In a gleaming line were twelve beautiful throwing blades. They rested on a harness with scabbards for each blade.

"Now, that is beautiful," I said. "I was expecting a sword or dagger. These are magnificent. Price?"

"A hundred and fifty script," she said. "This coin is worth twenty. So we knock that off of..."

"No, that's yours," I said. "Here's the rest. Not often I find this quality. The only thing I've found of this high quality is my razor. It's made with Old World tech, and its better grade metal than most anything I've seen. I think these may be Old World-forged, too."

I slid several Old World coins to her and slid my coat off. After a few minutes of adjustments, I had a harness with twelve blades over my shirt.

She saw the pistol I had taken from Corso in my waistband.

"He also had a holster that attached to the harness. It's under the cloth."

I lifted the cloth to find a leather holster that was worn, but matched the harness. After a moment, I had it attached under the left arm. The pistol slid into the holster easily, and I pulled the thong over the hammer to hold it snugly.

"Nice," I said. "One stop shoppin'."

"Now let me finish your tacos," the woman said and returned to stacking tacos.

"Never knew you to carry anything other than the razor, Kade."

"I got a feelin'," I said.

"That's a little ominous," he said.

"Yea, that's the feelin' I'm getting."

We left the woman's wagon with our hands full of tacos. I showed Wilson the proper way to eat a taco without losing the majority of it down the front of your chest. They were even better than I remembered. No industrialized ingredients; all Farm fresh. I was impressed, to say the least.

The harness felt different, but I would get used to that in short order. Now we had to find Grenwas. Then we would have to meet Drekk in Jaxom's. Or catch up to him if we missed the Caravan. Drekk would have some explaining to do.

"We still need Grenwas?"

"Yeah," I said. "I need some bullets for this gun."

"Bullets?" he asked. "That's even more ominous. You never use guns."

"They're forever runnin' out of bullets," I said, "but it may be handy at some point. Worthless without bullets."

"True enough," he said. "Too bad we don't have a chapter here. We could get ammo there."

"That's just weird," I said. "It's the Society of the Sword. Not the NRA."

"NRA?"

"Pre-Fall nonsense," I said. "Sorry, I get a little mixed up sometimes."

We rounded the corner as I finished my last taco. I could see Grenwas' wagon down the street. I also saw someone giving us a great deal more attention than I was comfortable with. The man turned and hurried into a building erected alongside the Scraper.

"Trouble soon," Wilson said. "Keep your eyes open."

"I saw him," I said. "He's a local, but it looks like he recognized us."

"Recognized you," he said. "No huge bounty on my head."

"You disappointed? I'm not. Expected as much."

"Shut up."

We reached Grenwas' wagon.

"Mathew Kade!" Grenwas exclaimed and shook my hand. "What can I do for you today?"

"Need some bullets for this," I said as I laid the revolver down on the counter he had erected around his wagon.

"Looks like a .44 caliber," he said and lifted it up to examine it. "Ruger was a good firearm in its day. Still holds up well."

"Got anything that'll fit it?"

"I sure do," he said. "I have a box of thirty cartridges that'll fit this. Five hundred scripts is the best I can do. High demand for these."

"I'll take 'em," I said.

Bullets are expensive. There's a booming business selling death in this Fallen World.

* * * * *

Chapter Six

We walked north toward Jaxom's Zone.

"Gonna be pushin' it to get there before Drekk passes through," Wilson said. "Might have to chase him down."

"True enough," I said. "That doesn't bother me as much as you might think. Better if we aren't right on top of the Scraper when we find him."

"Ya gotta point," he said. "Do ya even know how many guards he uses on his Caravan?"

"Probably twenty or so," I said. "Don't feel sorry for them. They work for Drekk knowing full well what he's doin'."

"Wasn't feelin' sorry for them," he said. "Just wondering how we would split the numbers."

"We'll be fair." I said, "Half and half."

"I can live with that." He chuckled. "He's probably got guns."

"We'll jump off that bridge when we get there, but I expect many guns."

"Me too."

"Good, you may not be so disappointed, then."

"Shut up."

I chuckled.

"Disappointment has a way of draggin' you down," I said. "You'll live longer if you don't have so many disappointments cluttterin' up your mind."

"I hate you, Old Man."

I laughed. "I guess I'm lucky your boss likes me."

"Still tryin' to figure that one out," he muttered.

We turned left at the next corner. The huts and shanties looked even more dilapidated than the ones in Zane's territory. This was Polk's Zone, and he was a greedy bastard who bled his people dry to support his luxury lifestyle. He was a pretty despicable guy. The problem for his people was that they couldn't leave and go to another Zone. They couldn't afford a Caravan and most local Zones wouldn't allow new settlers. They were trapped under the thumb of their greedy Warlord.

But he was the one with the guns, so what could they do?

The next Zone to the north was Jaxom's, but it was already after noon, and Drekk could already be there and gone.

"Nine o'clock," Wilson said.

"I see 'em," I answered.

There were four guys waiting in the shadow of Polk's Scraper.

"Looks like they're waitin' for someone," Wilson said.

"Definitely waitin' for us," I said.

"It could be a coincidence."

"What'd we just discuss about disappointment?"

He sighed as the men saw us and the furthest one out ran back into the Scraper.

"Now you're disappointed."

He sighed again.

"Just keep goin'," I said. "When I give the word, we'll attack."

"Gotcha."

We continued down the street and passed the guys, acting like we didn't see them.

We were half a block past the lookouts when there was a commotion behind us, and Polk's Guards poured out of the Scraper looking right and left.

"Shit," Wilson said.

"Coulda been worse," I answered.

More guys poured into the street from the side of the Scraper. There had to be thirty of the guards in the street. Then they saw us and pushed through the people in front of Polk's.

"Dammit!" Wilson exclaimed. "Don't say anything else."

"Run," I said.

We bolted.

"I hate running," Wilson said between breaths.

"Me too," I answered.

I heard gunfire just as it whistled past my ear.

"Idiots!" I muttered. "People packed in the streets ahead of us."

"I don't think they care who they shoot, as long as one of 'em is you."

"Rethinkin' that whole 'backin me up' thing yet?"

"Can't," his breaths were getting more pronounced, "more scared of her than them."

"Save it, Wilson," I said. "Just breathe. I have a plan."

"Oh shit," he panted.

I glanced back. They were falling further behind.

"Slow down a bit," I said, through my steady breathing. It pays to keep fit. Wilson was fit but he was huge. Harder to keep running than it was for me.

"Thought we were trying to lose 'em," he gasped.

"One more block," I said and we ran on.

Occasionally I would hear the whine of a bullet and a gunshot. We crossed into Jaxom's Zone and neared his Scraper. The group didn't halt at the border. Seems Polk really wanted this bounty.

I didn't see a Caravan in the streets in front of Jaxom's but there were a lot of people in the street. This usually happened as a Caravan pulled out from one of the Scrapers. He couldn't be far. He would have gone south at the next street.

I rounded the corner with a yell, "Eureka!"

The Caravan was right around the corner. There were guards surrounding the six wagons and I saw the familiar bulk of Hodipis Drekk right in the center.

I plowed through the surprised guards and grabbed Drekk at full speed. We tumbled over and behind the wagon to his left. Wilson was right behind me as we ducked down.

Thirty two of Polk's men rounded the corner as we ducked down, and they opened fire. Twenty-eight Caravan guards ducked and located the gunmen.

Thunder rolled through the city streets as sixty guns opened fire.

I giggled and looked over at Drekk as he struggled to a sitting position.

"Hodipis!" I said. "How the hell are ya?"

"What is the meaning of this?!"

"Oh," I answered. "We have some things to discuss, you and I."

The gunfire had stopped but the groans and screams could still be heard, plainly. I peeked around the wagon for a second.

"Looks like three guys left out there," I said. "Sorry 'bout your guards, Drekk."

I stood up, and my hands blurred as I launched three knives, one after the other.

"Polk needs new guards, too."

Drekk struggled to his feet to see the carnage that had been wrought in the streets.

"What have you done, you bastard?"

I turned back to Drekk with that dead look in my eyes, "The question is, what have you done, Hodipis Drekk?"

He tried to back step only to run into a wall named Wilson Poe.

"Maddy Hale."

His face paled.

"Tell me everything, Drekk," I said. "I've already seen Denton. I know that end of it."

"I d-don't know where she w-went."

"Where was she supposed to be? You wanted ransom but never finished up."

"Th-the d-damn Clowns…"

"You gave her to the Circus!?"

"N-no," he stammered. "I had a deal with the damn Clowns to hold her till the ransom gets paid! We done it a lot of times. They said the guy who was to deliver her didn't show, and the girl is gone!"

I heard thumping from the wagon we were standing beside. Muffled yells sounded.

"Hold him," I said and Wilson clamped down on Drekk's shoulder with a huge hand.

I moved to the back of the wagon and unlocked the door. I drew the gun from its holster and opened the door. Inside were three women huddled in a corner of the wagon. I said women but two were little more than kids, fourteen or fifteen years old. All three were naked and bruised, and I didn't have to guess what had been happening to them. Something stirred inside me, a rage, but not just anger.

How had we come down to this? A once-great civilization reduced to this.

"Stay in here for a second," I said. "I'll finish with Drekk, and we'll get you somewhere safe."

I walked around the wagon, and shot Drekk in the head.

Wilson looked at me with one eyebrow raised.

"Look in the wagon," I said.

Jaxom's guards rounded the corner, and I walked out to meet them. Jaxom, himself, was among the guards.

"Mathew," he said with a nod, "why are there over fifty bodies in my street?"

"Sorry about that, Jaxom," I said. "If it's any consolation, you have six Caravan wagons full of goods to move into your Scraper."

"That helps," he said, "but it's not really a reason why I have bodies littering my street."

"Short version," I said. "Drekk kidnapped the wrong girl. He had three more in his wagon who are gonna need treatment. I expect you to put them up until Teresa Manora gets here to collect them."

My words were a statement and not a question. He could see that fury stirring beneath my surface, and he didn't argue even for a second. He nodded.

"Everything else is yours."

"Generous," he said.

"I don't need a baggage train," I said. "You can use it here. I could use a couple boxes of .44's if you got any."

"I could scrape up a few," he said.

"I'll owe ya one."

Wilson walked up to Jaxom's guards. He pointed at three.

"Give me your coats."

Jaxom saw the look on his face. "Give 'em the coats"

Wilson strode back around the wagon. In a few moments, he returned with three forms huddled together. He walked up to Jaxom.

"Take care of these ladies. If anything happens to 'em, the Society will be back in force. You understand?"

"I wouldn't let anything happen to them, son," Jaxom said. "I'm not that idiot next door."

"I used the shortwave in the wagons to call Teresa," Wilson said. "There will be a group of Knights here tonight to pick them up. The Society will take care of them."

"Understood, Knight," Jaxom said.

"I'm no Knight," Wilson said.

"You sound like one."

Wilson nodded and stepped back into his 'back up' position.

"You get me that ammo, and I'll be on my way," I said.

"Where to, if you don't mind my asking?"

"Polk just sent thirty-two men out to kill me," I said. "I think I'll pay him a visit. Then I have to go see a Clown."

"Circus is an evil place, Mathew," he said. "I'd be careful in there."

I nodded.

Jaxom was one of the better Warlords. He was tough, but he was also merciful. He didn't hurt people unless they needed it. I had no doubt he would keep those girls safe until Teresa arrived.

Mercy is a rare commodity in this Fallen World.

* * * * *

Chapter Seven

"So," Wilson said. "We gonna have a talk with Polk?"

"Oh, yeah."

"Good," he said. "That was about ridiculous."

"Worked out pretty well though."

"True enough."

"I do think he needs a lesson," I said as I retrieved my blades from the throats of three of his men. I spied the perfect thing. I picked up a two-foot-long piece of steel tubing one of his men had at his waist for a melee weapon.

"I see," Wilson said with a vicious smile.

I straightened up and turned back toward Polk's Zone. Flipping the tubing from one end to the other, I strode down the center of the street. Wilson walked by my side, glaring at any who looked at us. People scattered as we walked through. It didn't take too long to reach his Scraper.

I pushed through the doors of Polk's Scraper to find myself facing seven men. I cocked my head to the side.

"Thirty-two tried. Give it your best shot," I said, "or get out of the way and clean up the mess when I'm done."

They were looking into the dead eyes of a killer as I spoke. They moved out of my path.

"Wilson," I said, "keep these guys company. I won't be long."

He nodded.

I entered the elevator and pushed the button for the top floor. Warlords always took the penthouse for their quarters when the electric still functioned in the Scraper. Polk was no different. I exited on the top floor to see him standing across the room with his back to me. He was looking out the huge windows, overlooking the city.

"Is he dead?" Polk asked.

"I'm not."

He spun around, eyes wide with surprise, "Why those useless…"

He snatched the pistol from the holster at his side and fired. But I wasn't there anymore. I dove forward and rolled to the right. Then I lunged forward again. He shot once more and I felt a tug at my side as I dodged left. My side burned so I knew I was hit. It didn't matter, I was on top of him.

The pipe arced and he screamed as the bones in his arm shattered. Then a backswing crushed his left knee. He screamed louder.

Something moved behind me and I dodged to the right. My hand lashed out and snatched the arrow right before it would have planted itself in Polk's heart.

A form stepped from the shadows, staring at me in disbelief. It was a woman in a black leather outfit. She held a recurve bow in her left hand.

"Why did you do that?!" she almost screamed, "He deserves to die!"

"If you kill him, he won't learn anything."

Polk lay on the floor moaning.

"He killed my sister!"

I saw the rope looped around her shoulder and an idea struck me.

"Then he suffers for it," I said. "Give me your rope."

She approached slowly and handed me the rope.

I slammed the steel tube through Polk's shoulder and tied the rope to either end of the pipe. Polk screamed as I took the doubled end and tied it to his massive desk. Then I picked the screaming Warlord up and slammed him through the window he had been staring out of. The glass shattered, and he went over the edge. The rope went tight, and I walked away.

As I left the elevator, Wilson turned. He saw the blood on my side.

"You gonna live?"

"It's just a graze."

I walked over to the seven men, "Who is Polk's second?"

The third from the right nodded.

"You are gonna send a message to Teresa Manora. You're gonna request for her to open a chapter of the Society right here in this Scraper. The rest of you can go pull your boss back in his window, and you may even be able to keep him alive. Once that's done, you're on your own. I would suggest that you take any advice Teresa's people give. Don't make me come back."

Wilson and I left Polk's Scraper to find the streets packed with the poor and downtrodden. Polk was rough on his people.

"This zone will soon be under the protection of the Society of the Sword!" I raised my voice. "Teresa Manora is fair and just. She will help those in need and destroy those that would harm you. Your time under the heel of Kunley Polk is over."

I strode down the street, and the crowds parted for us.

"Guess she won't have a choice but to come in here now," Wilson said. "It's what she would want to do anyway."

"True."

"Stop when we get around the corner, and I'll take a look at that wound."

"Ok," I said. "Didn't want to show it to those folks."

We rounded the corner, and I sat on a stoop in front of a building. I shrugged my coat off and unbuckled the harness for the blades.

"Pretty deep." he said, "Needs stitches. We need to find a medic."

"I'll do it," a voice came from our left. It was the archer from Polk's quarters. "I was a medic in the Farmer's Guard."

I nodded, and she approached. She pulled a kit from her pack. She seemed pretty competent as she started threading the curved needle. The wound burned like hell as she stitched it closed. Then she pulled some salve from the kit and rubbed it on the area. The salve cooled the burn immediately, and she wrapped a bandage around my abdomen to cover the wound.

"Pretty handy," Wilson said. "And who are you?"

"We met in Polk's office," I said. "We had conflicting ideas of how to deal with Polk. We compromised and threw him out a window with a steel bar through his shoulder."

"I can always come back," she said. "And finish the job if I don't feel satisfied."

"Wilson Poe," he said with his hand outstretched. "How are ya?"

"Bella Trask," she said grasping Wilson's hand.

"The Bella Trask?" he asked. "The one that cleared the way for Wilderman?"

"Yes."

"That was impressive work," I said.

"It was hard work," she said. "And I'm guessing you're Mathew Kade?"

"Most of the time," I said.

"You're the one who found the murderer of the Farmer's daughter?"

"True."

"They say you're bat shit crazy, over in Wilderman's Zone."

"Used to be," I said. "A little less so, now."

She nodded.

Wilderman was the head of the Zone where the Obsidian Corporation had its headquarters. When I left that place, I wasn't in the greatest shape, mentally. Several people had taken offense at some of the things I took with me, and it had been ugly. It was seventeen years ago and still people remember me in Wilderman's.

"What sort of trouble are you into?" Bella asked.

"Kidnapped girl," I said. "Started with a shopkeeper. Sold her out to a Caravan Master who had a deal with the Clowns to hold her until the ransom was paid."

"Had?"

"He can't make deals anymore," Wilson said. "Hard to do that with a bullet in your brain."

"I see," she said. "So, now the Circus?"

"I need to sleep before I go deal with the Clowns," I said. "My place is not too far away. I'm on the edge of Steiner's."

"Probably a good idea," Wilson said. "We traveled all night last night. I can report to Teresa, as well."

"Then let's get to it," I said.

"If you could use another person, I would join you," Bella said.

"Clowns don't bother you?" Wilson asked.

"They are a disgrace."

"Yeah," he said, "but a damn scary bunch."

"Yes."

"You're welcome to join us if that's what you want," I said. "But this may get real ugly before it's done."

She nodded. "It's the least I can do after you removed the guards from around Polk."

"So be it."

We walked south toward Steiner's.

In all honesty, I wasn't looking forward to a confrontation with the Clowns. Right after the Fall, the Circus sprang up. It was a place where you could buy anything your black heart desired. If you wanted to shoot another person, one would be provided for the right amount of money. If you wanted to hunt someone down, someone was provided. If you wanted to have sex with a child, one was provided. Any twisted thing a person could think of could be bought at the Circus. It was a twisted abomination with occupants who should be in an asylum. And the Clowns were the guards. They were a fierce group of twisted bastards who would almost give the Knights a run for their money, one on one.

Problem was, there were about forty or fifty Knights of the Society of the Sword. There were close to a two hundred and fifty Clowns. They followed a core group of Clowns numbering thirty. Those thirty were some of the toughest bastards in this fallen city. Their numbers were why they haven't been eliminated before.

I hated Clowns.

"Any plans on how to go about this?" Wilson asked.

"I'll do some thinkin' about it tonight, and we'll see in the morning," I said. "I'm thinkin' a straightforward approach would be best. We need information from the bastards. You can buy anything from the Clowns. If they refuse, well, that's when we have to get creative."

"From what is known in Wilderman's," Bella said, "the Clowns will respond to money."

"That's what I'm countin' on," I said.

We reached Steiner's without incident.

"I expected another attack before we got here," Wilson said.

"And now you're not disappointed at the outcome, are you?"

"Oh my god, I'm startin' to think like you," he said. "Teresa should put a warning label on orders when they send us out to be in your general vicinity."

"Careful," I said, "you'll hurt my feeling."

"Feeling?" Bella asked. "You only have one?"

"Yep, and he's hurtin' it."

She just shook her head.

We approached an Old World building.

"Used to call these banks in the Old World," I said.

"I'm familiar with the term," she said.

We pushed through a door that used to be glass and crossed a large room filled with rubble and trash.

"Nice place ya have here," Wilson said.

"This is just the nice part," I said and opened a door on the left side of the room. Across the room was a huge metal door. "This used to be the bank vault."

I worked the dials on the vault door and swung it open. The inside was pristine. I motioned forward to my companions.

"Welcome to my home."

As they passed me, I entered and pulled the vault door closed. As the door clicked closed, lights turned on.

"You have electricity?"

"Made a deal with Steiner a long time ago. I run my place off his Scraper, and I mount the solar system on his roof. It's mutually beneficial so he had no problem."

On the other side of the Vault was a wooden door. I led them through it and we descended a set of stairs that turned back and forth down under the city. They ended in a small hallway with another door. We exited into a huge room with concrete floors and walls. They were very old walls except for two that filled huge, round holes at each end of the massive room.

"Is that an old subway car?" Bella asked.

In the center of the room was a train car. It was a luxury car from a train.

"I'd love to take credit for building this place, but it was mostly done before I found it. It belonged to Allen, the former Warlord. When Steiner took this Zone from him, he didn't even know this place existed. So I collapsed the tunnel from the Scraper to here and moved in. I did put the stairs in and made the new entrance in the Vault."

"Where's that door go?" Wilson asked.

He was pointing across the huge room to the reinforced metal door at the head of a set of concrete steps.

"Goes to the Tees," I said. "The tunnels that open on the sewer system."

"Why do ya even leave this place?" he asked. "Climate control, electricity, I bet you even got runnin water."

"Yep," I said. "Even a water heater."

"Oh my," Bella said. "Hot, running water?"

"The baths are that way," I pointed to the back corner where I had erected some of the partitions from an old place they used to call Chinatown. The material was a sort of paper stretched between frames of wood. I had found it interesting. The paper had crumbled, so I used white fabric I found in an Old World hotel.

"Do you mind if I use them?" she asked. "I haven't had a hot bath in so long."

"Go ahead."

She headed to the back with her pack in hand.

"This place is amazing," Wilson said. "Wonder how many of these sort of places are scattered around the city?"

"I've only found the one," I said. "Although I have found a lot of caches scattered around."

"Always wondered how you always had coin."

"Found a lot of that over the years."

I hung my coat over a fork of a coat rack I had found in an old building. Then I loosened the buckles and removed the knife harness. There was a lot of blood on my shirt and a jagged hole where the bullet had ripped it, so I threw it in a trash can by the door.

I entered the kitchen and opened the cooler. I pulled out a pot, carried it to the burners, and left the pot of stew sitting there to heat up.

"A good meal and a night's rest before we hit the Clowns."

"You expect a fight tomorrow?"

"You know what I expect."

"We're all gonna die while the Clowns dance around us, naked?"

"That fits," I said. "I can't think of anything much worse."

"Humph."

"Indeed."

"That smells delicious," Wilson said. "What is it?"

"Stew."

"I smell carrots."

"Yep."

"Where the hell did you get carrots?"

"I have a small garden box on the roof," I said. "Bought some seeds from the Farmers last year. I sometimes can my own foods instead of trading the jars back to the Farmers. Just something I enjoy when I'm not on a case."

"That's a handy skill."

"True," I said. "I don't like to be completely dependent on the Farmers. I'm slowly building my own stores up."

"You think there'll be trouble with the Farmers?"

"At some point, there will be," I said. "They have too much power. It's just a matter of time 'til something breaks. You'd be smart to work toward the same independence."

"Teresa said something similar a few weeks ago."

"Have you ever met the Stead holder?"

"Nope."

"He's seventy years old," I said. "His rules are what the Farmers live by. How much longer do you think he'll live? When he goes, I don't like to think about the odds of getting another like him in charge."

"I see your point," he said. "What if they end up with a Blechley? Or a Polk?"

"Exactly."

"I think the odds are pretty good that the next Stead holder will be much like this one," Bella said from behind us. "I'm sure he is grooming his successor."

"That hasn't worked so well throughout history," I said. "Usually the successor who was given his rule is corrupted by the fact it was given to 'em."

"What history would that be?"

"Pre-Fall. Human history," I said. "You can hope for the best if you want, but prepare for the worst."

"He believes in expecting the worst so he's never disappointed," Wilson said.

"That's a sad view on life, Mister Kade."

"That's what I said," Wilson added.

"And you live your life in disappointment," I said. "For instance, you thought you would be the next one to use the bath. And now you're disappointed."

I headed for the back to soak in the hot water.

There are a few moments of peace in this Fallen World.

* * * * *

Chapter Eight

I awoke refreshed to hear Wilson snoring. My bed was in the train car, and I heard him snoring on the sofa outside the car. I shook my head and eased upright with a twinge of pain from the bullet wound in my side. It wasn't as bad as many of the wounds I'd taken in my life. There were scars all over my body from the various ways people had tried to kill me.

"Damn!" I heard Bella say from the door to the other half of the car. "You've been through the mill."

"Years of rough living," I said as I pulled a new shirt around my shoulders. "Could be worse."

"How's that?"

"Coulda killed me."

"I guess you have a point."

I pulled a pair of socks from a drawer and sat on the bed. I pulled the socks up and grabbed my boots.

"Where do you get all these things?" she asked. "That is an Old World set of drawers."

"Came with the place," I said. "Allen really made the place nice before Steiner killed him. I've added a few things, but mostly just useful things. I don't really care about the luxury. It was here when I got here so I'll use it."

We exited the car. The snoring stopped, and Wilson sat up.

"That may be the best night's sleep I've had in years," he said. "I see why Teresa likes you now."

"The bath would be enough," Bella said. "I'd have your babies just for that."

I laughed. "You're both welcome here anytime."

"Don't make promises like that," Bella said. "I'll never get back to Wilderman's."

"Teresa might get mad if you stayed here," Wilson said. "She's staked a claim on Kade. At least now we know why."

"Who is Teresa?" she asked. "You've mentioned her several times."

"Teresa Manora."

"The Teresa Manora?" she asked. "Matron of the Society of the Sword?"

"That's her," Wilson said.

"I take that back then," she said. "No babies for you. I think I'll be heading back to Wilderman's after helping you. I'm not pissing off that woman for the whole city."

"I can see that," Wilson said. "She ordered me to back him up, and I'm about to go face the Clowns rather than disobey her."

I chuckled.

"She likes puppies."

"Jesus, Kade," Wilson said. "I've seen her dogs. They're some sort of mutated breed. They're big as horses."

"She likes big puppies," I said with a shrug. "But they're puppies, nonetheless."

Bella laughed.

"What say we eat some more of that stew before we go?" Wilson asked. "What kind of meat was that? It was really good."

"You probably don't want to know," Bella said. "I've had rat before."

"That was rat?"

"Yep," I said.

He was silent for a second, "What the hell? It was the best rat I've ever eaten. Should I get it out of the cooler?"

I laughed, "Yeah. Let's eat well before we leave. We're all probably gonna die anyway."

"Aren't you just a ray of sunshine," Wilson said.

"Expect the worst…"

"Shut up."

"You're doomed to a life of disappointment, Wilson."

"That's ok," he said. "I think I can live with the disappointment. I'll keep my hopes, thank you very much. Now pass me some of that rat stew."

We left by the same route we had entered my house, and we once again headed west into the next zone. It was run by a man named Devin. He pretty much kept to himself but there were usually some cutthroats around his zone at night. We were traveling during the day.

"Should be fairly easy crossing Devin's," Wilson said.

"Probably get ambushed."

"Just keep those sorts of things to yourself, Kade," he said. "I don't need your negativity."

"Sure," I said. "But I just want ya prepared for what's about to happen."

"Ah, shit."

"Yep."

"Did we forget to tell you about the huge bounty on Kade's head, Bella?"

"I don't remember hearing anything about bounties," she said. "I'm assuming this group of bravos are here to collect?"

"That would be my guess."

The leader of the group of twenty stopped in front of the rest.

"Mathew Kade!" he said. "I'm about to collect… Gack!"

"What was that last?" I asked.

He made a gurgling sound. It's hard to speak with a knife sunk four inches in your throat.

He tumbled to the ground and those around him were standing with their mouths hanging open.

"Hell with this!" I said and my hands began snatching knives and throwing them. Eight were down before any could even react. Arrows began to sprout from several. Wilson had drawn his sword but decided to hang back as the missiles kept flying.

Three managed to flee down an alley.

I walked out to the moaning group and retrieved my knives which I cleaned on their shirts and sheathed them.

"Interesting conversation that was," Wilson said. "A little brief, don't ya think?"

"I'm tired of trying to talk these dumb asses out of tryin'," I said. "Gettin' rid of idiots helps strengthen the gene pool."

"So why did I run through a zone and a half yesterday?"

"They had guns."

"They weren't very accurate with 'em," he said.

"You're just mad cause you had to run."

"Well, yeah," he said. "What's that sort of thing gonna do to my reputation?"

"Not as bad as sitting there with your thumb up your butt while we handled this bunch."

"I took care of most of Corso's bunch," he said. "You owed me one."

"That's how it is?"

"Boys, boys," Bella interrupted, "don't you think we should move along before we have to answer a bunch of questions?"

"Probably right," I said. "Come on ya big baby. I'll try not to make ya run anymore."

He sniffed and sheathed his sword.

I laughed.

We continued on our way after I stopped and retrieved a revolver from the leader.

"What are the odds?" I asked. "It's the same caliber as the other one. I could be a gunslinger."

"That's a pretty good name," Wilson said. "You make that one up?"

"Kids these days," I said. "Pre-Fall stuff."

"Figures."

I shoved the pistol into my waistband. Another might be handy.

We headed south as Devin's guards passed us heading north in a hurry.

"Late to the party," Wilson said as we continued on.

"Typical," I said.

"There is a great deal of chaos in the central city zones," Bella said. "Wilderman keeps his zone under control for the most part."

"They say Kathrop keeps hers under control, too," Wilson said.

"She does," I said. "Been there a few times. Difference from the local zones and hers is like night and day. Steiner's is probably the only one that's safe to travel at night, locally. Kathrop has a booming nightlife. There are some incidents, but she comes down on the culprits like a hammer."

"Maybe I should visit there sometime," Wilson said. "Would like to see a place where people walk around at night without bein' attacked by cutthroats and bravos."

"You should visit Wilderman's, then," Bella said. "He has much the same sort of control over his zone. They don't have the party nightlife that Kathrop has, but it's safe to travel, night or day."

"It would be an interesting place to visit," I said. "But you'd get bored in a week when no one picked a fight, and then you'd have to come back home."

"Maybe I'd like to settle down."

"Wilson, people like us don't settle down," I said. "Maybe, what we can do, is make a situation where others might be able to."

"That's what the Society stands for," he said. "It's one of the first things they teach us when we get there."

"Teresa is good people," I said. "She had a rough time after the Fall, but she's tryin' to make a difference. Maybe it's time for a difference."

"Comin' up on Franco's zone," Wilson said. "He shouldn't be a problem. He spends most of the time hiding in his Scraper from the Circus freaks. I think he's just waitin' for the Circus Clowns to come and absorb his zone."

"Heard about the last time the Circus expanded," Bella said. "They crucified anyone who objected to the merge."

They had lined the streets with crosses and stakes. Half had been crucified, the others were impaled on the stakes. It's a horrible way to die, and it instilled a terror of the Clowns that does the work for them now.

"Figured the Circus would keep expanding 'til they meet something to stop 'em," I said. "They run into the Society if they expand north. I expect 'em to go south when they try to grow again."

The streets were quiet. Which, in a normal zone would be ominous, but here the day was quiet. The night was when all the freaks came out. Franco may have been the Warlord of the zone, but it was in name only. His zone was already run by the Circus. He just didn't realize it.

"You see that?" Wilson asked.

"Yeah."

At the corner of the Scraper stood a Clown, almost as big as Wilson. His face was painted a ghastly white with a huge red smile painted over his mouth. Once this paint was a sign of joy and fun. Now it instilled terror in those who looked upon them.

We strode past the Clown toward the Circus. His eyes followed our progress and he pulled a two way radio from his colorful shirt.

"They know we're here," I said. "At least we won't have to hunt 'em down."

"I'm so relieved," Wilson said.

"Joy," Bella agreed.

"When we get to a meeting, Bella, stay as far back as you can. These guys are fast. If you shoot, shoot at one that's not lookin' at ya. If they see it they'll catch it or bat it aside. They're that fast."

"Gotcha," she said.

"Wilson," I said, "if it comes down to a rumble, use the length of that blade. Don't let 'em in close."

"Right."

Clowns began to enter the street from the south. All of them painted and wearing brightly colored clothes. The weapons didn't look bright or colorful. There were swords, clubs, massive hammers, and several guns amidst the thirty-eight Clowns that arrayed themselves in front of us.

"Looks like we're a few Clowns short of the Circus." I giggled.

Who said you can't laugh a little in this Fallen World.

* * * * *

Chapter Nine

"Mathew Kade," one of them said and stepped forward.

"Blinky?" I asked. "Is that you?"

The Clown chuckled. "Most people just start screaming. I think I like you."

"Oh, look," Wilson said. "You've made best friends with a Clown."

"You, I don't like."

"I'll try to contain my disappointment," he said.

"Told ya," I said. "Now you're disappointed again."

Wilson let out a long sigh.

"I've got questions to ask you, Clown," I said. "If your boy gets any closer behind us, he's gonna have a bad day."

A slight frown crossed his face and a minute shake of his head stopped the large Clown we had seen on the way through from moving any closer.

"Nothing is free at the Circus."

"Then I'll swap question for question."

"We deal in script," the Clown said. "But there are some things I would like to know. Deal."

"Maddy Hale," I said. "What happened?"

He grimaced.

"I already know you have a deal with Drekk to hold his victims until ransom is paid. What happened to the girl?"

"She disappeared in transit from Golon to the Circus. We lost two of our agents in the process."

"She was never here?"

"Question for question."

I nodded.

"You worked for Obsidian. Rumor has it you were in the imprinter when the nukes dropped. Is this true?"

"Yes," I said. "She never made it to the Circus, so where did they disappear?"

"Their path would have been Simms, Overton, Jeffreys, Kort, Dozet, and here. Dozet never saw them, Simms did. It happened in Overton, Jeffreys or Kort's zone."

"Is it true that multiple imprints dropped in your head and drove you crazy?"

"Yes. How do you know about what happened at Obsidian?"

The change of my questions set him back a little. He figured he would get more about the girl. I had enough for that but his knowledge of Obsidian bothered me.

"The majority of what you see here are imprinted. Corporate Guard."

"Are you trying to piss me off, Clown?" I asked in disgust. "How does a Corporate Guard become this…abomination?"

"I'm going to treat that as a single question," he said. "We're doing our job."

The job of a Corporate Guard is simple. Protect Corporate Heads. The ramifications of what the Clown had just told me were ominous. One or more Corporate Heads were behind the Circus.

"How many imprints did the machine dump in you? Are they accessible?"

"I'll also treat this as one question," I said. "Also the last question. It dropped the database. Now, I'll give you a warning."

His eyes had narrowed.

"You tell your boss that I said he or she is a disgrace. They were part of a civilized world, there's no excuse for becoming...this," I said. "Pray your path doesn't cross mine again; the next time I come to the Circus, I'll burn it down. In answer to the last question, yes."

He took an involuntary step backwards. He knew a lot about the imprint database. Enough to be scared.

"You're gonna take that shit from this piece of..." A voice came from the left edge of the group of Clowns.

"Shut that idiot up, Funboy!"

Two Clowns closed on the outraged Clown. He snarled and grabbed his knife with amazing speed and hurled it.

I caught it and hurled it back. The two Clowns closing on the knife thrower caught his limp form as he sank backwards with his own knife handle jutting from his right eye.

"You want to dance this dance?" I asked, staring out of the dead eyes of someone else. "We can dance right now."

"Back off, guys," the Clown said. "Kade and his companions are leaving."

"Smart choice, Clown," I said with a smile that made the man flinch.

We turned east and walked away.

Kort was the closest zone to where we were, so that's where we were going. We walked almost the length of the zone before Wilson said a word.

"I've never seen anything like that, Kade," he said. "Clowns don't back down, ever. What the hell were you talkin about? Imprints, databases? Who the hell are you, Kade?"

"Old World shit, Wilson," I said. "I'm just a leftover from a dead civilization."

"What's an imprint?"

"Old World tech," I said. "There were worse things than Clowns, back then."

"I still can't believe they backed down," he said. "I expected to die right there."

"See, you're not disappointed at the outcome," I said. "That's what I've been sayin' all along."

"See what I have to put up with?" he asked Bella. He was getting his composure back.

"You could leave," she suggested.

"Then Teresa would probably cut me up in tiny little pieces."

"I guess you're just doomed," she said.

"What excuse do you have?" he asked. "You can leave anytime."

"And lose the chance to use that enormous bathtub again? I think not."

"That *was* pretty nice," he said.

I chuckled and continued into the territory of a Warlord named Oliver Miz. He owned a single block with one Scraper. He was harmless, He spent his days fretting over which of his neighbors was coming to swallow his territory. Franco, Tully, Dozet, or Xeno.

"The first thing we have to do is spread out and ask questions in Kort's zone," I said. "They would have been a small Caravan with closed wagons. The prisoner or prisoners would have been hidden from sight. May have been as small as one wagon and guards. Shoulda asked what sort of group it was while questioning the Clowns."

"We could go back," Bella said.

"No, thank you," Wilson said.

"Probably not an option," I said. "I made a promise."

"Yea, I heard that," Bella said. "I've got matches."

"It's a blight on this city," Wilson said. "Which is saying a lot, as screwed up as this city is."

"The Circus's day will come," I said. "We have enough to find what happened. We just have to ask questions. And keep an eye out for more of Blechley's bounty hunters."

Miz's zone was busier than Franco's. But there were no Clowns on the street so people weren't hiding wherever they could. The Clowns were known to be mean, twisted freaks. No one was safe when the Clowns were on the streets.

"No reason we should start askin' questions before Kort's zone, is there?" Wilson asked. "Do you trust the Clown's information?"

"Actually, I do," I said. "They lost men so it would benefit them to learn where the threat is. And for a bonus, they get to send us in first."

"I'm not sure if I'm happy doin' the Clown's work," he said.

"Me neither," I said. "But we're doin' my work, not the Clowns'. I wouldn't give one shit about their men if our girl wasn't a victim, too. It would actually serve the bastards right to lose men when they do things like this."

We turned south and crossed into Dozet's zone. There were still plenty of people out in the streets but there were a lot more bravos leaning on walls or signposts.

"Keep your eyes open," I said. "More of the unsavory sort here."

"None of 'em want any of this," Wilson said. "I think the body count over the last few days has begun to trickle down."

"I see a lot of 'hell no' comments on their lips," Bella said. "Reading lips is one of those handy skills I picked up."

"That would be a handy skill," I said.

"It's useful."

"When we hit Kort's, we should split up. We need to cover most of the zone, and it would be quicker if we split," Wilson said.

"I'll hit the Scraper," Bella said. "I spend a lot of time with that sort in Wilderman's."

"I'll take the bars," Wilson said.

"Alright," I said. "I'll work the street."

"Sounds good," Bella said.

I saw a fruit stand beside the Scraper and turned that way. I pulled a quarter from a pocket and smiled at the lady behind the counter. She saw the coin, and her eyes widened.

I normally don't deal with the vendors from the Scrapers. I'm not interested in giving money to those that already have it, but I needed bargaining power on the streets of Kort's zone. This would buy more good will than Old World coins.

I left with a fairly large sack of apples and pears. There were some plums and peaches in the mix as well. I was guessing there was a small orchard on top of one or more of the buildings in Dozet's zone.

We crossed into Kort's without incident.

"Meet back in two hours on the other side of the zone," I said. "We should be able to find anything if it happened here by then."

"Sounds good," Bella said and headed straight for the nearest of the two Scrapers in Kort's.

Wilson nodded and headed down the street toward a ramshackle building built near the mouth of an alley.

I walked down the center of the street. After I passed the Scraper, I began walking near the right side. There was an old woman sitting near a stoop to one of the smaller buildings. She looked wary as I closed the distance between us.

I reached into my bag and pulled an apple out. I handed it to the woman.

"Hello, Gran," I said. "I need some information. I'm not from this area, and I wondered if you might know the best place to find out what's been goin' on around here."

She pulled a small blade from her side and sliced a small piece of apple. She ate the piece with a look of joy.

"You should talk to Rega," the woman said. "She sets up shop down the alley behind the next building. She hears more than any of us considering the particular thing she sells."

I chuckled, "I'm guessin' it's something most men tend to look for."

I saw her favoring the right side of her mouth as she chewed the apple. I reached back into the bag and pulled out a soft plum.

"Much obliged, Gran," I said and handed the softer fruit to her.

I stood up and walked onward, down the street. I may have gotten lucky. One of the most informed people in a zone would be the one who provides pleasure.

I rounded the corner and headed down the alley. There was a large building that opened on the alley. It was six stories tall and by no means a Scraper. But the one who owned it wasn't considered poor, either. The door was flanked by two large individuals.

"I'd like to speak to Rega."

"She's not seein' anyone," the larger of the two rumbled.

"It's important," I said. "Ask her to see Mathew Kade."

I flashed an Old World coin and the smaller of the giants eyes widened.

"I said…"

The other interrupted him. "I'll check with her."

He turned and entered the door. I stared at the remaining guard, and he stared at me. I pulled an apple from my bag and began eating it. His eyes followed the apple.

"No fruit, lately?" I asked.

"Not 'til the Farmers come back through."

I threw him an apple. He looked at me with suspicion, and I just shook my head. Generosity isn't a common thing. I had almost finished my apple before the guy returned. He stopped and whispered something to his partner. The partner had a flash of disappointment cross his face but he nodded. They both started into the street toward me.

The expression on my face hardened, and I set my bag down. They charged, and I stood up with a pistol in each hand. Two shots thundered in the alley and a wound blossomed in the forehead of each man. The backs of their heads exploded onto the wall they had been standing before.

"Two more, Blechley," I muttered.

I set my bag of fruit behind a crate that sat on the corner of the building and loaded both pistols. One went in the holster and the other in the waistband. Drawing my straight razor from its small pouch, I stared at the door a moment.

Then I kicked it in. The door slammed inward, and I was through it in a flash. There was a man with a club just inside, and I flashed by him. He toppled over as my razor crossed his abdomen. I ducked under the arms of the next one and turned to pull his head back. The razor snaked out again to cross his throat.

Then I was moving again. I rolled forward as a sword flashed over my head. My razor flashed out, once more. It sliced across the inside of the man's leg, severing the Femoral Artery. There had only been three in the hallway. Standing at the other end was a woman who had been quite beautiful in her younger years. She still had some of that beauty but the life she led had been rough on it.

"Rega, I presume?"

She was staring in horror at the toppling bodies of her men. I stepped forward three steps and stopped. I closed my razor and placed it in its pouch. I cocked my head to the side as if I was listening to someone.

"I see," I said, and my hands flashed. The pistols came up and I fired through the doors on each side of the hall as I stepped forward. A shot boomed from the left but it hadn't been pointed at the door any more.

The muzzle of the right pistol touched her chest and pushed her backwards to the door that she had stood in front of. She gasped as the barrel burned her flesh.

"Time for us to talk."

"Please don't kill me."

"Don't beg," I said. "If I was planning on killin' ya, you'd be dead."

"Anything..."

"I'm gonna ask you some questions, you're gonna answer 'em. Then I'm gonna hurt you for costing seven men their lives."

There was a look of sheer terror on her face. Terror is a high commodity in this Fallen World.

* * * * *

Chapter Ten

Bella and Wilson found me sitting on a stoop near the border of Kort's zone and that of Moreau. No one goes into Moreau's zone and comes back out. It's like some black hole that sucks in anyone who goes in. The only ones who do are the Farmers. They don't talk about Moreau's zone.

"Found out where it happened," I said.

"Have anything to do with the gunshots I heard?" he asked.

"Maybe."

"Figures."

"I saw a local Madam brought into the Scraper with a large piece of wood through her shoulder," Bella said. "Looked like a table leg."

"I don't know what you're talkin' about," I said, "but I learned that the Clowns were hit in Overton's."

"The shoulder, eh?" Wilson asked. "That sounds familiar."

I just looked at him.

"I'm just sayin'," he said.

"So... Overton's?" Bella asked.

"Yeah, he's a couple zones to the north," I said. "He's a mean bastard. But he's not stupid enough to hit the Clowns. If it had been him, the Clowns would have already been in and killed everyone."

"That sounds about right," Wilson said.

"Then we need to go to Overton's and see if we can find out who it was that hit the Clowns," Bella said.

"That's what I'm thinkin'," I said. "We need to go north through Jeffrey's zone."

"Jeffrey," Wilson said with distaste. "He's a bastard. A Slaver. The Society really doesn't like this guy, and he doesn't like us."

"Think we can make it through Jeffrey's without you pickin' a fight?" I asked.

"Yeah, but I don't know about whether we can get through without him pickin' a fight."

"That's his funeral," I said. "He picks a fight he'll deserve what he gets."

"I'm guessing it involves something broken and shoved through his shoulder," Bella said. "I'm detecting a pattern."

"Don't know what you're talkin' about."

"Yeah…sure."

We headed to the north. Jeffrey owned two Scrapers and a small plot that used to be a park. He grew a lot of his own food and didn't rely as heavily on the Farmers. But it also gave him an attitude. Plus his booming slave trade. He wasn't a blight as severe as the Circus or Derris, but he was indeed another of those blights on the city.

It was like the city got a little more dark and dirty as we crossed into Jeffrey's. It was more of a psychological darkness. We didn't speak as we strode up the street toward the first of the Scrapers. This was the one Jeffrey lived in. The other housed his slave auction. People came from around the city to buy and sell their slaves.

If the girl hadn't been held by the Clowns, Jeffrey would have been number one on my list of suspects. He would rather bathe in acid, though, than piss off the Clowns. They were one of his best customers. The various twisted shows the Circus put on for the rich and depraved needed a supply of people to feed through that grinder.

I still had a hard time seeing Corporate Guards as Clowns. How far the mighty had fallen. In the old days, Guard was the best job slot an Agent could get. Protect the Heads. They rarely traveled, so the Guards were home most of the time.

The skills Clowns had for battle were so much easier explained with the fact that they were Guards. There weren't many who could match a Corporate Guard.

"There are a few, though," I muttered.

"What was that?" Wilson asked.

"Nothin'," I said. "Talkin' to myselves."

"This place disgusts me."

"The world would be a better place without such as this," Bella said.

"Very true," I said.

"So far so good," Wilson said.

"We'll get hit."

"Damn, Kade," he said. "Just once, look on the bright side."

"That just ends in disappointment."

He let out a long sigh. It wasn't hard to figure out why. The busy street was becoming much less crowded as people began darting out of the way of the group of men that approached us. There were easily, seventy-five men.

"Ah, shit," Wilson said.

"Disappointed?"

"Shut up."

The man in the lead approached us by himself.

"Mathew Kade, I presume?" he asked.

He was a tough-looking dark-skinned man. Six feet tall, and he carried several pistols.

"I'm guessin' you're Jeffrey," I said.

"True," he said. "The Clowns sent word to me you were on the way in this direction."

"Guess they caught your interest with the bounty?"

"No," he said. "Oddly, the advice I got from the Clown was to help you in any way I can. And under no circumstance should I attack your party."

He fell in beside me as we walked north.

"Really?"

"If it had just been anyone telling me this, I wouldn't think much of it," he said. "This came straight from a Clown, a high-ranking Clown. Clowns never preach caution, and I felt it would behoove me to listen when one does."

"That is a little surprising," I said. "What are your intentions?"

"I intend to escort you through my zone to the next one," he said. "There should be no misunderstandings, this way."

"Did the Clowns tell you what I am investigating?"

"No they didn't."

"They're probably embarrassed," I said. "Several days ago they had a group of their agents escorting a wagon with various captives toward the circus. Someone hit that group. Everything disappeared. One of those captives is a girl I have been hired to find."

"I can see why they wouldn't advertise something like this."

"The thing is, Jeffrey," I said with dead eyes staring into his, "if you had a hand in this, we're gonna have a conflict of interests. People don't tend to survive those conflicts."

"Number one," he said, "and I'm pretty sure you've already figured this out, I wouldn't hit a Clown's agent for all the script in the world. My guys are tough as leather but the damn Clowns are monsters. Anything like that happened in my zone, I would know. I keep apprised of the groups traveling my zone."

"My information says it happened in Overton's," I said.

"That's not all that surprising," he said. "Overton isn't much. He sits in his Scraper while chaos reigns outside of it. I can tell you one thing."

"What's that?"

"This group traveled north through my zone three days back. It never returned through my zone. If it was taken in Overton, they traveled another direction from there."

I nodded. We were nearing the border into Overton's. He stopped, and his men waited.

"Good luck with your hunt, Mister Kade," he said. "I can't help but wonder why a Clown would warn me off about such a small group."

"They want to keep doin' business with you," I said. "They couldn't if you were dead."

"Very high opinion of yourself," he said. "That mildly offends me."

"That's good," I said. "If you're offended, you're still breathing."

I turned from the Warlord and walked into Overton's zone.

"That was different," Wilson said. "First the Clowns, then Jeffrey. Who the hell are you, Kade?"

"Rumors abound in Wilderman's," Bella said. "I never thought I would actually be working with him."

"I'm just a leftover from a world that fell," I said.

My mind wandered back toward the past. The missions, the war, the death and destruction I had left in my wake.

"A world that needed to fall," I added. "We brought the Fall on ourselves. It's not a better world that we have, now. Maybe, in time, it could be made into a better one if…"

Wilson slammed me sideways as I heard the thunder of a gun. His body rocked with the impact but he kept pushing me to the edge of the street. His body rocked again as another shot hit him. Then we were under cover of the wall. I pulled him behind a wagon parked at the side of the street.

The shooter was on top of the building we were against.

"Son of a bitch," he cursed, "bastard got me."

"Looks like one in the leg, one in the side," I said. Something was beginning to boil inside me. I tore my coat from my shoulders and pushed it against the wound in his side. Bella rolled into the spot behind the wagon.

"Look after him," I said.

She nodded, and my eyes went cold and dead. I launched myself toward the wall and upwards, my fingers grasping protrusions where you would think none could be found. Up the wall I scaled. I caught a window sill and launched myself upwards. I shot over the top and made three steps before the gunman even knew I was there. He spun around and my right foot slammed into his chest like a piston. I caught his rifle as it flew from his hands and spun it around. I shot him three times before he hit the ground five stories below.

I wasted no time, and went over the edge to reverse the path I had taken to the top. I dropped from window sill to window sill and landed lightly on the ground below. I reached Wilson.

"How is he?"

"The one in his side is rough. He's not going any farther with us."

"Neither are you," I said. "I'll finish this. You get him to Steiner's and back to the Society. When I'm through, I'll meet you there."

"What about backup?"

"They better get more."

"They?"

"Yeah," I said. "They have no idea what's comin'. And when I'm done, I'm gonna have a word with Blechley."

I handed her a handful of coins. "Hire who you need to get him home."

"Home," he mumbled, "Teresa…kill me."

"Tell her I'll be along, shortly, Wilson," I said. "You saved my life back there. You've done your job. Now it's time for me to do mine."

I should have killed Blechley. For some people, mercy is wasted in this Fallen World.

* * * * *

Chapter Eleven

Rage was still boiling just below the surface as I watched Bella with two guys she had hired to carry the stretcher with Wilson leave to the west. Steiner's was the next zone over so she shouldn't have any trouble. I turned toward the east. Rega had said it was done by some freelancers close to the border with Payne. I strode down the middle of the street and people sidestepped as I neared them.

I stopped as I neared the border. An old man sat on a stoop. He was carving a piece of stone. There were quite a few chips around him so I approached.

"Might you sell me some info?" I asked.

"Maybe."

"Ya been out here for a few days?"

"Been here for weeks."

"A wagon and some guys got hit here a few days ago."

"Saw what happened, I did."

I slipped a coin into his hand. "Tell me."

"Won't do ya no good," he said. "It was that cult, down south. Moreau, his name is. People go in there, they don't come back. If they do its cause they workin' for him."

I nodded, "That's what I needed to know. Take another for your troubles and your silence."

He nodded as I slipped him another coin. Then I turned and walked into Payne's zone. Moreau's was the zone below Payne. I'd never been into Moreau's for obvious reasons. It was unknown whether it was like Derris' or something else. It was rumored to be some sort of cult. If you go into Derris' you'll get eaten. It's unknown what happens in Moreau's if you don't choose to join his cult. People just quit going into the zone.

The skies were darkening from their normal burnt red to black; night was closing in. Perhaps that was a good thing. A little darkness might be just what was called for.

I stopped about halfway down through Payne's when I saw a wagon with a fire and a grill. An old woman was grilling meat on skewers. I didn't bother asking what sort of meat it was. It didn't smell like pork so it was safe to say it wasn't pork or human. That was good enough for me. I also saw some sort of bird on the grill.

"Too small to be chicken," I said, pointing at the bird. "What is it?"

"Pigeon," she said.

"I'll take that and one skewer of the mystery meat."

She laughed but pulled a skewer from the grill along with the pigeon.

"Two script," she said.

I slipped her two of the plastic chits that ended up with the name "script" after the Fall. They were used to buy food from the Farmers and became the currency of choice years ago. There had been one attempt to counterfeit the chits about ten years back. The Farmers placed a permanent ban on the zone. That zone was empty ten years later because the Farmers won't supply that zone again. Permanent ban. No one can move into the area for lack of supplies. Neighboring zones couldn't supply the zone or they would have been banned as well and left to die.

Never pays to mess with the Farmers.

I took my meal over to an empty stoop and sat with my back to a wall. I would need to wait for about an hour to take advantage of the shadows as the sun set. Chewing on a piece of pigeon, I thought about what had to come. If the girl was in Moreau's, she was indoctrinated into his cult or possibly disposed of. It depended on the time it would take to convert someone. There had been ways to brainwash a person before the Fall, and I expected there were some who remembered the techniques.

Most of those techniques were pushed aside with the imprint tech. Obsidian Corporation had been the original developer of the tech but it had spread to the rest of the world fairly quickly. Lots of money changed hands and, suddenly, the world had been a whole new place. Schools were replaced with imprint tech. Who would take the time to learn things, when they could have it imprinted straight into their minds?

Of course, things went sideways. The cost of imprinting was high, so the rich became the educated. The poor learned the hard way. It was discovered that a lot of the education programs weren't permanent. The joke was on them, I suppose. Many lost their imprinted knowledge. It seemed that Obsidian had sold faulty tech to the majority of the world. They, alone, held the permanent imprint system.

Oh, the glory days of Obsidian. This had begun the Corporate Wars. The Fall of the world followed as the nukes rained down. Obsidian versus the World. There were things I had done for Obsidian that made me sigh in relief as the nukes ripped great holes in our cities.

Damned if I didn't survive it. Who would have thought that?

The shadows were deep enough, so I stood and headed south toward Moreau's. I wouldn't have expected it, but I missed the banter between Wilson and me. The majority of my life has been spent alone with the mess that rattles around in my head. Wilson had been a pleasant distraction. I found that I genuinely liked the man. His wounds weren't life threatening if Bella could get him to Teresa.

He shouldn't have pushed me out of the way. I could take the punishment much better than he could. Some of the alterations from before the Fall made me a lot tougher than most. But he had, and when this was finished, Blechley was going to learn a final lesson.

I reached the border and slipped into the shadows of the buildings to disappear. There were people in the streets, just like Payne's zone. But there was a tension in the air. You would think something like that couldn't be seen, but most things like that are visible through something more than sight—intuition, perhaps. The use of all the senses in a passive reading of the world around you. I could feel a sense of desperation in the people who lived along these streets. There were booths set up to sell food or goods, just as any other zone.

I slid, silently through the shadows toward the Scraper closest to the border. There were two, but this one was much larger. I stopped to survey the surroundings.

"You should leave," on older man said from the booth in front of me. His back was to me and he never raised his head from the cookware he was cleaning. "Leave before the Guard finds ya, boy."

"Can't," I said back, softly. "Have to find someone who disappeared into this place a few days ago."

"Ya can't help 'em, boy," he said. "Moreau's got 'em now."

"You saw 'em?"

"It's where any of the young go," he said. "I was too old for his tastes. I was told to sell these and if I tried to run they would kill my daughter. She's in the Scraper."

I was beginning to feel that rage building again.

"They come through the streets every so often with our family members. Just to show us they live. I saw Frea two days ago. She saw me but I didn't see any sign of it. She didn't know me."

I felt a hollowness in my stomach. Something was majorly wrong here. I looked around toward the various people I could see. All were old. None of the people were less than sixty years. Where were the others?

"I still have to find her," I said.

"A girl?" he asked. "A red head?"

"Yeah."

"It's a pity. She was a beauty. They're hard on the beautiful. Ugly and you can still be a Guard. The beautiful are for one thing inside the Scraper."

That hollow pit stayed in my stomach.

"They'll catch ya, son," he said. "But I'll wish ya good luck, anyway. Maybe ya can get her outta there."

"Thanks for the wishes," I said with the rage touching the surface. "But if they catch me, they'll wish they hadn't."

"I hope you're right, son," he said. He never lifted his head, and his eyes never left his work.

I slipped along in the shadows toward the Scraper. When I reached the side of the Scraper, I scaled the wall to the third floor, where I found a sliding window that wasn't locked. I was inside in seconds and found an empty room with a bed.

The door opened, and I backed into the shadows. The door closed, and a light came on. A pretty girl of about fourteen stood there looking at me with a throwing knife in each of my hands.

She didn't even blink. I saw no fear, no surprise. Her eyes were filled with adoration.

"May I please you?" she asked as she slipped her loose white robe from her shoulders.

Something ugly twitched inside me. I had seen that look before. This wasn't brainwashing, it was much more sinister. I had seen this tear our world apart once. Moreau had an imprinter and my mission had just become a great deal more than just saving a single girl.

"No, thank you," I said.

Tears sprang into her eyes and I shuddered in rage.

"I'm not pretty enough," she said.

"You're beautiful," I said and saw her tears slow. "And I would love for you to please me when I return. I must go for a while and finish my job. Wait for me here."

The smile changed her face to radiance, and I knew that Moreau would suffer this day.

I had lived the imprints of thousands. This was worse than the rape of a body. This was a rape of the body, mind, and soul.

I walked openly out the door and down to the lobby where I knew there would be Guards.

"Take me to your Warlord!" I yelled as I entered the lobby. "He can't just steal my wife and not face me!"

The Guards closed and I put up a token fight, bloodying a nose or two. If Moreau had recovered some of the lost imprint tech, something would have to be done. What better way to find it than to get an escort.

There are things that should never be recovered in this Fallen World.

* * * * *

Chapter Twelve

I was dragged to an elevator and pushed inside. Five Guards joined me, and one pushed the button for the penthouse. Old World or new, they always wanted to be at the top.

"My wife..." I muttered.

"Shut up," one of the five commanded as he backhanded me.

I restrained myself. Not yet.

The elevator stopped, and I was pushed out of the small compartment into a lavish suite. They dragged me toward an extremely obese man who sat on a throne of sorts. It was a huge, padded chair.

"Who might this be?" he said. I could see his jowls shake with the movement of his mouth.

"He claims to be searching for his wife."

Laughter rolled from the fat man.

"Then, by all means, let's reunite them!" he said. "What is her name?"

"It's Maddy," I said, "Maddy Hale."

He bellowed his laughter, again. "The new one? Oh. This is going to be wonderful!"

He pointed to one of the men, "Bring the new girl to me!"

The Guard left and was gone for a few minutes. He returned, followed by Maddy Hale. She was in one of the white, flowing robes.

"Maddy!" I yelled.

"May I please you?" she asked me.

The fat man bellowed his laughter.

"Come here, girl!"

She turned and almost ran to him.

"This is what is going to happen," he said with an evil glint in his eyes. "First, we're going to strap you into this machine."

He pointed to a chair with straps that had a helmet hanging above it.

"Then your little darling, here, is going to service me right in front of you. Then she is going to service all twenty-five of my Guards."

He waved his arms, indicating the twenty-five Guards in the penthouse.

"Then we are going to turn on the machine, and you are going to come out of it with your only waking thought being to pleasure us. Then you will take your turn and service each and every one of us."

I decided it was the perfect time to call in the reinforcements.

My head sagged for a second then I stood erect with the guards around me.

"No. This is what's going to happen. In ten seconds, I am going to break this man's arm. Then I'm going to incapacitate all of your Guards, from the right side of the room to the left. I'm not going to kill them because they are victims, just as much as she is. And when I'm done, I'll deal with you, Tubby."

"What the hell?!" he exclaimed. "Who are you!?"

"Just consider yourselves lucky," I said to the Guard on my left. He was the one who had backhanded me. "Be happy he didn't send Gaunt. My name is William Childers, Obsidian Special Forces."

I snapped the arm of the man on my left. Stiffened fingers sank into the one on the right and he toppled, trying to draw a breath. My elbow punched the side of the next one's neck hard enough to drop him into unconsciousness. I span around and put stiffened fingers into pressure points on the other two that left them paralyzed. They toppled backwards.

This had taken two and a half seconds. I spun again and launched myself forward toward the ten guards on the right that were just realizing something was happening. I had put down four more before the first gunshot boomed in the room.

I felt a tug at my leg but ignored it and ripped the gun from the hand of the man who had just shot me. I threw it and it slammed into the throat of his partner. Then I dislocated both of the man's arms as I twisted them backwards with a pop.

I moved on to the next. His shot went wide as my foot sank into his solar plexus. He was done. The next three took stiffened fingers to pressure points.

I heard the guns and felt the tug of another hit in my side. I didn't slow down. I was among the ones on the left and they would have trouble shooting me without hitting their friends. The guns still fired and three of them fell from friendly fire. I felt the bullet go through my shoulder just before I throat punched the last man.

I turned to Moreau who cringed.

"Time for a change of regimes, fat man."

I dragged the blubbering Warlord from his throne and over to his own imprinter. I strapped him in and dropped the helmet down. A vacation printer. I felt a swell of relief as I saw what type of imprinter it was.

These had been used to give someone a month of being someone else. The imprint would fade. He'd been re-imprinting whenever it was running out. I flipped the switch on the side and Moreau's begging stopped. I raised the helmet.

"May I please you?" he asked.

I turned to the Guards and retrieved my weapons then I returned to Moreau. I unstrapped the former Warlord from the chair. There was a mark tattooed onto his arm so I drew my razor and cut it from his arm. He cried.

I walked to one of the Guards I had paralyzed. I hit another pressure point and showed the Guard the mark I held in my hand.

"Master?" he asked. "Orders?"

I pointed at Moreau. "Doctor his arm and chain him to the wall. His sole purpose is to pleasure every Guard in the Scraper. He will do this every day. You will make sure it is done."

"Yes sir."

I looked at Maddy Hale who stood beside the throne with a blank stare.

"May I please you?" she asked as I approached. I showed her the mark.

"Master," she said with complete adoration.

"Come with me," I said.

"Will I be pleasing you, Master?"

"Not yet," I said. "Soon."

I returned to the imprinter and removed several parts, including the limited database. All that made it work was removed, and I placed the parts in my pockets.

I led Maddy to the elevator, and we descended to the third floor where we returned to the room I had left the girl in.

"Master," she said "May I please you?"

"Come with me," I said.

She followed along and we descended to the lobby.

"Orders?" the first Guard asked as he saw the mark I held out.

"Gather every guard in the zone and report to the penthouse. Orders will be awaiting."

Moreau was in for a hell of a month. All of his men would deprogram before he would. They would retain the memories. He may survive that, he may not.

The girls followed me out of the Scraper. We walked north up the street. I stopped at a stand that sold cookware. The man looked up from his work. I handed him a flap of skin with a mark on it.

"Show this and no one will interfere with you," I said. "Go find your daughter."

"I can never repay you son," he said.

"Use that wisely," I said. "Stay away from the penthouse. There will be a chapter of the Society of the Sword moving in here. Give that to the leader and go…or stay. This zone is changing. May be worth watching."

"The imprinter?"

He was old enough to remember the imprinters.

"Destroyed."

"Who are you, son?"

"Mathew Kade."

"I'll remember it," he said and turned away. He almost ran toward the Scraper.

"Alright girls, let's go."

"Will we be pleasing you?"

"Soon enough," I said.

We walked out of Moreau's zone to the astonishment of those inside of Payne's zone. No one approached. They stayed out of my way. It was the first time I had ever traveled at night that I didn't have to defend myself. We walked, unharmed through Payne's, then Overton's, and on through Steiner's to the warehouse that was the home of the Society.

The guard at the entrance recognized me immediately.

"Kade," he said. "You're bleeding."

"I'm ok," I said. "They're not."

He chuckled.

"I need you to take these two ladies to Teresa," I said. "I have some unfinished business to take care of.

"Protect them," I added. "Especially from themselves. You'll understand in a minute."

"Will do."

"Girls, go with him."

"Will we be pleasuring you?" they asked simultaneously.

"I see."

"Tell her it's imprint tech. It'll fade, but they'll need help when it does."

"I will."

"Wilson make it back in?"

"Yeah," he said. "Too stubborn to die, anyway."

"True."

I nodded at the Squire and strode back into the night. There are more than just blights in this broken place. Sometimes there are beacons in this Fallen World.

* * * * *

Epilogue

Simon Blechley awoke with a start. There was a wetness on his face. He reached out and turned the lamp on beside the immense canopy bed. He looked up to see the canopy sagging as it dripped on his face.

He wiped his hand across his face and it came away red. He started to scream just as the canopy split and the heads of all of his lieutenants cascaded down over him.

His screech was cut short as a hand seized his throat.

"Hello there," a voice whispered to him. "I don't think we've been formally introduced."

"K-K-Kade?"

"Not today, Simon," the voice answered, "Stephen Gaunt, at your service. We have so much to talk about."

* * *

I walked across the floor to the vault I had built into the solid concrete of the platform. I turned the dials to open the vault door. I pulled the various pieces of the imprinter from my pockets and lay them on a shelf. Then I took the database from another pocket and placed it on a shelf with the other five.

Some things never should have been created and never should be where people could get to them.

I left my vault and began to doctor the wounds I had received. The quick healing from the alterations was a great boon to someone in my line of work.

Perhaps I would soak in the huge tub for a while.

* * *

K ade had been on her mind a lot lately.
SSWWSSSHHH
Too much for her comfort.
TTHHSSSSS

Kade. How was he still alive? Especially after the last days. And why did it even matter to her? But it did, didn't it?

SSHHAAPP

The head of the practice maniq went flying as she twisted the katana blade at just the right moment. She didn't stop moving as the sword came back around and ended up in the scabbard at her side without seeming to slow from the killing stroke. She loved the katana. It had been her mother's before the Fall and rested in a place of honor with its twin when not on her side or across her back. She placed it in the wooden wardrobe and closed the dark-grained door with a smile. For some reason, the thought of Kade gave her the same feeling as the thought of her mother. Well, not exactly the same, she thought with a wry grin.

"One of my weaknesses," she said quietly, "of which I have far too many."

A throat cleared across the room, and she came back to full realization of her surroundings and out of the heightened awareness of the fight. While in the practice session, she felt and saw everything around her. She had felt Poe as he came up to the door and patiently stopped to wait for her to finish the bout. She had immediately dismissed him as a threat and continued on to contend with the maniqs that attacked her from the floor and ceiling. Seven this time, a good workout coming right after the half hour of parkour training in full armor.

"What's up, Wilson?" she asked the big man. He was recovering from his wounds nicely.

"You have a visitor from the Tee's, ma'am." Poe rumbled with head bowed.

The Tee's were a tunnel system that ran beneath a large part of the city. After the bombings that led to the Fall, it had been blocked off. That was the story that everyone believed. The Society of the Sword knew better. She had known of the system for several years now and had dealt with the Mardins that inhabited the dark damp labyrinth. She did an occasional favor for them and provided certain foodstuffs they had no access to, and they provided information and safe passage when needed—when it did not endanger their secrecy.

"Must be important for them to send an emissary above ground. Any idea what it's about?" She leapt effortlessly up from the sunken training area, plucking a damp towel from the rack on the way.

"No, ma'am. Only that it was of interest to you and that you would want the info immediately."

"Well, let's go see what's so important," Teresa Manora, Matriarch and absolute leader of the Society of the Sword said with a small smile. "Maybe they want a chapterhouse opened there."

"That's possible," he said. "Nothing would surprise me after Blechley's one remaining lieutenant came in asking for a chapterhouse when he couldn't find all the pieces of his boss. But I think it's unlikely since I don't think Kade has a beef with the Tee's."

"Blechley deserved it," she said. "I swear, Kade's like a great big cat. He brings what he thinks are gifts to my doorstep."

"Sounds about right," he said. "We have four decent sized zones to run, now. Kinda makes you wonder what will happen when he goes on another rampage."

"Who knows?" she answered as she approached the door to the meeting hall and motioned for Poe to enter. "Shall we?"

* * * * *

Broken City

Chapter One

I heard the mechanism begin to turn on the vault door, and I was moving. Not many people know the combination to my home, and I was going to be prepared if it wasn't one of those few.

I recognized the light step of Teresa and sat back down in the huge armchair that the previous owner had graciously left for me. The straight razor slid back into the pocket where it usually rested. I winced a little as I twisted and stretched the skin around the latest bullet wound.

Gettin' sloppy, boy, Childers chided at me from inside my head. *Need to exercise more.*

And the tacos? Stephen Gaunt's precise voice asked. What were you thinking?

"Quit squawkin'," I muttered, "both of you."

Teresa Manora stepped through the door from my entrance and looked at me with an eyebrow raised.

"Arguing with yourselves?"

"They're givin' me a hard time about getting shot again."

"I happen to agree with them," she said.

I'm not even sure why Teresa has anything to do with me. I'm bat shit crazy, and she's probably one of the most powerful people in the central city zones. Not to mention beautiful and one of the best users of the katana she carried I had ever seen.

Her blonde hair was pulled back in a ponytail so as not to impede her vision, and she wore black body armor that couldn't disguise the curves underneath. The light step was silent as she glided across the floor toward me. Any noise she had made was for my benefit as she had entered.

I stood back up, and she was in my arms, our lips connecting. We stayed like this for some time.

I took a deep breath as we parted and looked toward the train car in the center of the huge room.

"Unfortunately," she said after a long sigh, "I came with another purpose in mind, this time. Although we might be able to get to that a little later."

"Promises, promises," I said. "So what, besides my charming personalities, has brought your lovely self to my humble abode?"

"Don't speak in Gaunt speak," she said. "It's disturbing."

I chuckled.

"The Mardins have sent an emissary to me," she said. "They have a problem and wanted my advice about how to handle it. I suggested they hire you for a job. I came to see if you were healthy enough to take on a case so soon after the mess with Moreau."

"It's possible," I said. "Depends on the job."

"Investigating a string of murders that run from one end of the city to the other."

"Gotta love a good old-fashioned murder investigation."

"They are particularly vicious murders," she said. "If you want to take the case I'm sending a few Squires down to assist you."

"I almost got Poe killed, last time," I said. "You sure you wanna send more?"

"Blechley almost got Poe killed," she said. "And I understand he's a bit torn up about it."

"True enough."

"If you're interested," she said, "the emissary is still at the Chapter House."

"Yeah," I said. "I think I am."

"Then get dressed and let's get this show on the road."

I chuckled and entered my train car. There were two large rooms to the train car. I had them both set up as bedrooms. They were lavish rooms since they were built before I had taken over the place. The former Warlord had built it before Steiner had killed him and taken his Scraper. Steiner hadn't known about the secret getaway so I had taken it.

I took my shirt off and unbuttoned my pants. Teresa's hands slid around my waist.

"On second thought," she whispered in my ear, "I think they can wait a little while."

Our lips met again when I turned around, and we surrendered to the moment and tumbled into the huge bed. We lost ourselves in each other for a time. Both of us have memories of terrible things we have done and terrible things done to us. But we could forget all of that for a while and just be together. Perhaps that's why she stayed with me. She found someone who was even more broken than she was.

We lay there looking at the ceiling, afterward.

"How the hell did you do that?" she asked.

"One of me is a very high-priced Courtesan," I said. "She knows all the right spots."

"She?"

"Not all Agents were guys," I said. "I got the whole data base."

"How many are there, really?"

"I don't know."

"Must be a hell of a thing."

"Not so much, anymore," I said. "The Kade persona pretty much took over. The rest took a back seat, and they all gain from the life experiences as we go. It's a jumble sometimes, but we all get along well now. We've had seventeen years to get used to each other since the royal rumble in my head found a winner."

"So that's why you know how to do so many things," she said.

"Yep. If you need somethin', I got an app for that."

"App?"

"Never mind," I chuckled. "Old World humor."

"Figures."

"I think a bath would be nice before we go," I said. "Care to join me."

"You didn't think I would come to your place and not use that enormous bathtub, did you?"

"You just use me for my appliances."

"My secret is out," she said and kissed me quickly.

She slid out of the bed and walked out of the train car. I thoroughly enjoyed watching her do that. I enjoyed the bath even more.

Despite the fall of civilization as we know it, there are times when I realize it's ok to have a moment of joy in this Fallen World.

* * * * *

Chapter Two

I took a new shirt from the closet and a new trench coat. My last one had taken a lot of abuse. I had several because the one before that had been mostly destroyed as well.

There was a lady who traveled with the Farmers who made them for me. Every couple of months, she would bring me a new set of clothing. She always tried not to charge me but I would always insist. She was the mother of a young girl who had been raped and killed. I had found the person responsible for it.

Teresa came back in the bedroom carrying the harness that held my weapons.

"You should use body armor," she said.

"Restricts my movement," I said.

"Yeah, yeah."

I slipped the harness over my shoulders and buckled the straps. I had added another holster to the harness to hold the second .44 I had picked up during the last case. There were some different guns in my vault but the six shooters were good weapons. Ammo was hard to come by, so it paid not to have an automatic. By the time I had shot twelve times, they would be dead or close enough that I would need the blades. There were twelve throwing knives made of Old World metals and the ever present straight razor I had used for years.

I went to the cabinet and took several sacks down and put them in various pockets. I opened one.

"Jerky?" I asked and held the bag out to Teresa.

She pulled a couple of pieces of dried meat from the sack.

"Do I want to know what kind of meat it is?"

"Nope," I answered. "It's not human. That's all you really need to know."

She shrugged and tore a chunk off with her teeth.

"Not bad," she said, after chewing a moment. "Not too hard to chew, either."

"There's an old Survivalist in here," I said while tapping my head.

"Survivalist?"

"Old World," I said. "We're all Survivalists now. He knew how to make good jerky."

"You sure you're up to this?"

"I heal quickly."

"Poe's gonna be pissed that he gets left out of this one," she said.

"He'll get over it," I said. "I almost got him killed last time. He should be tryin' to stay away from me."

"He was doing his job, Kade."

"I should have killed Blechley the first time I dealt with him," I said. "Instead, there's a hundred or so people who died because of that damn bounty."

"You can't retrain Humans to be Human if you kill them all," she said. "You tried to give him a chance. That's something you should do. I'm not saying to let it go on and on, but a chance to be a Human again should be there."

"You make my choice sound noble," I said. "It wasn't. I thought it would be fun to see what happened."

"That's what you tell yourself," she said. "I know better. I've seen who you are, Mathew Kade. Sure, you have all those people inside of you, but I've seen you walk the streets and give to the poor. I've seen you help the helpless. You were paid to find Hap, not walk in and take on a whole Zone to free him. You did that because you couldn't let what was happening continue. The same with that girl, Maddy."

I snorted as I opened the vault door to leave my home.

"You still think you're that guy who worked for the Obsidian Corporation," she said. "He did some terrible things for people who didn't deserve the service he gave. You may not see the changes in yourself, but those of us who have watched you over the last ten years have seen it."

"Hmph."

"You keep telling yourself what you want."

We walked out of the old bank building. There were people in the streets. Some were operating small stands. Across from the bank was a shack where the sound of a hammer on metal sounded a rhythm as Soba plied his trade as a blacksmith. We had lost a great deal in the Fall. Factories used to do what Soba did and much more. Soba made several things. He used light metals to make bowls and plates, heavier metal to make some tools and weapons.

I walked over and stepped into his shop.

"Kade!" he said as he saw me. "It is good to see you, my friend."

"How are ya, Soba?"

"Doing well after the contract you got for me with the Farmers," he said. "I never thought I would be making horse shoes."

"True," I said. "Not a lot of horses in the city."

"I still am amazed they would give me the contract when the have their own blacksmiths."

"I've seen their guys," I said. "They have three good blacksmiths. The youngest is nearly sixty years old. They use apprentices to do most of the work, now. You're lucky you spent the time before the Fall doing the Fairs and things. You've got ten times the experience of the apprentices, and you're better than at least one of their main guys. I wouldn't be surprised if you didn't land a lot more work from 'em in the future."

"You don't say?"

"You might even look into some apprentices now to be prepared."

"I don't have the script to work apprentices, yet. Perhaps after this contract is filled, I can."

"I know some people with a little script," I said. "I've been talkin' to a few and they would like to do a little investment. Would you be interested in that?"

"How big of a bite would they want of my business?" he asked. "I don't want to be stuck working for someone else, here. I built this forge."

"Ten percent," I said. "They'll provide the script to get your shop moving and to support apprentices and guards. They want a little input on the contracts. Not much, just suggestions. Ultimately, the business is all you. They may be able to steer some contracts your way."

"And you vouch for these people?" he asked. "If you trust them I would be willing to do it. But, only if you trust them."

"I trust 'em."

"Then my answer would be yes, my friend."

I reached into my right coat pocket and pulled out a sack of coins. I extended it to a wide eyed blacksmith.

"You were that sure of my answer?" he asked. "They sent script with you?"

"This will get you a start," I said. "I'll be your go between with these folks, and we'll talk more later on. I have a case at the moment, and it's gonna take me out of the zone for a bit."

"Jesus, Kade!" he said as he looked into the sack. "There's a lot of script, here."

"Just a start, Soba."

"I'll hire some guards, first, I think."

"I would suggest a couple of Squires from the Society."

He looked in the sack once more, "Yeah, I think so."

"Two will be on the way over in less than an hour," Teresa said from behind me. She had been quiet throughout the whole conversation.

Soba's eyes widened even further when he saw her and realized who she was.

"Ma'am," he said with a respectful nod.

"All right, Soba," I said. "I'm off, and you'll have guards very shortly. Keep that under wraps until they get here."

"That I will do, my friend."

"Tomorrow," Teresa said, "I would like to see you about a contract for a few weapons. If you have the time to meet me."

"At your convenience, ma'am."

"Perhaps early," she said. "So it won't interfere with your work day."

"Gladly, ma'am," he said. "I'll be here at sun up."

"Agreed."

We exited the shop of a very excited blacksmith.

"Investors?"

"Yep."

"I saw you get that sack of coins from your vault before we left."

"Hmph."

"Yeah, you're a bad guy. Keep telling yourself that."

"Yeah," I said. "How big is the weapon contract you're after?"

"We need some basic short swords for the novices to start with," she said. "Perhaps a hundred or so."

I chuckled.

"He'll have a heart attack," I said. "Break it to him gently. That's more weapons than he made the last year."

"He's good, isn't he?"

"Oh yeah," I said. "There's not many better. The Farmers have two, and Wilderman has one who's great. Soba is probably number four in the whole city on quality."

"If he's that good, there'll be more after that."

"He is."

"Then he'll do well."

We walked up the street toward the building that housed the Society of the Sword. It had been a large building of a modest ten stories but it had covered a great deal of space. Teresa and her folks had built defenses around the building and had done a lot of remodeling inside. She had close to two hundred inhabitants who lived on the premises. Close to a hundred of them were novices who had come to learn how to defend themselves. Most of those were poor, but some were from wealthy families in the Scrapers. The Society had grown a great deal in the last five years. They hadn't opened other Chapter Houses until recently though.

People traveled to her compound to become part of the Society. If they passed her vetting process, she would start their training.

When a person graduated as a Knight of the Sword, they were one of the toughest fighters in our broken city. Knights traveled the city when they chose to, and they sought their own path after leaving the Compound to start their life quest.

Teresa had taken a lot from the medieval history I had imparted on her. Knights and Quests, something most people don't know anything about from before the Fall and long in the past. She tried to form her Society with the best of those things and discard the worst.

Teresa would train almost anyone in basic skills to survive in this fallen world. Some would take the Oath of Allegiance to the Society and become Yeomen. These would train for a future as a Knight. The wealthy paid to have their children trained, and Teresa trained the less fortunate for other fare. Some would work the compound as cooks, cleaners, and such.

"Ma'am," the sentry nodded toward Teresa with respect.

His eyes met mine, and he nodded toward me. "Kade."

"Michael," I said. "How's the wife?"

"She's the same as always," he said. "Crazy."

"They're all crazy," I said with a grin.

"Some are crazier than others." He chuckled.

"True enough."

Teresa looked at me with one eyebrow raised.

"What?"

She shook her head and walked through the gate. I shrugged and followed. As we made our way toward the center of the building, we passed many of the inhabitants of the Chapter House. All looked to Teresa with the utmost respect. You don't get that sort of respect unless you are something pretty special.

Considering the hell she went through right after the Fall, it's amazing she could become the person she is today.

I saw a familiar face and stopped.

"Maddy," I said.

She had been walking down the hallway with her head bowed. She hardly ever looked into someone's eyes.

She saw me, and the expression on her face went from sadness to wide-eyed joy. She ran straight to me.

"Kade!"

I hugged the girl who had been captive of the Warlord, Moreau.

"How are you holdin' up, girl?" I asked.

"So much better, now."

She noticed Teresa and nodded to her. "Ma'am."

"I never got to thank you for what you did for me, Mister Kade," she said, turning back to me. "I only got free of the imprint a few days ago. The Matron has been helping me accept what happened and grow from it. She is an amazing person."

"I know," I said. "Have you seen your father?"

"He's coming tomorrow," she said. "I'm so scared of what he'll think of me."

"He'll think he's too happy to have you back than to judge you for what you had no control over."

"I hope so," she said.

"Have you given thought to taking the training courses, here?"

"I have," she said. "If Dad is ok with it, I want the training. No one is going to make me a victim again."

I saw the smile on Teresa's face at the girl's words. She would make sure the girl knew enough to protect herself.

You're only a victim if you choose to be in this Fallen World.

* * * * *

Chapter Three

Teresa had a conference room where she met with future clients who wished to hire the Society for various jobs. I saw a pale man sitting in one of the chairs around the large round table. He wore dark lenses over his eyes. I recognized the form of dress. I'd met some of the Mardins when I built the escape tunnel from my home. They live in the Tees, the tunnel system underneath the city. Below them was the sewer and they kept the system working in return for people from above staying out of their territory. Occasionally they would hire some from above to work in the Tees, but never very deep.

I nodded to the representative. "I understand you would like to hire me for a job?"

"You come very highly recommended, Mister Kade," he said. "I have been told that you are a very good investigator."

"I've investigated a few murders over the years," I said. "Found a few items, recovered a few kidnappings. What can I do for you Mister…?"

"Fraans," he said. "There have been a series of deaths in the Tees. We are at a loss as to who is behind them. We would like to hire you to find the one responsible."

"To be clear, when I find this guy, do you want him alive to face charges?"

"We want the killings stopped," Fraans said. "If you bring him to us alive, we will charge and execute him. If you kill him, the killings stop. Either way is fine with us."

"What can you tell me about the murders?"

"They are particularly violent," he said. "I have pictures of the latest one."

"Pictures?" I asked. "It's been a while since I saw anyone who had a camera."

"You would be surprised at what is found underground in this city."

"Not really," I said. "I've seen some pretty odd things up here. The Tees having all sorts of things from the old world doesn't surprise me at all."

Fraans nodded and pulled a briefcase from beside his chair and set it on the table. He opened it and pulled a small stack of photos from the case and slid them across the table to me.

I winced as I saw the first one. There was blood everywhere. Pools and splatter. The body was that of a woman. She was pale like Fraans and, from what I could tell, not much older than Maddy Hale. I'd seen many cuts in my life and these weren't cuts. She had, literally been ripped apart. The amount of strength to do what damage had been done was staggering. This wasn't a normal killer. I would have thought it a group if not for the next picture.

There were footprints in the blood. But it was just one set. I thumbed through the rest of the pictures.

"Ok," I said. "I'll take the job. Twenty-five thousand script. Payable when the job is done. I don't find him, you don't have to pay."

"Very high," he said. "But the part where we don't pay if you fail to find the killer is unusual. Most people want their script up front.

What would happen if you did a job, and the client decided not to pay? The job would have been done already."

"Ask Blechley, he crossed me. Ask around."

He chuckled. "Just playing the devil's advocate, Mister Kade. I am well aware of the recent events. And events that aren't so recent. The deal is more than fair. You will have full access to our territory during your investigation."

"I need a map of the Tees," I said. "I have a map of the city, but not the Tees."

"We will have an escort for you…"

"I don't intend to get lost down there if our escort is gone for any reason."

He nodded. "Understood. I wouldn't like to be lost above ground in unknown territory."

"Alright then," I said as I stood up. "You get the map, and I'll get my supplies ready."

He nodded. "Thank you, Mister Kade."

"Save that for when I find this guy."

Fraans stood and nodded toward Teresa. "Thanks once again, Matron."

"It is the least I can do." She stood and shook hands with the Mardin. "Your people helped a poor outsider when no others would. I haven't forgotten."

He nodded and left the room.

"That's where you hid after The General?" I asked.

"Yes."

"I had wondered," I said. "Figured you'd tell me someday."

"It was a dark time," she said.

"I'd say so."

She stepped close, and our lips met again.

"I'll go get Michael and Lindsey," she said as we separated. "I'm sending two Squires with you."

"That could be interesting," I said with a chuckle.

"Shouldn't be boring." She laughed.

She walked out of the room, and I sat back down to look at the pictures again.

See the marks on the torso? The voice in my head belonged to Samuel Gladson, a former homicide detective. *Those are claw marks.*

"Some exotic weapon or somethin' much worse," I muttered.

I saw something like this before the Fall. Be careful.

I could see what he remembered in my head and suspected that the detective was probably right. They hadn't caught the killer back then. The killings stopped when Gladson had gotten too close. If it was the same guy, this fallen world was the perfect hunting ground for him. There's no telling how many deaths he'd caused in the last twenty years after the Fall. The city was fractured into all of these mini kingdoms and someone could slip through the cracks much easier than in the Old World.

"What are the odds this is the same guy?" I muttered.

I'd say, pretty damn good.

I stood up and pushed the photos into an inside pocket. Leaving the room, I headed down the hallway to the armory. I wanted some bullets for my pistols. The Society kept one hell of an arsenal.

As I turned a corner I almost ran into a human wall.

"Wilson," I said. "How's the leg?"

"Getting better," he said. "I hear you're takin on another case. The boss won't let me come."

He looked disappointed.

"You probably won't fit in the tunnels anyway."

"That's a nice new coat, there," he said. "Be a shame if somethin' happened to it."

I laughed. "Wish you could come, big guy. Instead I get the Tanziks."

"Serves you right," he said with a laugh.

"Expected as much," I said. "So I'm not disappointed."

He laughed again. "Maybe I got that backwards. Maybe it serves them right."

"I have no idea what you're talkin' about."

"Hmph."

"Got anything new in the armory?"

"Funny you should ask that," he said. "I have somethin' that will probably help in the Tees."

I followed as the big man turned and led the way to the armory. He didn't limp as badly as I expected. Wilson was a healthy guy, and he healed pretty fast from the shots.

We entered a room with weapons in every corner and in racks set up along the center. There were swords, axes, daggers, hammers, clubs, and a cabinet in the far left corner with guns displayed inside.

Wilson led the way to the cabinet and opened it. He pulled out an old automatic pistol with a long magazine. On the end of the barrel was a silencer. I hadn't seen one of these since the Fall. I didn't even have one in my vault. He handed me the pistol.

"Nice," I said.

"It's got a sixteen-shot magazine," he said. "It's a nine millimeter, and I have three boxes of rounds for it. All yours for the small price of your eternal soul."

"They don't call me a soulless bastard for nothin'."

"I thought I might be too late for that," he said.

"How about if you give it to me, I won't tell your boss you're tryin' to sell her stuff?"

"Sounds fair."

"I think we have a deal." I removed a holster from the case that looked like it was made for the pistol. Looking closer, I saw the brand of auto. It was a Sig Sauer, a very good Old World gun company.

It took a few minutes to get the holster attached to my harness, but it would be a handy asset in the enclosed space of the Tees when I would need a gun. The boxes of shells I added to the pockets of my coat.

"Keep addin' weapons to that arsenal and you won't be able to move," Wilson said.

"Probably right," I said as I twisted to test movement. "Better leave the other two here."

I removed the two .44s and the holsters from my harness. I twisted a bit, and it felt much smoother.

"I hate to admit it, but there is such a thing as too many weapons."

"I know how hard that was to admit," Wilson said. "Now if you were a little bigger you could carry that and a five foot piece of steel on your back with little effect to performance."

"Yeah but you're such a big target. You get shot more."

"You cut me deep, Kade."

"Did I hurt your feeling?"

"I'm devastated."

"I'll try to live with the guilt."

"Hmph."

I just stared.

"I see how it's gonna be," he said. "Got any ideas about these murders yet?"

"Yeah, I got a couple thoughts on it," I said. "But I need the map of the Tees before I can really tell."

"Pretty brutal," he said. "Even for this screwed up world."

"Saw something like it before the Fall," I said. "They never caught the guy, back then. There were some pretty horrible people back then. I know, cause I was one of 'em."

"I think you're too hard on yourself," he said.

"Got a lot to atone for."

"If you say so."

I heard voices in the hall outside of the armory.

"Can't protect the boy from everything," a man's voice said.

"I'll damn well protect him if I want to," a woman's voice answered.

"You know what it's like out there."

"He's four years old!"

"Never too young to start learning," Michael said as he opened the armory door.

"Get this straight, Tanzik," Michael's wife, Lindsey said. "There will not be a sword in that boy's hand until he's at least twelve."

"But…"

"That's all I'm saying on the subject."

Michael grunted.

Wilson looked at me and laughed aloud.

"Shut up," I said.

He laughed again. "Good luck, buddy."

He turned and walked out the door.

"What do you think, Mathew?" the small woman asked. "Shouldn't a child get to be a child before we start hammering him with training?"

Michael Tanzik was about average in height and weight, being a couple inches less than six feet tall. Lindsey barely reached five feet. She had flaming red hair and the temperament to go with it.

"I thought that was the last you were goin' to say on the subject," he said.

"Is your name Mathew?"

"Nope."

"Then I was talking to someone else."

"I told you," he said as he looked at me. "She's crazy."

She pointedly ignored Michael and looked at me, waiting for an answer.

"Kids do learn quicker than adults…"

"So now you're ganging up on me," she said. "I'll go get Teresa, and then we'll…"

"On second thought," I said, "I believe I should stay out of this one."

"Probably a wise choice," Michael said.

"Hmph," she said and turned away from us to start looking for ranged weapons.

"We're in tunnels," Michael said. "Cramped spaces."

"Shut your pie hole, I know what I'm doing."

"Only pie shuts my pie hole."

"My foot in your ass will shut it too," she said from across the room.

"You can't kick that high."

"You really don't want to find out, dear."

He chuckled and took a pair of short swords from a rack. They resembled what I remembered as a gladius like the Romans used. I think one of my personalities was a history professor.

"These should do nicely in a confined space."

"Should," I said.

Lindsey had found a compact crossbow with a quiver full of bolts. She took them and moved down to a rack of blades. She picked a pair of long daggers. They were not much shorter than Michael's swords. They each donned sheathes and belts then sheathed the blades.

"May want to stock up on some travel food," I said. "No tellin' how long this is gonna take."

Lindsey nodded, "Maybe I can find some pie to shut his hole with."

"If you're lucky."

"Traitor," he said to me.

"Crazy is ok, buddy," I said. "But crazy with weapons…hell no."

"I see your point."

"I'm right here," she said.

"Wasn't there some kind of medication in the Old World for it?"

"It went pretty quick after the Fall when they couldn't make any more."

"I guess the supply got very limited after that," he said. "We just have to make allowances nowadays."

"I'm right here," she said again.

"Maybe we can find some sort of natural remedy," Michael said as he walked out of the armory with Lindsey.

I laughed as the door closed behind them. People will always be people, and some things still haven't changed so much in this Fallen World.

* * * * *

Chapter Four

Fraans returned after about three hours, and I met him again inside the conference room. He had brought a rolled up map with him.

"I need you to mark the places where all of the killings took place," I said as I rolled out the map.

He pointed to a spot on the map of tunnels.

"This was the first one," he said. "It was pretty gruesome, but death is common in the world we live in."

I marked a red x with a brush. "What I wouldn't give for a sharpie."

"A sharpie?"

"Old World stuff," I said.

We lost a lot of the little things that make life easier in the Fall. Now we used things like the old stylus pens of the ancient days with ink bottles, or we use brushes and paint. If there had been any markers and pens left, they had dried up years ago.

Fraans looked at me strangely, then pointed to another spot on the map. "This is the second one we found, although it was an older killing. The room it had been done in was off the beaten track. Seldom visited because of the location."

I painted an x on that spot as well.

"This was the third we found," he said, pointing to another room in the tunnels. "This is where we began to be alarmed. Death is common, but this was something else."

Another x and I was seeing something, or rather, Gladson was seeing something.

"Two others have been found since then," he said. "One here, and another here."

He pointed the spots out as he spoke, and I marked them with x's.

"We Mardins pride ourselves with being more civilized than the surface dwellers," he said. "It pains me to think one of our own is this brutal."

"All civilizations throughout history," I said, "have had their psychopaths. But I don't think this is one of yours. Look at the spacing of these murders."

I moved to our right and unrolled a map of my own. It was a map of the city. It was an old world map that I had added boundary lines of the Zones I knew.

"The first was here," I said, pointing at the zone above the first crime scene. "Then, here… here… here… and the last one, here."

"They're scattered all over the place," Fraans said.

"I think he is moving across the city. If you look at the zones, you see the oldest happened in Krell. Krell is a semi-safe zone. Then he moves up to Platis. If he had headed straight east, there would have been Royles, and it's a no-go zone. So the choice is north or south. He is living in these zones for a month or so and moving on. Platis is pretty big, and the second one was way to the north of the zone. Now he turns east, the next three zones to the east are pretty chaotic. So he travels through and sets up in Morgan."

I pointed to the third murder, right under Morgan's zone.

"Now, Morgan is also a semi-safe zone, so he stays his month or so. Then he kills and goes south. North is out of the question. There are three zones there that are perpetually at war. You enter one of these, and you're drafted and put into the meat grinder. You'd think a person could sneak off, but they shoot anyone who tries."

My finger traced south from Morgan's. "Gord is chaotic, so he continues south through Placer and then east to Trilla. He sets up there for a month or so and kills this one."

I pointed at the fourth murder site.

"Here's where it throws a monkey wrench in my theory," I said. "The fifth is in Yarborough. It should be in either Dunn or Gallis. Considering you'd go through Dunn to reach Yarborough, my guess is there may be a scene you haven't found, yet. Or he killed up top that time. Either way, I need to go there and see. If there is, we have a pattern. We can predict where he may strike next and intercept him."

There was a look of respect in Fraans's eyes. "We would never have put that together. Perhaps we need to take more notice of the surface."

"There's too much access to your territory not to take a notice of the surface."

"We are aware of the surface," he said. "We walled off the tunnels under Derris' zone just to your west. They are savages and cannibals."

"It would do your people a service to cultivate the relationship you have with the Society. They're aware of the surface issues and can relay this to you. You have ways of travel that would benefit the Society as safe routes through the city. It would be a mutual benefit, and there is no one better suited for it than Teresa's people. They may even work with your security."

"It has crossed our minds to do something like this," he said. "Years of hiding in the Tees, as you call them, has made us cautious."

"You've already got ties with her," I said. "Wouldn't be too large of a step to go further."

"After this is through, I will bring it to the King's advisors."

"I have to say, it's impressive that you guys have developed such a large territory. You work together where the surface folks constantly fight amongst themselves."

"It wasn't like that in the beginning," he said. "It took ten hard years to unify the Tees. The result was a group of advisors, who used to be individual zone leaders. They report and advise the King, who carved his kingdom with a sword from the chaos that was."

"We could use a little of that up top."

"I understand you have already begun," he said. "I hear that you have brought three zones under the influence of the Society. This might worry the Advisors and the King."

"It wasn't what I set out to do," I said. "They attacked me, and I removed them. The Society can offer safety to the people in those zones, so it made sense."

"Of course it makes sense. It made sense fifteen years ago, when Grady O'Neal rose and took the lead of the Tee that belonged to Mardin. He built from those original Mardins and spread to eventually run the majority of the Tees under the city. There are still some he doesn't run. There are some that are walled off from any way of entering, such as Derris."

"The surface will be much harder to unite," he continued. "There are many more people on the surface than in the Tees. But consider the future if such a thing could be accomplished. Unite this broken city, and it would be a great start to uniting this fallen world."

"I'm no hero," I said. "I was just doing my job. I don't dream of uniting a city. Just surviving it."

"I see," he said. "I wish you the best of luck with your endeavors, Mister Kade. Your guide should be here by now. You wish to go to Dunn?"

"Yeah," I said. "We need to check my theory before we proceed any farther."

"Then I will take my leave, and Portus shall lead you anywhere you need to go in the Tees."

"I'll get this done as quickly as I can, Fraans," I said. "Hopefully we can get to him before he kills again."

Fraans turned and left the conference room.

I looked at the maps for another minute and rolled them up. We'd know soon enough if I was right. I heard the door open again, and a pale man of about five and a half feet walked in. He nodded at me.

"Portus, I'm guessin'?"

"Yes," he answered. "I am at your disposal."

"The first thing we need to do is to go to Dunn."

"Not too complicated," he said. "We have to divert around the area under Derris."

"Fraans mentioned that Derris had been walled off," I said. "Let me get my escorts, and we'll get on our way."

"I will meet you in the basement," he said. "This lighting bothers me greatly."

"I imagine it does."

I followed the Mardin out of the conference room, and we went in separate directions. I made my way to the commons, the area in the center of the Chapterhouse that was open and used for training. That's where I would meet Michael and Lindsey.

"I'm not sayin' I want you to cook," I heard Michael say as I walked out into the commons. "I just want you to learn how to cook a few things."

"What!?"

"There's surviving the Fall, and there's barely surviving the Fall."

"Just what do you mean by that?"

"If we survived on what you know how to cook," he said, "it would be barely surviving."

"Why you old bastard," she said. "Maybe I won't cook anything anymore."

"We'd all be better off," he said. "Little Sammy is probably traumatized already."

"Sammy likes my cooking just fine!"

"Then why does he go over and eat at the Kord's all the time?"

"He's friends with the Kord girl."

"I'm just sayin'," he said. "The boy came home with a sack of leftovers yesterday. I caught him eatin' 'em in the back room."

"He said he wasn't hungry," she said. "Come to think of it, you weren't either."

"He brought a lot of stuff from the Kord's."

"You and he both…"

"Woman can cook a rat's ass and make it taste good."

"You son of a…"

"Hi guys!" I yelled. "Ready to go?"

Michael turned and walked toward me as Lindsey cursed under her breath.

"Sure thing," Michael said with a grin.

The two Squires followed me back into the building and down through the stairwells to the basement entrance to the Tees. Lindsey was still muttering under her breath as we followed Portus through the metal door and down into the dim light of the Tunnels.

"Guys, this is Portus," I said. "Portus, this is Michael and Lindsey Tanzik, Squires of the Society."

He nodded to the couple, who nodded back.

"We're headed to Dunn," I said. "We have to test a theory about the killings. If I'm right we may be able to guess where he hits next and be waitin' for him."

"That would be nice," Lindsey said. "Catch him before he kills again."

"That's what I'm hopin' for," I said. "Let's take it slow through here, Portus. We need to get our eyes adjusted before we do much travelin'."

"Understood," he said. "We'll go slowly until we pass by Derris. You should be ok long before we reach that far. I can inspect the walls as we go. Any Scouts are required to check the walls anytime we are in this area."

"That's understandable," Michael said. "Derris' bunch are savages. They've been pushed back enough times on the surface to quit tryin' to break out of their zone."

"One of these days, someone's gonna have to clean 'em out of there," I said. "Have to wait till Wilson gets better, though. I promised he could go, too."

"Better take more than just Wilson," Michael said with his eyebrow raised.

"They'll probably attack our zone before then anyway since I promised he could help."

"Why would you even think that?"

"Expect the worst," I said. "You'll never be disappointed."

"Poe told us about you," Lindsey said. "That's a pretty crappy outlook, Kade."

"I don't walk around disappointed."

"Yeah, he said that."

Both of them were looking around the area suspiciously.

"What?"

"He also said if you brought the subject up, something bad inevitably follows."

"I have no idea what you're talkin' about."

I heard running footsteps, and my straight razor jumped into my hand. A woman ran from the darkness ahead and saw Portus. She skidded to a halt.

"Scout! They've broken through!"

"What?!"

"They're in the Tunnels! E-Branch!"

"We don't have any forces over here!" he said. "Are the charges still good?"

"Yes, sir," she answered. "We have thirty people down beyond the charges!"

"There's nothing we can do," he said.

"There's somethin' we can do," I said. "We'll hold 'em long enough to get your people out of the area. Then we can blow the charges."

"You would do something like that for us? It is suicide."

"Poe's gonna be so mad," I said. "Get your people out."

I ran straight toward the faint sounds ahead of us. I slowed as we neared the sounds of metal clashing. I could see the metal boxes that held the explosive charges that Portus had spoken of.

"You don't have to do this," I said to my companions.

"We are Squires," Michael said.

Then I heard the scream.

I launched myself down the tunnel system at the fastest speed my augmented body could attain.

I began laughing as I ran. There are worse things than savage cannibals in this Fallen World.

* * * * *

Chapter Five

I saw the branching tunnel the noise was coming from and rounded the corner. I took in the scene as I left the ground to rebound from the wall to slow my speed. A group of pale Mardins fled toward me. The tunnels behind them were packed with half-naked, screaming savages with makeshift weapons.

I palmed the Sig and pulled the slide to load it in one smooth motion. The silencer took most of the sound from the shots but it was still far from silent. The slide sounded and the muzzle let some sound out, still.

I watched as head after head blossomed with the impact of the bullets.

The eighth shot hit the eighth head when Michael and Lindsey rounded the corner. Michael's hands blurred as his twin swords seemed to leap into his hands. He shot forward and leaped over the heads of the fleeing Mardins. He landed with his swords dancing around him. Lindsey was just seconds behind him with her blades flashing.

Wilson Poe was a Yeoman when he had accompanied me on my last case, and he is a deadly fighter. A squire is in another league, altogether, and the savages hit an immoveable wall of steel. As one of the savages got too close to Lindsey, I shot it in the head. Seven more shots and seven more dead exhausted the magazine, and the Sig dropped to the floor.

I stepped closer and my hands blurred as I began throwing blades. The final blade sank into the throat of the last of the savages.

"Wow," Michael said. "He wasn't kidding."

"If you don't mind," Lindsey said to me, "Let's not bring that up again."

"I'm not disappointed," I said. "Are you?"

She looked back at the heap of dead cannibals. "Not at this particular moment."

There were howls from deeper into the tunnels, and I felt something I hadn't in a long time. It was the indignation the righteous feel at the sight of evil. I had been that evil in the world before the Fall. I still wasn't sure what I was in the fallen world. But I knew I would not let this blight upon our city take one more life this day.

I walked forward and let my coat slip off behind me, "If anything comes down this tunnel besides me, kill it."

"What?"

I launched myself forward and dove over the pile of bodies just as the horde of cannibals came screaming into the other end of the tunnel. I looked down for a second and my razor slipped into my hand. When I looked back up, it was someone else's smile on my face.

"Oh, Mathew," Stephen Gaunt said breathily, "you take me to the most wonderful places."

I glided across the tunnel toward the screaming savages.

"Hello, my pretties."

They charged the spot where I had been. Three landed without moving. I had slit three throats with one swipe and rolled to the side. Then I was moving once more into the darkness.

"This won't hurt," I whispered in the ear of a barely human woman. "Long."

My razor slid around her throat from behind as my left hand pulled her chin up. Then I was gone again. The razor would slip out and a Femoral artery would be severed, a set of tendons sliced, a throat cut. The screams of rage became screams of pain. Then screams of terror.

"Don't run, my little darlings."

The Security forces of the Mardins arrived in less than thirty minutes, a very quick response considering the distance they had covered. Michael and Lindsey hadn't come into the tunnel, even after the noise had ended. I understood. Stephen Gaunt can be a bit…well…terrifying. They were still the first in when the Security forces arrived. I think they expected me to be dead since I hadn't come out of the tunnel. I was standing in the center of the broken wall that had been keeping Derris' savages out of the Tees. The whole tunnel was littered with bodies.

"Jesus, Kade," Michael said.

Lindsey handed me my coat and the Sig.

"Thanks," I said.

"Would have been a shame to wear that in here," she said, looking at the mess. "Good choice."

"I thought so," I said. "Wilson already threatened to mess it up. Didn't want to give him the satisfaction of seein' it done."

The Security forces were staring at us with wide eyes.

"Three of you did all of this?" their leader asked.

"He did all this, himself," Michael said. "We helped with the bunch out there."

"One man did this?"

"That's debatable," I said.

"What do you mean?"

"Never mind," I said. "A little Schizophrenic humor."

He looked at me in confusion.

"Just... never mind," I said. "You should have plenty of time to set charges and blast this tunnel without having to blow the other charges. They're not comin' back here anytime soon."

He nodded.

"Have you seen Portus? He's supposed to guide us to Dunn."

"He's standing by the charges, prepared to blow the tunnels if needed."

"We'll go meet him there then."

I walked around the staring fighters and drew the Sig. I ejected the magazine and pulled one of the boxes of shells from my pocket. As we walked back along the path we had taken, I reloaded the magazine with sixteen bullets. The thing had already proven its worth.

"I'm definitely gonna see if Teresa will sell me this," I said. "I love it."

"I had a Sig, before the Fall," Michael said. "Very nice gun. One of the best in its time."

"How old were you?" I asked.

"Twenty-two when the bombs fell. Had done a tour in OCAF," he said.

Obsidian Corporation Armed Forces was where I had begun, as well. But quite a few years earlier. They pulled most Agents from the armed forces. Some of the younger Agents had been pulled from other places. A few were even from prisons.

"I was three when it happened," Lindsey said. "Teresa found me when I was sixteen and pulled me out of a zone in the East. They were about to do some evil things, and she walked in and destroyed the place with three Knights. Well... they're Knights, now. I don't think she had set up anything quite yet. I think it was the next year she started the Society and moved into the Chapterhouse."

I had just moved into my new home under the bank when Teresa had moved into Steiner's.

"Officers told us about Agents, back then," Michael said. "They could be anyone, anywhere, and always on a mission."

"Teresa told us when we became Squires," Lindsey said. "You're at the top of the allies on the trusted list."

"What was the mission when the bombs fell?" Michael asked. "Most of the Agents died, but the few who survived were stuck in the role they were playing at the end."

"I was in the imprinter," I said as we rounded the corner to see an anxious Portus standing under the explosives with a torch ready to light the fuse. "It dumped the whole database into my noggin."

"Holy shit."

"Where are the fighters?" Portus asked.

"Guarding the breach," I said. "You won't be needin' to blow that."

I pointed at the metal encased explosive charge. He pulled the torch away from the fuse.

"I think we can continue our mission but you can check with your boys, first, just to be sure."

He nodded and sped down the tunnel toward the breach. I squatted down with my back against the wall. I pulled a sack of jerky from my coat.

"Jerky?" I held the bag out. Both reached in and took a piece.

"This is what I'm talkin about, woman," said Michael. "If you could learn to make this, our son wouldn't be trying to sneak out to eat at the Kords'."

"You just be careful, you old fart," she said. "I may use arsenic in the next dinner I make."

"Probably taste better," he muttered.

"What?!"

"Nothin'."

"I thought so."

"One of these days…" he muttered.

"Pow! Right in the kisser!" I added.

Lindsey looked at me with narrowed eyes.

"Sorry, Old World joke," I said and laughed. "Used to be a show on TV so long ago…"

I was looking into confused eyes.

"Never mind."

We lost a great deal in the Fall.

"I can teach you how to make the jerky," I said as I started chewing on a piece.

"Don't you even start," she said.

"Just sayin'."

Anything more would be kicking a hornets' nest. Some things truly haven't changed in this Fallen World.

* * * * *

Chapter Six

We sat down and chewed on the jerky for a while in silence. Portus came back around the corner with a paler face than he left with.

"Is his face paler than before?" Lindsey asked.

"I wouldn't have thought that possible," Michael said, "but damned if it isn't."

"Y-you were correct, sir," Portus said. "We can proceed to Dunn."

"Lead on," I said.

I rose to my feet, wincing as the gunshots from Moreau's goons shot a surge of pain to my brain. During the fight, Gaunt had ignored the pain as the adrenaline had filled me.

"You get injured?" Michael asked.

"Just a twinge from the gunshots I got a couple weeks ago."

"Teresa said you'd gone and got shot a couple times."

"Gettin' sloppy in my old age."

"Did you bust anything open?" Lindsey asked.

"Nah," I answered. "Just achy, now. It'll go away soon enough."

"That's what you get for jumping in the middle of a mess like that," she said. "That's what we're here for."

"True, Kade," Michael said. "Teresa will kick both our asses if we let you get all messed up."

"I needed to let Gaunt out to play," I said. "He whines if I don't."

"Gaunt?" she asked.

"One of the personalities from the data base?" Michael asked.

"Yeah."

"You can access them?"

"Most of 'em," I said. "The stronger personalities are the easiest to access. Some of the others are vague but I can draw from their experience."

"That's the damnedest thing I've ever seen."

"Was a little rough for the first few years."

"I imagine so," Lindsey said.

We passed several people as we walked down the tunnels. A pale woman led four children in the opposite direction, and I paused to hand her a small pouch.

"Somethin' for the kids," I muttered and continued down the tunnel. I caught a glance back as we turned into a branch tunnel and saw her giving the kids pieces of jerky.

I kept referring to the map I had seen of the tunnels. I didn't look at the physical map but the one that I had mostly memorized. I had studied the local tunnels closely while looking the map over. So far, it seemed to match what was in my head.

I didn't like being at the mercy of someone else when it came to where I was located. I'd explored the city to a great extent and knew where we were at the moment.

"I'd say we're under Devin," Michael said. "Possibly under Blechley."

"You mean Holden?" Lindsey asked.

"Well... yeah, now that you mention it," he said. "I heard Blechley came to a gruesome end. Know anything about that, Kade?"

"I have no idea what you're talkin' about."

"I heard something about finding him in many pieces," Lindsey said.

"Pinned to a wall," Michael said.

"With all of his parts arranged in alphabetical order," she added.

"He must have done something pretty bad for someone to do somethin' like that," I said.

"Must have," he said.

"Can't say I can feel sorry for the bastard," Lindsey said. "Maybe he insulted his wife's cooking one too many times."

"I doubt it," Michael said. "From what I heard, he had excellent cooks."

"I bet you snuck over there and ate dinner a few times."

"Had to," Michael said. "There's only so many peanut butter sandwiches and noodles a man can eat."

"What?!"

"Damn the Farmers and their peanut butter. I hated it long before the Fall, and I almost forgave the ones who dropped the bombs when there was no more of the stuff."

"You ate it," she said.

"The Kords were over in Wilderman's…"

"You son of a…"

"So, Kade," Michael interrupted, "what was that jerky? It was spectacular."

"The key is in how you cut the meat. If you cut the sinew out and just leave the meat it makes a tender jerky. Even if it's rat jerky. I have some pigeon jerky here, too. Wanna try it?"

I handed him another small sack. He pulled a piece from the sack and bit off a chunk. Lindsey reached in and took a piece.

"Damn that's even better than the other one," she said.

He passed the sack back to me, and I nudged Portus. He turned and reached into the sack for a piece.

"Very good," he said as he chewed the meat.

We passed the sack around as we continued down the dim tunnels.

There was a sound ahead of running water, and Portus rushed forward. We found a pipe with a strong leak around the next bend.

"Oh, this is not good," Portus said. "I have to report this. If you can remain here for a few moments, I will report and be right back."

"Can you report when we get to where we're going?" I asked.

"This is part of the Accords."

"Then go," I said. "We'll be here."

Portus took off at a dead run.

"Accords?"

"Yeah," I said. "The Accords were written up about ten years ago. It was an agreement between the Mardins and the zones above. The Mardins would upkeep the water and sewage under the city, and the zones above would leave the Mardins alone. That's why some folks don't even know who the Mardins are. And they take the Accords very seriously."

"I could see where it would be important," Lindsey said. "If we lost the water up top, there would be utter chaos. No one would be safe. What little order we have in place would be gone in an instant."

"The city would consume itself," I said. "Many people don't know it, but we owe the Mardins as much as we owe the Farmers. Without the Farmers, the city would have self-destructed long ago. Same with the Mardins. I hate to even say it but we also owe Dynamo a great deal for keeping the electricity up and running."

"Yeah," Michael said. "He knows it, too. Although, of the three, the electric is the least important. Much of the city gets by without it. The Scrapers are populated by those who have electric, and it's created an upper and a lower class."

"True enough," I said. "The Scrapers aren't nearly as nice without the power."

"And Dynamo charges a tax for his services. The Mardins and the Farmers don't. They just want to be left alone."

"Worlds of difference between him and either of the others," I said. "We try to make our zones self-sufficient, but, in all honesty, a city can never really be self-sufficient. We'll always be dependent on someone else."

"True," Michael said. "We've got our water towers and solar grids but they would never support a whole zone for an extended amount of time."

"And there's just not enough room to grow enough food for the whole city, which brings us back to the Farmers, the Mardins, and Dynamo."

I heard running feet, and Portus came back into view, followed by three other pale-skinned Mardins. He stopped in front of me.

"We can continue our journey, Mister Kade."

I nodded and followed him again toward the west. The pipes along the walls seemed more important than they had before. We take for granted a great deal in this Fallen World.

* * * * *

Chapter Seven

We continued west under the zone of Jade, a woman who had been part of a criminal organization before the Fall. She had carved out her own little slice of the city almost immediately after the Fall and had held it, successfully, for twenty years.

Next to the west was Paris. This zone had gone through no less than ten warlords in the last twenty years. I expected Jade to get tired of the chaos and move in, but she never made any advances to expand her territory.

The tunnels angled to the southwest for a while and crossed under The Saint's zone. He called himself Saint but he was far from a Saint. He was a cold-hearted mercenary. He had trained soldiers under his command and had expanded three times since the Fall. Perhaps he was the reason Jade had left Paris' zone alone. It was a sort of buffer zone between her and The Saint.

We would almost reach Wilderman's before reaching Dunn. The tunnels all looked close to the same, and I could see getting lost in them very easily. My eye was drawn to the pipes running along the tunnels.

"A lot of patched pipes down here," I said motioning toward a six inch pipe with a clamp around it. "No one knows how close to the edge we really are."

"I saw at least ten of those clamps since we left that leak," Michael said.

"We are ever vigilant, my friends," Portus said. "We live by the Accords."

"I knew of the Accords," I said, "but never really saw how important that one agreement was."

"The life of this city is flowing through these pipes," he touched one of the pipes, almost reverently. "We protect this life with our own."

I nodded to the man.

"We have reached the edge of Dunn," he said. "This area is less populated than some of the others, due to a breach in the tunnels into the sewer below."

I could smell the difference as we neared our destination.

"I need you to organize a detailed search of the area," I said. "If he hit down here, we need to find the scene. I'll go up and see if he hit up top. According to his pattern, there should be a body in this zone."

"The search is already underway," Portus said. "We started as soon as you established a pattern."

"Good," I said. "Where's the nearest surface access?"

"Right this way."

We heard the commotion before we started to climb the ladder. Running feet and several yells.

"May not need to go up in Dunn, after all," Michael said. "Sounds like someone found something."

A pale-skinned man ran around the corner to skid to a halt before Portus.

"We've found it, sir," the man said.

"Lead the way, Sarto."

We followed Sarto back deeper into the tunnels. Several twists and turns later we stood before a door. The stench was almost unbearable from the sewer but my nose detected more than just the sewer. It was a familiar smell to Gladson.

Decomp, he said in my mind.

"It's in this room," Sarto said. "We didn't go in after we opened the door. It was pretty obvious this was what you were looking for."

"Alright," I said. "I'm goin' in to examine the scene. You guys wait for me to get a good look before comin' in."

I twisted the lever and pushed the door open. The smell of the decomposing body was stronger. Stepping into the room was like stepping into the past life of a homicide detective. Gladson had entered many rooms like this one.

The torso was in the center of the room in two pieces. I snarled as I saw the blood splattered in several directions. The arms had been ripped off and slung into a corner. You could tell by the blood patterns that the victim, a pale-skinned man, had been alive when they were ripped off. One leg had a similar blood pattern. The victim had died after the leg. The other leg had been torn off as well but the blood spray was different.

Not many of his victims lived through the legs being torn off, said Gladson in my head. Never understood how they were kept still between the acts, though.

"Some sort of drug, maybe," I muttered.

The rest of what had been done occurred after death. The torso had been disemboweled and the spine had been broken, leaving two halves of the torso. The head had been twisted off and spiked to the wall, directly in front of the door opening so that it would be the first thing seen when the body was found.

It would have taken enormous strength to do something like this. Possibly an Agent? But what sort of Agent would do this? Gaunt is a psycho, but would even he do this?

Not randomly, Gaunt's voice echoed in my head. I could do this, but it would be for the shock factor on my targets. Not just for the kill.

"This guy isn't an Agent with any of the personalities in the database," I muttered, "which probably means he's not an Agent. Unless a Clown were ordered to do it."

"What's that leave?" I asked myself. "Cyborg?"

Most of the Cyborgs were gone, now. Their technology was so hard to upkeep, they died shortly after the Fall.

I stooped low and looked closely at the abdomen. It looked like an animal had torn it open.

What if it was a Geno Freak? Gladson asked in my head.

"They died out years before the Fall," I muttered.

The Geno Freaks were a fad that had swept through the youth about ten years before the war. They would do illegal gene splicing with animal DNA to give themselves cat's eyes, fox ears, and a multitude of different things. It was illegal because it didn't work. Sure you got the eyes or ears or fur-covered body, but you also received a lifespan of about four years. Needless to say, Geno Freaks were a short-lived fad.

"There just aren't many humans with the strength to do what's been done here," I said. "Whatever it is, it's gonna be a handful when we catch it."

"Alright, guys," I raised my voice. "You can clean it up. I have all I'm gonna get here."

Michael and Lindsey were the first to enter the blood-soaked room.

"Damn," he muttered.

"This is pretty gruesome," she said. "Hard to believe one person did it. Only one set of prints in the blood, though."

"A damn big set of prints," he said.

"Yeah," I said. "This guy is big. Probably as big as Wilson Poe."

"That's big," she said.

"Stronger than anyone has any right to be," Michael said, looking at the body. "Ripped the arms and legs off with his hands. Those aren't cuts."

"Agreed," I said. "Let's let these guys clean up. We need to head back east. This proves my pattern is correct. There are three possibilities for the next attack. All three are stable zones near Yarborough."

"You have somewhere figured where we can possibly catch him before he kills again?" Portus asked.

"Yeah," I said. "I needed to prove my pattern to be sure."

We exited the room and let the rest of the Mardins in to clean up.

"Where shall we begin?" Portus asked.

I squatted down and pulled the maps from my coat. Spreading them both on the floor, I pointed at Yarborough.

"From here, he could go two zones to the north and stop in Morris. Or he could go straight east to Trew. But, if he's studied the zones any, I'd guess that he went three zones south to Plagis."

"Why Plagis?" Lindsey asked. "Both of the others are closer."

"The next few moves would answer that," Michael said, pointing at the map. "If he goes to Trew, there aren't any stable zones in that path for about six zones. If he chooses Morris, his next move is pretty easy. He'd go to Hiller. But after Hiller he'd have to cross the Warzone."

"I can see the problem with that one," she said. "No one wants to cross the Warzone."

Three zones were in a perpetual state of war with each other. There were about twelve zones that were always in a state of war near these three. It wasn't a very safe place to cross. Some days you could cross the area without incident, others, you may end up between a hundred or so warriors battling in the streets. It was a good place to avoid.

"So Plagis would be the smartest for him to set up," Michael said. "That's if the man has prior knowledge of the area. He may be just traveling till he hits a stable place."

"The path he's already taken says he has some prior knowledge," I said. "He's avoided a couple of bad routes by going the way he's going. He's planning his moves well ahead. This city is the perfect hunting grounds for someone like him. All the different Warlords and zones. If he knew how well the Mardins were connected, he never would have picked them as victims. He thinks in upper zones."

"I think you're right," Lindsey said.

"We know a little about the guy, so far," I said. "He's a loner. He doesn't associate with others, they're just prey to him. If he was social, he'd be someplace like the Circus, where he could do this sort of thing for clients. They do some twisted shit in places like that."

"Makes sense," Michael said. "He's not one of the rich, or he'd just buy slaves and do his thing where he lived."

"He's a wanderer," I said. "He may take jobs as a warrior for the Warlords, but he doesn't stay very long. A month's pay would keep him fed and then he'd move on to the next. No one would turn down someone with his strength if he requested work as a fighter."

"He's also a coward," Lindsey said.

"How's that?" Michael asked.

"If not, he'd have joined one of the Warlords in the Warzone. He could kill as he pleases and be paid for it."

"Might have a point there," I said. "Too much chance of gettin' killed by some lucky shot during one of their skirmishes."

"He's a psychopath," Michael said. "He gets his jollies from killing the helpless."

"The drugging of his victims backs that," I said.

"Drugging?"

"If you noticed the blood patterns, they show a distinct lack of struggle from the victim. I think he drugs 'em in some way."

"I'm really not liking this guy," Michael said. "I'm thinking I'm gonna enjoy killing the bastard."

"Just remember the strength this guy has," I said. "It's not completely human."

"What? Like a Cyborg?"

"Cyborg, Agent, Geno Freak," I said. "There's something more to this guy than just bein' a twisted bastard."

"Geno Freak?" Michael asked. "Doubtful. They died out years before the Fall. Cyborgs are gone. Are Agents that strong?"

He looked at me with eyebrows raised.

"Yep," I said. "But none of the templates in the database fit this guy."

"An Agent from another Corporation?"

"Obsidian was the undeniable victor of the wars," I said. "But it's possible an Agent of one of the others survived. The problem is, this guy was killin' folks years before the Fall." I tapped the side of my head. "I got a detective up here who was after him a long time ago. He's seen this before. The whole scene. This guy was killin' people and leavin' 'em just like that room back there. It was close to twenty-five years ago. If this guy was an Agent from the other side, he would have been doin' corporate business during the war. Not killin' civilians."

"Twenty five years ago would put him in range of the Geno Freak theory," Michael said. "But surely, he wouldn't still be around now, would he?"

"It's possible one survived, but what would he have to be spliced with to live this long?"

"Maybe some sort of lizard," Michael said. "Some lizards can live long lives."

"That makes sense," I said. "Either way, he's gonna be a handful when we find him. He's strong enough to be a danger, but if he's a Geno freak, he's probably got the speed to go with it, and there's no tellin' what else. We need to be careful."

"No doubt."

"Regardless, we need to head for Plagis," I said, pointing at the spot on the tunnel map. "Portus, we need to get here."

"Yes, sir," he answered.

"And I'd increase forces in these two areas, as well," Michael added. "If we're right, he'll hit under Plagis. If not, it is highly likely he'll hit one of these two."

"I will contact the Patrol and let them know as soon as we get to a point where we have comm systems."

"Good," I said. "Let's get movin'."

Portus started back up the tunnel we had come down to get here, and we fell in line behind him.

If I had been an Agent back then instead of just a cop, Gladson said in my head, I'd have found this guy.

"Maybe," I muttered.

"What?" Michael asked from behind me.

"Nothin'," I answered. "Just talkin' to myselves."

He chuckled.

Agents only had one personality at a time, Childers said. It may not have helped to be an Agent when you pursued the guy back then.

True, Gladson admitted.

Many of the personalities in my head had just been regular people. Every Agent came from somewhere. Somewhere out there was a body that belonged to a former homicide detective who became an Agent. His body may be dead, or somewhere stuck as whatever it was programmed to be when the bombs fell. It could be a damn

Clown, for all I knew. It may even be Samuel Gladson, survivor of the Fall. His most current program would still be in the database. There could be any number of people out there that I have in my head, as well.

It worried me that there may be another Stephen Gaunt out there.

I'm mildly offended, Gaunt's voice said. But I often worry about the same thing.

I giggled.

"Did he just giggle?" Lindsey asked.

"I believe so."

"I have no idea what you're talkin' about," I said

"Must be an interesting conversation going on in there," she said.

"Sounds that way."

Sometimes a little crazy is all you need to keep sane in this Fallen World.

* * * * *

Chapter Eight

"What's that sound?" Lindsey asked.

I had noticed a clanking sound coming from ahead of us. There was a noticeable movement of air around us, too.

"We are nearing one of the ventilation stations," Portus said. "It is shorter to cut through the area than to go around."

We rounded a corner to find a large room with immense fan blades suspended far up into the shafts in the ceiling. I could see the huge electric motors above the fans. They were disconnected from the fan assemblies.

"Motors burned out?" I asked.

"About five years ago," he answered. "They are driven by the belts under the motors, now. We have five shifts that work the fans. Ten people per fan on each five hour shift."

"Hard job," Michael said.

"Yes," Portus said. "It is probably the most important job in the Tees. There are twenty of these ventilation stations in our territory. All but one are manually operated, now. One still has power but it is expected to fail at any moment."

"I can see the importance," I said. "Without the air flow, no one can survive down here."

"There are people already on the lists for hire as others finish their service," he said. "Every Mardin will serve at the Vents at some point in their lives. I did my service when I reached my eighteenth year. It was an honor to serve my people in such an important task. Most of us do our Vent service as we reach adulthood. Afterwards, we are considered Citizens and have the right to live in the Tees."

"Makes sense to me," I said.

"There are three Services," Portus said. "In a Mardin's life, he or she will perform these three Services. Each brings the Citizen to a higher level in the Citizenry."

"My guess would be the vents and water to be two of them," I said.

"That they are," Portus said. "The Sewer Department is the third. It is also the hardest of the three Services to do. But a Citizen can never be eligible to vote for or become an Advisor unless they have done all three. It is also the one we have to hire outsiders to help with. Some Mardins are happy without the right to vote. All are required to serve in one to stay in the Tees. Two give the right to be a Patroller. Three grant you the full citizenship."

"I like that setup, for some reason," I said. "To lead you must walk through the shit of a city."

"The Accords leave us responsible for the Water pipes and the Sewer flow," Portus said. "That is why they are requirements to become full Citizens. The Vents are what keep us alive."

"And the power?"

"Dynamo needs water, too," Portus chuckled. "We did not come away from the Accords with nothing, Mr. Kade."

I laughed.

"I would guess you guys can deal with the Farmers in any sector over your territory, too," Lindsey said.

"Most of them. We deal mostly while the Farmers are in Wilderman or Kathrop," he said. "Of course, it seems there is a growing area in the center of the city that is becoming safer and safer."

"Hmm," Michael said. "I wonder why that would be."

"I have no idea what you're talkin' about."

"Doesn't surprise me," Lindsey said.

"Are the Farmers anywhere near where we're headed?" I asked.

"They are in Kathrop over the next week," Portus said.

"That's a shame," I said. "There was a wagon with tacos the last time I saw 'em."

"I haven't had a decent taco in over twenty years," Michael said.

"What the hell is a taco?" Lindsey asked.

"Kids today," Michael said as he shook his head.

"Who are you calling a kid, you old bastard?"

"Someone who's never had a damn taco."

"I bet I could make a taco," she muttered.

"Oh my god, Woman!" Michael snorted. "You can't even boil water."

"Bite me, you damn fossil!"

I was trying not to, but I may have giggled again.

"You shut up, you giggling bastard!"

She stomped past me and fell in behind Portus.

"Sad part is," I said, tapping the side of my head, "there's all these people up here, and none of 'em know how to make a damn tortilla."

"Why didn't you ask the Farmer?"

"Cause I'm a dumb ass."

We turned south into a larger tunnel. There were steel tracks in the center where the subways used to run. There was a noise coming from ahead of us.

"Please move to the side," Portus said. "Cart is coming through."

The noise approached our position, and soon I saw a large cart with a load of dirt and rocks. The sides of the cart had handles protruding. Each had a Mardin behind it. They pushed the cart past us, and Portus returned to the center of the tunnel.

"We are excavating a collapsed tunnel that used to lead to the central hub of the railways."

"Surprised all the rails haven't been pulled up for the steel," I said.

"We use the rails," he said. "There are a lot of unused tunnels with rails that will never be used."

"You could pull in a good amount of Script with that steel," I said. "Perhaps you might put in a word to the bosses about the idea. I know a blacksmith who could use a good source of strong steel."

"That might interest the King," Portus said.

"Just let me know, and I'll put you in touch with Soba," I said. "He is really just gettin' started with larger orders, but the man is good."

"I will relay this to Gevik, my superior."

"Good."

"There's a noticeable lack of sewer smell down here, excepting the area under Dunn," Michael said. "It kind of surprised me."

"The sewers are ventilated in completely different systems than our tunnels. It is a common mistake from surface dwellers to think we live in the sewers."

"You're right about the rumors," Michael said.

"It does serve to keep fewer surface dwellers from trying to explore our territory."

"More light than I had expected," Lindsey said. "For that I am grateful."

"There's very little lighting here, Mrs. Tanzik," Portus said. "Your eyes are adapting to the darkness and finding more residual light than before."

"I just thought it was brighter, here."

"I was thinking the same thing," Michael said. "I think he's right, though. We probably are just getting better at seeing in the dark."

I smiled, behind the two. They actually agreed with each other every so often.

"We'll be near the southern edge of our territory when we turn east," Portus said. "We will have to be careful; we have incursions from the southern territories pretty frequently. Most of the Patrol spends its time on the borders of our territory, but numerous patrols have been pulled to cover the three areas you designated."

"It figures," I said.

"Don't you even say it," Lindsey warned.

"What are you talkin' about?"

"Expect the worst, and you're never disappointed."

"Damn, woman!" Michael exclaimed, and his hand hovered near the sword on his left side. "Now, you've already said it."

"It doesn't matter if one of us says it," she said. "It just matters if he says it."

I heard noises from the southern tunnels, and I smiled at her.

"Doesn't it?" she asked nervously.

I chuckled.

"You're shitting me! What was that sound?"

"It sounds like someone is having a spot of fun, ahead," I said with Gaunt's precise voice.

"Son of a bitch..." she muttered as Portus turned toward us in alarm.

I nodded toward the man. "We'll lend a hand, Portus. Follow as you can."

I drew the Sig with my right hand, and the straight razor with my left. Launching myself forward with my enhanced speed, I left the three behind, fairly quickly. The tunnel curved ahead, and I could hear the clash of weapons and the grunts of fighters just ahead.

Rounding the bend, I took in the sight ahead of me. There were eight Mardins in two staggered lines of four. In front of them was a tunnel full of pale-skinned attackers. They wielded swords, much like the Mardins did, but there was no organization to their ranks, which was why the Mardins had held their ground so far—they held a formation that supported one another.

I took aim and fired the Sig. One of the attackers in the front line lurched as a small dot appeared in his forehead and the back of his head blossomed with the exit of the bullet. One of the defenders took a blade in his side and staggered backwards. The man to his left in the staggered formation stepped forward and took his place.

The Sig coughed and the action slid again as the second of the attackers toppled backwards with a spray of blood from the back of his head. Two more times the Sig spouted fire, and two more of the lead attackers were slammed backwards.

Then a form shot by me at full speed. Michael had a sword in each hand and launched himself over the heads of the Mardins to land in the opening I had just created. His swords blurred, and blood sprayed in several directions. Lindsey shot past me and hit the left wall where the line had been weakest. She bounded over the Mardin to hit the wall with both feet and launch herself around in front of the Mardin. Her blade flashed as she rebounded behind the attacker in front of the Mardin, and he staggered as his spine was severed just below the spot where it joined the skull. She began to weave in and out of the startled attackers, and bodies slumped to the floor.

The two of them took the center in the Mardins' formation, and the surprised Mardins stepped forward to resume the staggered formation around the two squires in the center. Before our arrival the line had been pushed backwards several times. Now they stepped forward.

I shot two more times, and two more fell. They were on the right side of the tunnel, so I switched to the left and fired two more times. One fell but the other moved just in time to survive…for about a second. I fired a second round and achieved the expected blossom from his head.

Getting sloppy, old man.

"Hush," I said and shot a woman on the right side of the tunnel.

The lines stepped forward again, and I could see two forms in the back of the attacking mob. I fired four times and those two forms toppled. Two shots apiece just to be sure. Five more forms slumped along the front lines as Michael and Lindsey stepped forward again, flanked by the two Mardins.

They broke as someone screamed from the back, "Silas is dead!"

The mob seemed to vanish as they dropped weapons and ran. Two of them kept their weapons so I shot them in the backs of their heads. I would have let them go if they had dropped weapons.

"You shot those two in the back," one of the Mardins accused.

I popped the magazine from the Sig. Calmly, I began reloading the magazine with new shells from the pocket in my coat.

"They should have dropped the weapons," Lindsey said. "We don't let them live to fight another day. At least, not with the same weapons."

The Mardin started to say something else, until he looked into her cold, pitiless eyes. He turned and joined his Patrol around a wounded fighter.

"Lardes," one of them said to the man. "You can make it. We'll get you to the Medics."

"You have to guard the Tees," he said. "You can't leave the Tees unguarded."

"But you'll die!"

"Do your duty, Patroller!"

"We'll take him in," I said as Portus rounded the bend.

The Patroller looked at me with doubt.

"You heard him," Portus said. "I am a Scout. I will show them the way. Get us the stretcher."

The Mardin nodded and ran back the way we had come. He returned with a medical stretcher. It was from before the Fall. It looked like a rescue board from a helicopter. They eased the Patroller onto the stretcher, and Portus took one end. Michael sheathed his blades and took the other.

"We thank you," the Mardin said.

I nodded and followed Lindsey behind the two carrying the stretcher.

"Lesson learned," Lindsey said as she tried to get the blood off of her shirt.

"Don't even talk about it," Michael said.

"You should wear black," I said. "Then you can't see the blood."

"Black, hell." she said, "I'll wear red if we ever go anywhere else with you."

"Shoulda talked to Poe."

"Why?"

"He wore black."

I smelled alcohol.

"We're close," I said. "Smell the alcohol and vinegar?"

"Yeah."

"They're a couple of cleaners that are easy enough to make."

"I use alcohol at home if I can keep the fossil from drinking it."

"You'd have a lot less trouble keepin' him out of vinegar."

She laughed.

We turned down a side passage, and the smell got stronger. There was a stronger light source ahead. My eyes were blasted with light as we hit the chamber ahead of us. I narrowed my lids to keep the light dim.

"What is this?"

"One of the Patrollers was injured in a battle with Silas' forces," Portus answered. Two big Mardins closed and took the stretcher from Portus and Michael.

"You can wait in the outer tunnels," the doctor said.

"We are on a mission and will not be waiting," Portus said. "Please report to the Patrol about this man when you are done."

The doctor nodded her head. She looked to be about fifty or so. She must have just finished her Medical Degree right before the Fall, because it hung on the wall behind a desk on the left wall of the room. The Mardins had been extremely lucky to get a true Doctor to staff their infirmary. People knowledgeable in the medical field were scarce in this Fallen World.

* * * * *

Chapter Nine

We exited the infirmary and turned to the east. "We keep an infirmary close to all the trouble spots so we can get our men to it quickly," Portus said. "We have seven of the facilities set up. All the staff has trained under Doctor Killian, our head of the Medic Program."

"I'm guessin' that was Killian back there?" Michael asked.

"Yes, she was a licensed surgeon when the bombs fell, and she took cover in the tunnels with a small group of soldiers. With them was a man named Clyde Mardin. He set up the immediate area around them to hold off attackers and established the original zone in our territory."

"What happened to him?" Lindsey asked.

"He became ill and turned to a young soldier named Grady O'Neal to keep his people safe. O'Neal is the man who united the territory we call Mardin by both force of arms and diplomacy. They say no one can match him in battle, but I'm not so certain of that anymore."

He was looking askance at me. If he only knew. Grady O'Neal was a familiar name to me. He was a soldier and a hero in the War. He was the one who took the Rift. The Rift had been a strip of urban hell. It was an evil piece of civilization and home to a group of terrorists who had been responsible for thousands of civilian deaths.

Obsidian had sent in an Agent with the forces that went into the Rift. His name was Grady O'Neal. Apparently, he'd made a home for himself after the Fall. His was a personality I couldn't find much of after the dust up in my noggin. I knew he was there, but he was just a shadow in my mind. A lot of the personalities in there were like that. I could access memories and not much more.

The man probably was on par with William Childers, my Special Forces persona. Probably not anywhere near Gaunt, the Corporate Assassin.

"It would've taken a strong man to do what he's done, down here," I said. "He's done good things for the city, and he's in no danger from me."

Portus nodded.

"How much farther is it to Plagis?" Lindsey asked.

"It isn't too far, now," Portus said. "Then we must wait until the man attempts to strike."

"If he hasn't already done it," Michael said. "Seems it's been about a month since the last one."

"True," I said. "Let's hope he hasn't already killed again. We'd have to wait a month to catch him in the act after that. We might find him up top, but there's no guarantee."

"We'll find him above ground if we have to," Michael said. "It'll be harder without the support of the Mardins, but we'll do what needs done."

"No doubt," I said.

Running footsteps sounded in the tunnels ahead of us. A few minutes later a form came into view. It was a Patroller.

"We found him!" the man yelled. "We have him cornered in Tunnel Seven. There's no way out of there except through our forces."

"How many forces?" I said quickly.

"Fourteen patrollers, sir."

"It's not enough," I said. "Catch up as quickly as you can."

I shot forward. They shouldn't have cornered him. It would be ugly. I consulted the map in my head. There were two paths to the area where they had him. I turned left at the next branch.

I was moving so fast, I had to rebound from the wall and back to the floor as I turned. They were wrong about exits from Tunnel Seven, according to the map. There was an entrance to the sewers down in the back of Seven. They were blocking him from the surface. I doubted they even thought of the sewer. Maybe he wouldn't find it.

I heard screams from ahead of me and drew the Sig. Turning another corner I found the tunnel ahead of me literally coated in blood. There were Patrollers, torn and broken, littering the tunnel. More screams came from closer, and I ran past the dead men.

I rounded another bend with the Sig extended and ready to fire. A shadow flickered on my right, and I turned toward it with the Sig. Something slammed into me like a battering ram, and the pistol flew from my hand. Huge hands seized my wrists and pulled outward.

He loomed in front of me and grunted in surprise as I pulled back inward with my arms. My foot lashed forward and connected. The huge man staggered and lost his hold on my wrists. I had kicked hard enough to push myself backwards from the Geno Freak.

It was pretty obvious that was what he was. There were scales on his clawed hands, and I could see yellow eyes staring at me.

"Geno Freak," I said.

"Don't call me that!" the huge man roared and charged in again.

I dodged to the left, and my hand shot out to hit a pressure point. It wasn't there. His hand grasped my wrist and yanked me toward him. With a violent twist, he tossed me through the air to slam into a tunnel wall.

"What are you?" he rumbled as I regained my feet.

I was starting to get mad. "I'm the guy that's gonna kill you."

We charged one another. His clawed right hand swept toward my side, and I twisted out of its path. My fist slammed into his throat. It felt like I had punched a wall when it hit the chorded muscle of his neck.

We circled back around for another pass. He didn't seem to have the same weaknesses as a regular person. That throat punch would have crushed a man's neck. He charged forward, and I let his arms encircle me so I could get close enough to grab hold of him. I realized my mistake almost immediately. His jaws spread wide and fangs pivoted from the roof of his mouth. His jaws clamped on my shoulder. I felt the fire as he injected venom through those fangs.

This must be the poison he had used on his victims. And I had just been dosed.

I grabbed around his ribs and squeezed with all of my enhanced strength. There was a crack as ribs broke inside the Geno Freak. His jaws released as he screamed. I twisted around and threw him across the tunnel to take his turn at being slammed into a wall.

He staggered to his feet. Instead of coming at me again, he ran out of the tunnel toward the exit to the surface. I launched myself forward to fall right on my face as the venom took effect on the left side of my body.

Two forms shot into tunnel.

"Damn, Kade," Michael said.

Lindsey helped me as I was struggling to regain my feet. I could feel the paralytic burning away by my enhanced system. I was shaking as my body poured adrenaline into my blood stream.

"That hurt." my voice was raspy.

"What the hell happened?"

"Definitely a Geno Freak," I said as the two of them supported me.

Portus and the Patroller ran in from the darkness.

"Dear God!" Portus gasped.

There were several surviving Patrollers in the tunnel. Most were severely injured. One of them was looking at me with open fear in his gaze. He'd seen the short fight between me and the Freak.

"W-what are y-you?"

"A guy that just got his ass kicked," I said. "Just like you."

He shook his head but didn't press the issue. There were more footsteps coming, and Patrollers came into sight. They began helping the wounded who were whispering to them as they cast sidelong glances at me.

"Looks like the rest of this is gonna be done on the surface," I said. "Now we pursue him up top."

Michael nodded.

I staggered forward as I burned through the paralytic that still filled my blood.

"We can't let up on him, or we'll lose him," I said. "We need to get movin'."

"You're not moving anywhere very fast," Lindsey said.

"It'll burn off," I said. "Let's go."

We moved slowly down the tunnel toward the nearest exit to the surface. Portus came up behind us.

"What will you do, now?"

"We're gonna find this guy and kill him," I said. "He's not gonna stop killin' folks, and it's gonna take someone like us to stop him. Tell your boss we'll finish the job."

"I will," he said. "You scared some of our men back there. What did you do?"

"Like I told your boy, I got my ass kicked," I answered. "Not gonna happen the next time. I know about that little trick, now."

"Good luck to you, Mathew Kade," he said. "And good luck to you as well, Mr. and Mrs. Tanzik."

"By the looks of things, we'll need all the luck we can get," Michael said. "I need you to do me a favor. Contact Teresa and tell her where we are and what the situation is. We may need the Society to keep its eyes peeled for this guy."

"It will be done."

"Thank you."

The steel door to the surface hung open from the hurried exit of the Freak. I limped through the opening, followed by two worried Squires. A fire was burning inside me as I thought of the monster we were pursuing. He was a relic left from a time best forgotten. I am one of those relics from the Old World. It was fitting one relic would be used to destroy another.

The cool temperature was refreshing, and I was glad it was nighttime after our prolonged stay in the dark. It would give us time to let our vision return to normal as daylight came.

Unfortunately, the night was the home of the predators that plagued this broken city. In the mood I was in, it may just be unfortunate for them.

I heard groans in the distance. "This way."

I limped towards the east. It wasn't far before I smelled the metallic scent of blood. There were three forms laying in the street. Only one was alive and in bad shape. His arms had been twisted so hard they were nearly unattached. He was bleeding profusely and had moments to live.

"Which way did it go?" I asked as he saw me.

His head turned, weakly to the east.

"There's nothing I can do for you," I said.

"I know," he gasped. Then he was gone.

"He'll be joining you soon," I muttered.

"He's gone off the edge," Michael said. "There's no telling what he'll do now."

"He'll kill anyone who gets in his way," I said. "He's hurt pretty bad. I crushed a few ribs."

"We have to find him as quickly as we can," Lindsey said. "There will be innocents in the streets come daylight."

I limped toward the east. My stride was getting stronger as my body worked on the venom. The bullet wound from my last case hurt, and I was pretty sure it had been damaged in the fight with the Freak. The bite wounds in my left shoulder burned, and I knew I could use some medical attention. But there was no time.

"We catch him tonight," I said.

We covered about half the block before shadows moved from the darkness.

"What have we here?" A blocky, shaven-headed man said from the front of a group of about fifteen thugs. "Aren't you a pretty thing?"

"Thank you," I said, "But I'm not really interested."

"You have one chance to leave this street alive," the bald man said, glaring at me. "Her."

"You don't," I said.

"Don't what?"

"Have that chance."

My hand blurred and one of the twelve blades on my harness sank into his throat. He gurgled and toppled backwards.

"Now, you all have one chance to leave this street alive."

The blades rasped as Michael and Lindsey drew them. I slid my razor from its sheathe.

There were still fifteen of them, and the numbers made them brave. They started to move closer.

"Ah, hell with it," I said and drew the Sig. I didn't even pause as I fired four shots. The front three men went down, and I stepped forward toward them, firing three more times. Three more fell, and the rest stopped approaching. I shot two more while they thought about it, and the rest fled. I stepped forward and pulled my blade from the leader's neck.

"Don't have time for this," I muttered and popped the magazine from the pistol.

We walked down the street to the east as I thumbed cartridges into the magazine. More shadows came from the darkness and closed on the fallen men. I glanced back as I walked and saw men and women pulling at various articles of clothing.

We sped up our pace as the venom burned away. The guys he'd killed had been fresh. He wasn't far ahead of us.

"Why is he going east?" Michael asked.

"Was the direction he'd been plannin' on," I said. "He's hurt and runnin' on instinct."

"And he's killing anything in his path," Lindsey added.

"We need to catch him."

I heard screams ahead and tried to speed up. It still didn't work.

"Go," I said. "Be careful. He's a damn handful."

Michael and Lindsey sprinted forward, and I stumped along after them. The venom was stubbornly slowing me down. I rounded a corner to see the Freak run into a Scraper. The Squires were right behind him. I felt a little more of the venom burn away, and I sped up. I shot through the door and stopped to listen. The sound of running feet came from the stairway.

"Figures," I muttered.

I started climbing. Following the noise, I climbed five stories. The sounds of a fight were coming from down the hall to my right. The door slammed open in front of me, and it seemed as if time slowed down. I took in the scene ahead of me.

Michael had sliced the Freak on his left and been slammed across the hall to hit the wall. I was familiar with that and knew it hurt. Lindsey closed from the right and sank a blade into the Freak's leathery hide. He grabbed her, and his mouth began to open wide.

Michael was back and his fist with the metal gauntlet he'd been wearing pounded into the Freak's mouth, behind his fangs. His other gauntlet slammed into the front and the Freak screamed as his fangs shattered.

He dropped Lindsey and punched Michael in the chest. Michael flew across the hall again and hit the wall with a thud.

Squires are a tough lot but the two of them were outmatched by the Freak's speed and strength. They'd done more than fourteen Mardin Patrollers could, but it wasn't enough. There's a skill taught to Special Forces. They can push their adrenal glands to the maximum with sheer will. It's dangerous and only used as a final measure. About thirty percent of the time it ended in the death of the soldier. An Agent is a little tougher, but it could still kill.

I willed the gland to full output.

All of the pain was gone as my body jerked. The venom was like an afterthought. I launched myself down the hallway.

The Freak took another cut from Lindsey and slapped her aside. He held her down with one huge hand and raised the other to rip his claws across her body. His hand descended, and I hit him at full speed.

The reason an Agent is as strong as he or she is comes from the enhancement of the muscle and bone. They are higher in density than a normal person. This makes an Agent heavier than their size. I would, if I was a normal person, weigh about one hundred and ninety pounds or so. With the density of my muscle and bone, I weighed about twice that.

My race down the hall sent that weight into the Freak at a high rate of speed. We both slammed into the windows at the end of the hall, and through the shattered glass we went.

"Kade!" I heard Lindsey's voice behind us.

The Freak clawed across my back once before impact, but I planted my knees on his chest. Just before impact I jumped with all my strength upwards. The force of the jump added to his impact and took from mine. I still landed right on his chest, and I felt the satisfying crunch as it collapsed under me. I also felt my left leg break. The adrenaline faded, and my racing heart was almost redlining.

I drew the Sig and placed it under his chin. After pulling the trigger three times, just to be sure, I rolled off of him.

I reached over and patted the dead man's shoulder, "Thank you. You broke my fall, nicely."

Darkness began to settle across my vision as I saw Michael and Lindsey running toward me. The darkness didn't bother me with the two of them there.

It's nice to have friends in this Fallen World.

* * * * *

Chapter Ten

I awoke in a bright room that looked distinctly familiar. I was in the Infirmary we had taken the injured Mardin. Or one that looked the same.

"That's gonna leave a mark," I muttered.

"That it will, Mister Kade." I didn't recognize the voice. I turned my head to see the speaker.

He was a short, stocky man, but I recognized the sort of man he was. The way he held himself. He looked as if he was ready to erupt in violence at any moment. Special Forces.

"You must be Grady."

"That would correct," he said. "It seems I have a lot to thank you for."

"Just doin' my job."

"Maybe so, when you killed the man who has been killing my people for some time," he said. "But you also stopped two attacks on my people that would have been quite devastating. The second time you even killed the man they called Lord Silas and his second in command, Yelvin. This single act has done my people a great service and paved the way to expanding our territory. Silas was a tyrant and a slaver. His second was just as bad. I have sent an offer to the third in line, who is a much more reasonable person."

"Buildin' empires?"

"No," he said. "I'm uniting a city. Well, an Undercity. The benefits will help the surface as well as our people. The Accords will extend through the southern zones of the city, almost to the Boroughs. There will be running water and working sewers through a large part of those zones that have only had sporadic success with those."

"Could do a lot worse than Mardins," I said.

"It could be a great boon to your quest to unite the city above as well," he said.

"I'm not on a quest," I said.

"Call it what you want, Agent. In the last two months there has been a change on the surface. The area around you seems to be coming under the influence of the Society of the Sword. Rumors abound of the reasons this is occurring. Certain Warlords have been removed and replaced with a Chapterhouse."

"I'm just doing the jobs I'm paid to do."

"I can see the way things are heading on the surface. It was becoming more and more violent. This quest that isn't a quest is a thing that could bring us back to a civilized place in this broken world."

"Like I said, I'm just doin' the job I get paid to do."

He nodded his head with a slight smile. "Speaking of pay, yours is in the bag on the table. We thank you for finding the killer."

I nodded.

"I understand you have a blacksmith who would be interested in a source of good steel. I will make contact with this man and possibly work out some arrangements. I could use several things a blacksmith can provide, and he is much closer than the Farmers."

"Soba is good," I said. "He'll be as good as the Farmers, given the chance."

"I will also be talking to Teresa Manora about a closer relationship with her Society. I feel it will be a power to be reckoned with in the future."

"You both can benefit from each other," I said.

"I believe you're right."

"I need to be on my way," I said. "Thanks for the medical."

"No, I thank you for the job you've done and the extra help you provided my Patrollers. I must be on my way, as well. I must meet the messenger I sent to the south. We will know shortly if my offer is accepted."

He shook my hand and turned to leave.

"Grady," I said. He looked back at me. "Remember the Rift? The world up there is much worse than the Rift ever got. It could stand some of what was done back then."

"It was a long time ago, in another world," he said. "I keep my people safe down here, Kade. But there might be a time when I can help in your quest."

"Ain't on a damn quest," I muttered. He smiled and walked out of the Infirmary.

Two other forms came from the shadows.

"Don't you even think of it," Lindsey said.

"You don't wanna know how to make it?"

"Just leave him alone about it."

"The kid might stay home more…"

"Don't even go there you old fart!"

"How you holding up, there, Kade?" Michael changed the subject.

"I'll live," I said.

"Killian said you had a broken leg, four broken ribs and your gunshot wounds reopened from before. Along with the bite the Geno Freak hit you with, there's the four cuts from his claws on your back. She stitched those up, nicely."

"Yeah, I think I'll take a break."

"You need to," Lindsey said. "How did you even survive that fall?"

"The Freak used his body to break my fall."

"Was awful nice of him," Michael said.

"I thought so."

"Ready to get outta here?"

"Definitely," I said. "Where's my coat?"

"Don't worry about that," Lindsey said. "Doctor Killian won't let you up, yet, so we're wheeling you out with one of her chairs."

"Let's get to it, then," I said. "If I'm gonna lay around it's gonna be in my big comfortable bed."

"Our orders are to bring you to the Chapterhouse," Michael said. "I don't think Teresa wants to leave you at home yet. Right now, you're not as scary as she is so we'll follow her orders."

Michael strode across the room to fetch the wheel chair.

"I love that old bastard," Lindsey said. "And he's right. She's much more terrifying than you."

I guess there are scarier things than a schizophrenic Corporate Agent in this Fallen World.

* * * * *

Epilogue

"Kade," Wilson Poe yelled from the front room of Teresa Manora's quarters.

"Come on in," I said.

"Teresa requested you join her in the conference room."

"Sure thing."

"Want me to wheel you there?"

"I guess," I grumbled. If she saw me out of the chair, I'd never hear the end of it.

He pushed my chair out of the office where I had been spending the majority of my time.

"Still won't let you go home?"

"Nope."

"You could sneak out."

"You think I would ever hear the end of that?"

"Probably not," he said as he pushed the door open and pulled my chair through.

"Probably has another job for me," I said. "I like some time between jobs to heal up. At this rate, I'll be a quadriplegic before the year is out."

He laughed and kept pushing me to my doom.

Pulling the door open, he pushed me into a conference room with nine people around the table. I knew all nine of the men in question, one way or another.

Zane stood up and pulled my chair to the table as Poe stepped out the door with a grin. I looked around the room at eight of the Warlords in the general vicinity, including Steiner, the Warlord of our own zone. Zane, Jaxom, Devin, Yamato, and Steiner were Warlords that had been in place for some time. Holden, the replacement for Blechley, and Safro, the replacement for Polk, were new to their jobs.

I chuckled as I saw the final member of this group. I first met him in the street of Moreau. He'd warned me to leave. I'd last seen him when I gave him the skin with the mark on it to control those under the influence of the imprinter.

"Moving up in the world?"

"I kept the mark and took over for a while to make it easier on the folks in Moreau," he said. "As the folks came off the imprinter, they recognized that I had treated them well and stayed. They made me the Warlord by election. I couldn't say no when they asked."

"Understandable," I said with a grin.

"The name's Kalib," he said.

"We requested you be here for a reason," Jaxom said.

"We all came together to create something, today," Yamato said. "An alliance of sorts. We are signing contracts to place our zones under the control of one person."

"Hell no…"

"Teresa Manora," Zane said.

"Thank God," I said. "You scared the crap out of me for a second."

Jaxom chuckled, "All of us have agreed to this alliance with one stipulation. Trust is hard to be given to such a degree, and we will only sign if this contract will be enforced by someone who is strong enough to remove anyone who breaks the contract. No one doubts that you could be that enforcer."

"We want your signature on the contract and your word that you will enforce it if necessary," Yamato said.

I find I can still be surprised in this Fallen World.

* * * * *

Seeds

Chapter One

I stared toward the west with a sick feeling in my stomach.

"They did it," I said.

"Damn fools," Pop said, shaking his head.

The cloud from the impact could be seen in the distance.

"They're far enough away to mean we might survive," he said.

"People are gonna run," I said. "They'll follow their first reaction."

"That's the truth."

"There's nowhere to run to."

"Also the truth."

"I'll gas up the truck," I said.

"Reckon we need a few things."

"Yep," I said as we watched the world fall.

* * *

"What about the raiders?" Pete Dalten's voice was filled with fear.

Pop's voice was deep and calm. "We'll deal with them if we need to."

"What are we supposed to do, Kendrik?" Dalten continued. "We're farmers. We're not soldiers."

"Look out there, Pete," Pop said, pointing toward the door. "We have something the whole damn country is in short supply of. We knew months ago the time would come when we would have to defend it. We have the guns, and you've all been trained to shoot. Did you think it was a game?"

He shook his head in misery.

I placed my hand on his shoulder and squeezed lightly. "We can do this, Pete."

He shook his head as he muttered, "Easy for you, Pratt."

"Death is never easy," I answered. "It's ugly. I never wanted that to be something I've done. But it is and I have no illusions; it will have to be done again."

Five years I was Obsidian Infantry. Five years of fighting before I finished my tour. When it was done, I'd laid down my rifle and joined my father on the farm. I lost two brothers in the war before it had all ended with the bombs. My elder brother, Kolby, died the first year I was in. He had always seemed invincible to me, but the war with JalCom had proven otherwise. And Jimmy? Well, he hadn't contacted us since the Fall. It was hard not to count him as lost. He'd been on assignment to who knows where. We'd tried to convince him to stay home and work the farm with Pop, but he was a Pratt.

We'd all gone to war. Pop fought against Dellik Unified. Kolby and I had fought against JalCom. And now Obsidian Corporation had come into conflict with the last big company in the west, Teledyne. The whole continent was under the control of the two Corporations. No one knew who launched the first nuke, but the world went to hell when that happened. Teledyne and Obsidian, followed by the overseas Corporations, launched everything. How that had come to be the decision was hard to fathom. The center of what had once been the United States of America was a radioactive wasteland.

Over the six months that followed, we learned that the southern half of the Eastern Conglomerate was completely destroyed. Billions of people died. It was unknown how far west the destruction went.

Before the mushroom clouds had finished climbing through the sky, Pop was planting corn.

The meeting went on for some time before Pop dropped the gavel on the block. There is only so much that can be said. The time for preparation was upon us.

I exited the hall to find a familiar figure waiting for me.

"Thanks, Zee," Neave said. "Thanks for trying to calm my dad."

"We're as prepared as we can be for trouble, Neave."

She slid under the crook of my arm and walked close beside me. "He's scared. We're all scared. All, except you and Kendrik."

"We're scared, too, Neave," I said, pulling her close. "But we can't let fear keep us from doing what we need to do."

"There's no going back to what we had before, is there?"

"I'm afraid not," I said with a light squeeze of my left arm that circled her waist. She used to walk on my right but now I needed my right arm free to be able to draw the pistol holstered on my side.

I was under no illusions about what was coming. Stories from people fleeing the city to the east about the savagery they had escaped were enough to make me open the trunk I had in the attic. Guns were second nature to me after the war, and the .45 caliber automatic was the same one I had carried while the fighting with JalCom had been at its highest.

"I just wish…"

"I know," I said. "We all wish we could go back."

"I'm not sure your dad does," she said. "He never was very outspoken until after."

"Don't ever doubt that he would rather be minding his own business and just growing corn," I replied. "He set aside the life of peace he'd wanted to do what was necessary."

"He just seems to be in his element, now."

"He's a natural leader," I said. "He led men in combat in the wars. He gladly laid that mantle aside afterwards. He'd be happily growing vegetables right now if it weren't for the Fall."

"What are we going to do about the raiders?"

"We're going to kill them, Neave," I said quietly. "And it isn't going to be pretty."

"There's no other way, is there?"

"There's not," I answered. "When they come, we'll kill them."

We neared her father's truck.

"I could stay."

"I have to go scouting tonight, baby," I said.

"Then I'll be back Tuesday."

"I'll be here," I smiled and pulled her in close.

Our lips touched, and I heard someone clear their throat behind me. She pulled back and looked past me to see her father.

"You couldn't wait a few more minutes?"

He shrugged.

She kissed me again, quickly. "Tuesday, Zebadiah Pratt."

"Tuesday, Neave Dalton," I returned. "I'll be waiting for you."

I watched her climb into the driver seat of the truck, and Pete got into the passenger side. Two younger boys climbed into the back of the truck with rifles. No one travels unarmed in this Fallen World.

* * * * *

Chapter Two

"Easy, boy," I said softly as Dagger side-stepped. "It's just a log."

Dagger was a little high strung, and we needed to spend the time riding him to work some of that out of the big black gelding. I knew he would make a great trail horse when he got used to it. When we had been training the others to shoot, Dagger and the other trail horses had been near. I'd been accused of mistreating them when that started but it was necessary. They needed to be able to handle the gunfire. I had no illusions about what we were going to face when others found us.

I pulled Dagger up as I looked off to the East. The sun was setting behind me but there was enough light to see the smoke from a campfire.

"Looks like I get to walk a while."

I jumped off Dagger and tied him in a copse of trees where he could nibble on the grass close by. This was another thing we had done as soon as the bombs dropped. We began training the horses for future use. Up until then, they had been pets of some of the residents near the town. When they ran they left the horses. We took them.

Dagger was just as happy to munch on the grass.

I drew the .45 and worked the action, ejecting a bullet. Catching it before it hit the ground, I ejected the mag and slid it back in. The action had been smooth, and I holstered the pistol. As I made my way toward the fire in the distance, I checked the other .45 and the mags stashed all over the vest I wore.

A little while later I slid along the ground toward the fire. I could smell the group of people almost as far out as I smelled the smoke. With several rivers and streams in the area, there was no excuse for the filth.

As soon as I could make out what was being said, I halted.

"…bunch of farmers."

"Did you see where the food was stored?"

"They got silos of corn. Saw them using those big combines to harvest it."

I grimaced. The combines had just been running over the last week. We had conserved all of the diesel to run them. After the harvest was done, they would be dead. But we would have a great head start on stored grains. We may be harvesting by hand next year, but we wouldn't go hungry this year.

Pop had gotten Garrick to start rebuilding the old water wheel on the mill. It had been shut down for years after the big mill upstate had opened. The old mill was local, and we would grind the wheat and corn into meal and flour. We talked about turning some of the lowlands into a place to grow rice.

"What about women?"

"Oh, they got some sweet lookin' cherries. And kids for the Lieutenant and that group."

"Guns?"

"Lot of em carryin' but I don't think they're particularly experienced."

"We'll hit em tomorrow," the voice that had been questioning said. "I want that cherry that we saw in the truck. Make sure she ain't damaged."

I may not be the brightest crayon in the box, but I always was the first in my platoon when it came to picking a fight.

"Tomorrow?" I said as I strode into their camp. "How about now?"

The .45 from my belt was in my hand, and I put a bullet through the forehead of the guy who had been asking questions. Another slammed through the chest of the scout. Raiders were scrabbling backward, but I felt little mercy as I emptied the .45 and popped the mag out. The other mag slammed home, and I racked the first round into the gun. One shot rang out, and I felt a tug at my arm as it barely clipped me. The shooter staggered and fell as my next round hit him in the chest.

All too soon there was no one left to shoot, and I stood in the center of their camp, breathing hard from the adrenaline that had flooded my body during the short fight.

Around me were twelve dead men. The barrel of my pistol sizzled as a drop of rain hit it. I looked to the darkened sky just as the rain began to fall. Perhaps it would take some of the smell away. The smell of blood, feces, and unwashed bodies permeated the air.

I was untying the picket rope from Dagger when the headlights of several trucks came within view. I looked at my watch. They were from the direction I had traveled from so I knew it was one of ours.

"Probably Pete and his boys," I muttered to myself. "Hope Neave isn't with 'em."

Her father's place was the closest farm to where I was, and I didn't really want her to see what I had just done. I wasn't sure if she was ready to see that.

I rode Dagger back toward the raider camp. This was something else he would have to get used to. Death would be all too common in this new world we had to face.

He was pretty skittish as we neared the dead raiders. I could tell he didn't want to go closer, but it needed to be done. My plan had been simple. I needed to get rid of the bodies, which would be a lot harder without the horse. Now that the trucks were coming, that wasn't the case, but I needed to get Dagger used to the dead.

I picketed him close to the camp and began searching through the raiders' camp. The rain had become a drizzle, and I could see the moon through the clouds. I had a pile of guns laying close to the smoking wood that had been their fire. There had been some serious hardware in that group. If they had been experienced with the weapons, I would have been toast.

I was laying the last gun into the pile when the trucks arrived and forms piled out of them.

"Grady," I said to the first of the farmers who stepped into the headlights.

"Zee?" he asked. "What the hell happened? We heard a lot of gunfire."

He gasped as he saw the first of the bodies. "Jesus, man!"

"You're bleeding," Doc said as he stepped into the light as well.

"It's a scratch," I said.

"Still need to let me look at it."

More of the men came from the darkness. Pete was among them. As they really got a look at the camp, I heard one of them gagging. Tony, Pete's oldest son threw up.

"There's twelve of them," Pete said. "Did you do this?"

His voice was accusing.

"Yes," I answered. "Yes I did."

"Why?" was the only thing he could seem to force out. He was scared, he was disgusted, and he was innocent.

"Heard their plans," I answered. "Couldn't let 'em do what they were goin' to."

"You can't just murder someone because they might do something!"

I was standing in front of him. "Do you want to hear what they planned? Well, let me tell you!"

I pointed at the first guy I shot. "This guy here ordered his guys to hit your place tomorrow morning. Now, the orders didn't include killing everyone. They were going to take all the kids back for some pervert they called the Lieutenant. And this piece of shit was going to keep Neave for himself!

"Now, would you rather have this fight on your doorstep, or would you rather I took care of it where your children didn't have to see it? This is the world we have to live in now, Pete Dalton! I don't want it to be, but it is! I went through the wars; I know what people will do when they're not held in check by the laws. I've seen men and women do things that would make your blood run cold. Now I've done what needed to be done. You don't like it. I don't like it. Deal with it!"

I turned away from Pete and found Doc and Grady standing right behind me.

"We need to dispose of the bodies," I said. "I think the old lead mine should do. Let's get 'em in the trucks and clean this place out."

"They can do that," Doc said. "You are coming with me in the other truck. We have to see about that 'scratch' of yours that is still bleeding."

"We'll take care of it, Zee," Grady said. "Tony will bring Dagger back in."

I grimaced. "Alright... alright."

The burning was starting in my arm as the shock wore off.

Doc pushed me up into the back of the truck. "Gary, get up there with him. You don't need to be a part of this grisly mess."

I sat down and pressed the spot where the bullet had went through my arm, wincing. The truck started, and Doc drove us back toward the farm. The ride was quiet, and I was feeling a little spooked by the way Gary watched me the whole way with a wide-eyed stare. I think he had finally seen what I'd been telling people since the bombs dropped.

Innocence would become a rare commodity in this Fallen World.

* * * * *

Chapter Three

"This is a little more than a scratch, Zee."

I shrugged.

"Quit moving," Doc said and pulled a syringe from the drawer. "Gonna need some stitches."

"How much of that do you have left?"

"I have some."

"Keep it for someone who needs it more, Doc," I said.

"Gonna hurt like hell to stitch without it."

"I deserve it for being a dumb ass," I said and braced myself for him to work on my arm.

"Probably so," he answered.

He was right, it hurt like hell, but I knew those meds would be needed in the future. We didn't have any way to replace them. The Hospital had already been cleared out. Our small supply had come from a veterinarian clinic. The first thing stolen from the Hospitals had been the pain killers. We were lucky to have found the antibiotics and the antiseptic we had.

I felt a little woozy by the time he had stitched my arm.

"That sucked," I said.

"You've been shot before," Doc pointed at a puckered scar on my back.

"Couple of times," I said. "Never patched up without the painkillers though."

"That's your own damn fault," he said.

"I didn't want to waste it after being dumb enough to let that guy get off a shot."

"Not dumb because you attacked a whole camp of raiders?"

"No," I said. "That needed done. But I should have assessed them better. I'm out of practice. They never should have gotten a shot off. They were amateurs. Dangerous, but they shouldn't have posed that much of a problem with surprise on my side. I realized a second too late that the one who shot me already had his gun in hand when I walked into camp."

"Twelve men, one with a gun in his hand?"

"Yeah," I said and reached for my shirt. "Should have shot that guy first, but the other two really pissed me off."

"I'll try to remember not to piss you off," Doc said with a grin.

"How do people go so far down in such a short time?" I shook my head. "It's been right at six months, and these people are talking murder and rape as if it was commonplace. Planning to murder Pete and rape Neave, not to mention giving the kids to some guy called the Lieutenant…"

I heard the intake of breath from behind me.

Neave had stepped into the doorway as I was speaking.

"I didn't believe what they said until right now," she said. "They said you killed people."

"I did," I said. "They were going to hit your farm tomorrow morning. I'm guessing you heard what they had planned. Your father looked at me much the same way you are looking at me right now. I understand."

I finished buttoning my shirt and walked by Neave to exit the infirmary. We had set it up almost immediately after the bombs dropped. Every piece of medical equipment we could find had been brought back. When we found Doc, we brought him back as well.

"Zee!" Neave yelled from the door behind me.

I stopped and took a deep breath. It hurt like hell to see the horror on Neave's face as she looked at me.

"There was no other way?"

"There was," I said. "I could have snuck back from the camp and come to your place where we all could have waited until tomorrow and fought them off together. But then the kids would have been in danger as well as the rest of you. Out there, I was the only one in danger, so I chose to keep you and the others safe. If that makes me a monster, then I guess I'll just have to live with it."

Her hand settled on my shoulder.

"You're not a monster, Zee," she said. "We all need to wake up to the world as it is now, and it's just harder for some of us."

"I know it is," I said. "That's why there are people like Pop. People like me. We fought in the wars so others wouldn't have it on their doorsteps. Well, now it's on our doorstep. I look out there beyond those fields, and I'm seeing Hannibal and his barbarians at the gate. The world has gone mad, and we have to be something different than we were before if we're to survive what's coming."

"There'll be more?"

"Count on it," I said. "There are things we need to do, now. They have to be done soon. We won't survive if we stay scattered on all the different farms. We have to consolidate."

"How do we move away while the silos are filled with corn?"

"That's the million dollar question," I said. "We need more people."

* * *

"Knew it was comin'," Pop said as he threw a bale of hay into the wagon.

"Yeah," I returned. "Remember those looks when I came home?"

"I remember," he said. "Got those same looks when they looked at me. They'd see the action on the vids and got that look for days after when they looked at me. It goes away after a few days."

"This is different, Pop," I said.

"Right on our damn doorstep," he muttered. "Still can't get 'em to back the plan."

"We need 'em to listen," I said. "I don't know what more I can do to demonstrate what we have coming. They all saw the damn raiders in that camp."

"They saw dead raiders, son."

"I couldn't let 'em hit the farm."

"I know," he said. "But I'm afraid it'll take one of their raids to get in before they'll see it."

"Can't let it happen if I can help it."

"Not sayin' to let it happen," he returned. "But there'll be one of the raids that gets through, and I just pray we don't pay too high of a cost for the kick in the ass these folks need. Until then, we just gotta keep workin' on the fortifications."

I looked back toward the house at the rock wall that was slowly raising around the place.

"Grady's not doubting what's coming," I said as I watched the group maneuvering another large rock into place.

The rock wall had started a week after the bombs dropped. Pop had seven people working for him at the time, and they all fell right in with the work. Grady didn't even hesitate when Pop said we needed a wall.

I threw a bale onto the wagon for Sam to stack. This would be the last of the bales. When the fuel ran out, we would have to start storing it loose like they did in the old days. My arm hurt as I threw the bale.

"Quit it, boy!" Pop said. "Let it heal."

"We don't have time," I said.

"Take the time." His voice had slipped into command voice, and I almost jerked to attention.

"Yes, sir."

"Get up there and drive the damn truck."

You never forget the bark of the sergeant, even in this Fallen World.

* * * * *

Chapter Four

"Whoa boy," I said to Dagger. He settled a little. The horse was getting better. He was probably the best of the herd. He got more ride time than most of them because he was my favorite, and I couldn't work with the arm healing so I spent a lot of time out scouting. All of the riding had built muscle on him, and he was a damn tank.

I raised the binoculars and faced toward home. Nothing seemed out of place so I swung toward the Daltens'. Then past them to check Walter's place. My swing stopped and moved back a little. That was a lot of dust.

"Vehicles," I muttered. They were moving toward Pete's.

My blood froze in my veins, but I remembered to send the signal. Red flare was emergency. I angled it up and toward Pete's so the others would know what the target was then I kicked Dagger in the ribs.

"Run!" I yelled. "Run, boy!"

He almost lost me as he launched forward. Normally we would steer down the aisles in the corn field but I pointed him straight at the target and gave him his head. Dagger loved to run and I would need that love of running to have any hope of reaching the farm in time.

This was a second planting of corn, which we hoped would come in before winter. It had been a gamble but what wasn't a gamble in the world we lived in. Running toward the Daltens' was a gamble as well but Neave was there, and I intended to be.

I leaned forward over his neck. "Run like the wind, boy."

I swear he heard me. I think he actually sped up.

I could see the roofs ahead of us when I heard the gunfire.

Dagger exploded from the cornfield behind a ragged truck with eight men crouched behind it. They would pop up and fire toward the house. I could see a body halfway across the clearing toward the house. I was almost certain it was Condy. Rage filled me, seeing the seventeen-year-old boy laying too still to be alive, and I dropped the reins which were tied together down on Dagger's neck. Both guns flew to my hands, and I opened fire on the men who faced away from me.

Now, there's a reason I usually use a single gun at any given time. Shooting two-handed is hard to do with any accuracy. You would always see it in the vid shows but that was a show. There is a time for it. When you want to send as much lead as you can in the general direction of your target, go for it. I was on the back of a running horse—what was I going to hit anyway?

I still hit two of them. Dagger saw the enemy and slammed into one of them as he came to a stop. He didn't hesitate as he stomped the fallen man. I leapt from his back to tackle another as he turned toward us. My empty pistol crunched into his face as I landed on him.

He screamed as I brought the pistol down a second time. The screams stopped.

I was moving again just as Dagger went for a second guy. The bearded raider in front of me raised his gun to point at the horse but my arms circled his head. With a snap, his head twisted sideways.

A shot boomed, and Dagger screamed but he didn't slow down. A second victim died under his hooves. My gun dropped, and I pulled the knife sheathed at my back. It sank to the hilt in another raider's neck. The last one behind the truck aimed his gun toward me, and the top of his head exploded as a shot from the house took him out.

The second vehicle, a sedan with metal armor started up and shot back toward the way it had come. I retrieved my .45 and ejected the mag. I slipped another mag in before holstering the weapon. My second was reloaded as well. Then I eased toward Dagger who stood trembling.

"Damnit boy," I said. "You're a badass."

He bumped me with his head.

I started inspecting the big black horse. There was a nasty groove on the side of his neck.

"That was a close one, brother."

I heard one of the raiders gurgling behind me so I turned and looked at him.

The knife had really done a number on him. Looking back toward the body of Condy, I drew the .45 and put a shot between his eyes.

Looking back up and toward the house, I could see Neave's pale face staring wide-eyed out of a window.

There was a dead raider where the second car had been, but I walked to where Condy lay. There was a large bullet hole in his chest. It would have been quick, at least. Dagger followed me. He sniffed the body and pushed at the boy with his nose. Condy had really loved the horses. Dagger blew air through his nose and laid his head against my arm.

I knew the horses had become part of the family, but it was gut wrenching to see the sorrow in Dagger. Condy had been part of his herd.

Looking west, I could see the plumes as the farmers closed in. Looking east toward the fleeing dust cloud, I knew today was the day Pop had been talking about.

"Zee?" I heard her voice from behind me. "Is it over?"

"No, Baby," I answered. "It's just beginning."

I looked back to where she knelt beside her cousin, tears flowing from her beautiful blue-grey eyes. I looked back toward the direction the raiders had come with hate in my heart. It hurt to see her cry.

"We need to get inside." I placed my hand on her shoulder. "They may turn around."

"What about Condy?"

"I'll bring him in."

She returned to the house, and I pulled the boy from the ground and placed him across my shoulder, remembering other days carrying my brothers off the field.

"Come on, boy," I said, and Dagger followed me toward the barn. I was pretty sure that Dallas and Fin didn't need to look at the body of their brother.

Dagger followed me into the barn. I placed Condy inside the cleanest of the stalls and went to the cabinet where the first aid supplies were kept. We didn't have much, but the antibiotic salve would help keep Dagger's wound from infecting.

I looked to the door as I saw Pete step into the barn.

"We should have listened," he said. "I…"

"We don't need to go into that, Pete," I said. "But we need to prepare for 'em to return."

"You think they'll be back?"

"Probably before the day is out."

"After losing nine men?"

"Especially after losing men."

He looked doubtful.

"In something like this, people will follow the strongest person they can," I said. "Now the guy who is in charge can't afford to show weakness. It's the nature of the sort of groups that have the raider type of mentality. If he doesn't step on us quickly, his position becomes much less secure."

"How do you even know these things?"

"We didn't just fight JalCom when I was in service," I answered. "Overseas we saw a lot of the Warlord types. Down deep they're all the same. They rule with strength or fear, and it's hard to keep that sort of thing rolling without raiding others to keep your people focused on an enemy instead of looking at your head to go on a pike."

"You knew this was going to happen."

"Yes," I answered. "I've dreaded the day for the last few months. There was no way of knowing when or where it was going to happen, but we knew it would. I'm sorry it was here, Pete."

"I wish I had listened," he said, softly.

"The important thing right now is to prepare for the next attack," I said. "We need all of the guns you've got placed and we need to fortify anything that we can before they come back."

"What can I do?"

"First we go to the house and see if there's any spots we can reinforce."

After leaving Dagger in the rearmost stall Pete and I crossed the clearing toward the house. I waved at Grady as he climbed the ladder on the side of the corn silo to find a good spot to lay in wait. He knew it wasn't over.

Entering the house and looking around for a moment, I stopped in front of Gary, Neave's youngest brother. It was easy enough to tell which of the people inside the house had been the one to shoot the guy who had been aiming his gun at me. Gary was in the corner, holding the rifle close. His face was pale, and I had seen that look in many a young soldier's eyes. I, myself, had carried that look one day nine years ago.

I squatted down in front of him. "Thank you, Gee. You saved my life out there."

"How did you know?"

"I've been there, boy," I said. "It's never an easy thing."

"Grady got the other one," he said.

"Grady's been there too," I said. "He was a deputy before this all happened."

"How can I feel this bad?"

"You should always feel bad when you have to take a life, Gee."

"You killed all those men out there in that camp," he said. "Then more here. Do you feel bad?"

"Yeah, I do," I said. "But I have to be strong for the others. You can do this, Gee. Be strong for your family. If you need someone to talk to, I'll always be here for you."

He nodded and took a deep breath, "Yes, sir."

"Okay, I want you to set up in that window over there and keep a sharp eye out for dust on the horizon. You see it, you let us know. Remember, you saved lives today, too."

I watched the boy take a position beside the window, peering out of the lower right corner. I saw in that youngster a lot of promise and one less victim in this Fallen World.

* * * * *

Chapter Five

It was almost sunset when Gary jumped up from his perch. "There's dust!"

I moved to the window to look out toward the incoming vehicles.

"That's at least four," I said.

"At least," Pop agreed.

"Shit," I muttered quietly so the others wouldn't hear.

"Grady and Ray don't have a chance of extracting if things go bad," Pop said.

"I know," I said. "We need that vantage. I can't ask them to do it though. I'll go relieve Grady."

He nodded. "I'll take Ray's position."

We both exited the house quickly and climbed the respective silos.

"You know I can do this," Grady said.

"I know but if they need to retreat I want you with 'em."

"You should be with them, Zee," he said. "I know what happens to the guys up here if you have to pull out."

I knew he was right.

"You and Kendrick both need to be down there anyway," he said. "Not one of us can hold a candle to either of you in hand-to-hand."

"If you see the flare, you get your ass down from here," I said.

"Yes, sir," he said.

I looked at the dust cloud getting closer and climbed back down the silo. I met Pop at the door.

"Ray told me to get the hell off his silo," Pop said.

"Yeah, Grady did too."

We slipped back into the house.

"Gonna be ugly fightin' in the dark," he said.

"True."

"It is what it is," he said and parked on the left side of the window Gary was manning. "You did good, earlier, boy. Ready to show these fellas what it means to face farmers?"

"Y-Yes, sir!"

"Alright, son," Pop said. "When you aim at moving targets, you lead a little and keep it low. He ain't runnin' if you shoot his damn legs out from under him. If they're chargin' you'll not get much aiming time."

"Yes, sir."

I smiled as Pop kept giving Gary little tips. Everyone looked at Pop to lead us and that position made any words carry much more weight. They looked at Pop as a sort of ruler. Mostly, they looked at me with fear. They knew what I had done to a raider camp of twelve. And they had just seen what happened when Dagger and I hit these raiders. Somehow Pop didn't give them that feeling, even though he was probably the best fighter in the whole group. We had sparred many times.

Then the roars of the engines came within hearing.

"Get ready," Pop said.

I took position to the left of the front door. The walls had been reinforced with wood planking and six inches of sand between the planks and the previous walls. Bullets wouldn't be coming through the sides of the house, at least. I remembered the vids of gunfights where the people hid behind walls. It was ridiculous. I knew what those walls were made of.

I counted four vehicles as they tore into the clearing and spread out in an arc.

"Do I shoot?"

"No, Gary," Pop said. "Wait a bit and let's see how they try to do this."

"Yes, sir."

"We've lost the light," I said.

"Yeah," Pop said. "They got headlights pointed in at us."

All we could see were shadows behind the lighted vehicles. A lot of damn shadows.

"You in the house!" a voice yelled. "We have a couple of ways we can settle this. You see, my boss just can't let people go around killing his boys. Now he gave me specific orders. I am to bring him the head of the crazy bastard on the horse. I don't know names, so that's as detailed as it gets. Now here's the deal. You give me Crazy Horse guy and I'll let you keep half the food and half the women."

"Let me think about that for a second!" I yelled. One of the shadows had been still for a little bit, and I put a round from the Winchester right into the spot I figured his head occupied.

"Son of a…!"

Shadows began to drop below the tops of the vehicles.

"You killed Garvey!" another voice said.

"Was he the one who asked for my head?" I yelled.

"Yes, you son of a whore!"

"Good!" I returned.

"I'll burn your… Who the hell are you?"

I was guessing he was interrupted.

"What are you…"

Then there were screams. A lot of screams.

"Jesus," Pete gasped. "What is happening?"

Some of the screams turned to pleas, and some just cut off abruptly. Then it was silent.

One form moved forward into the light. "Don't you shoot me, Grady Conners. Nor you, Ray Donovan."

I knew that voice as well as I knew my own.

"Jimmy?"

"Hey, Zee," the voice returned. "These fellows are through. Mind if I come in?"

I met him halfway across the clearing and swept my little brother into an embrace.

"We thought you were dead, little brother," I said. "God it's good to see you."

"Good to be home, brother."

Pop was there and wrapped arms around both of us.

"Both of my boys are alive!"

There just may be some hope, after all, for this Fallen World.

* * * * *

Chapter Six

"Jesus Christ, Zee," Grady said. We were looking at the raiders after Jimmy had gone through them. The best I could tell when my brother had come out to meet us, he was unarmed.

"Shit, Zee," Ray said. "This guy's head is completely backwards."

I was looking at a man who was folded in the middle. It wouldn't have been as odd if he hadn't been folded backwards. His spine had been broken. I looked at another with similar injury as the one Ray was looking at.

"I've been a deputy for ten years, Zee," Grady said. "I've never seen anything like this. This guy's chest is just crushed."

Ray's face was pale as we picked up a body that was just connected at the waist by skin and a few muscles.

"One guy, did this?" he asked. "How is that even possible?"

"I saw something like this in the war," I said. "It's possible."

"How?"

"I have to talk to Jimmy, first," I answered. "Not really mine to tell. It was classified material."

I looked off to the west where we had seen the mushroom clouds. "Nothing is really classified anymore, but I still need to talk to him about it first."

"Okay, Zee," Ray said.

As we picked up the bodies, I heard both of them making guesses as to how this could be done by one man. Cyborg was the one that they agreed the most with. Neither of them had ever seen what was left of a JalCom company in Egypt. There were close to three hundred soldiers in that company. Obsidian had ordered us to withdraw from the area and they sent in an Agent. One Corporate Agent had done this to that company of soldiers.

I was almost positive that my brother, James Alan Pratt, was an Agent.

I had applied to become an Agent when I enlisted. They had denied me because I lacked of moral ambiguity. They didn't think I would be able to do what they demanded of their Agents. I accepted that and joined the infantry. What really confused me was how Jimmy could have been accepted. He was always the altruistic one of us. He dreamed of heroes, flying around the world saving the day. His comic books still filled a closet in Pop's house.

Another body was lifted into the back of the truck. It had to be lifted carefully since both arms were dislocated and the skin was on the verge of splitting.

"Damn it, Jimmy," I muttered.

We spent the majority of the day disposing of thirty-four bodies. Only one of the newest raiders had a bullet wound. The nine previous raiders had been placed in the barn. All of them were loaded up and dropped down the old mineshaft. Now there were forty-six bodies at the bottom of the old lead mine. Condy would be buried with his family at the graveyard beside their farmhouse.

"How many more?" I said under my breath.

"What?" Grady asked.

"I was just wondering how many more will be at the bottom of this shaft before we get this place in good enough shape not to be a target."

"What else can we do, Zee?" he asked. "They send more, we kill more. Some of us die in the process. You know, without Jimmy, we'd have had some deaths of our own last night."

"We need to send a message," I said. "That map you found in the glove compartment of the car is pretty detailed."

"They've been scouting us for a while," he said.

"I think it's time we returned the favor," I said. "They had their HQ marked on the map as well."

"The others aren't gonna be happy if we go hit these guys."

"Pop would approve of it," I said. "But there's no need to get him involved, yet. I want to go and scout the place first."

"I'm going with you," he said. "We have all the kids and regulars moving to the compound tomorrow. A lot easier to defend with the wall."

"We'll be out a week, at least."

"Yeah, a couple days walking to get there and a couple days back."

"We could take one of their vehicles part of the way. The dust shouldn't be too bad for the first twenty miles or so since the roads are paved."

"That would take a couple days off the trip," I answered. "How much fuel was in the car?"

"It's still got over a half tank."

"That should be plenty to get us close." I nodded and continued, "If the other roads are paved, we might get even closer before kicking up too much dust."

"That crazy horse of yours is going to be pissed when he doesn't get to come with you."

"He's not only my horse."

"No one else wants to ride him after yesterday," he said.

"He's a badass," I said. "If he wasn't a gelding, I'd breed him to every one of the mares."

"You just like him because he acts like you."

"I have no idea what you're talking about."

"Sure," he said and climbed into the driver's seat of the truck. "Let's go back this thing into the lake and wash all the blood out of it."

"Probably be a good idea."

* * *

The truck cleaned up well, and we parked it in the barn at Pop's.

"I'll get the car out and make sure it's in decent shape," Grady said. "Sure you don't want to run it by Pop?"

"I will if no one else is near," I said. "I know he'll approve. Not so sure about the others."

"I'll be ready and waiting at dawn."

"See you then," I said.

I started toward the house and saw Jimmy sitting on the front porch looking out over the corn field. He just sat there until he saw me. Then he smiled. His smile was off, and I couldn't tell why for a moment. Then I saw it. His face smiled but his eyes weren't part of it. I had a suspicion that something was broken in my little brother.

Sitting down beside him in the other rocker Pop kept on the porch, I asked, "How classified is your status, Jimmy? Can you even talk about it?"

"Six months ago it was classified," he said. "Now I guess nothing is. Obsidian is gone. There were thousands of Corporate Heads, now dead. There were a few that escaped with some Guards but the corporation is done. I'm guessing you figured out what I am?"

"Yeah," I answered. "How it's possible, I don't really understand. I applied when I enlisted and was denied."

"That was before the imprinters went online."

"Imprinters?"

"After they started the imprint program, you didn't need to really have the right mindset for the job," he answered. "They gave it to you."

"They changed you?"

"Somewhat." He shrugged. "What they did was pulled your personality out of your body and replace it with the one needed to do the job. When you return, your old self is reloaded."

"There's got to be more to it," I said. "I can see the difference in you but you have yourself in there."

"When the bombs dropped, I was in the imprinter," he said. "I was halfway through the imprint when my imprinter shorted out. I have all of my memories of life as Jimmy Pratt and the skills and emotion package of the Agent."

"What does that mean?"

"I got no emotions, Zee."

"What the hell?"

"It could have been worse," he said. "The guy in the other imprinter had it much worse. His shorted out and dumped the whole database into his head. He screamed for three days. I was about to put him out of his misery when he just shut down. His body was running but his mind was off."

"Jesus."

"I have all the memories of what I should feel, so I helped keep him fed."

"That's where you've been?"

"Yes," he said. "Some of the Obsidian medical personnel finally showed up to care for the guy so I came home because it's what Jimmy would do. I need you, Zee. I need you to be my handler. I need someone to keep me from doing things when there is no memory of how I should act."

I looked into the dead eyes of my brother and realized that, no matter what your situation, there can always be worse fates in this Fallen World.

* * * * *

Chapter Seven

"Decided to bring back-up?" Grady asked. He was a little nervous around Jimmy.

"He doesn't want to be too far away from me at the moment," I said after I explained the situation. "So many ways to slip up around old friends. We're not telling everybody what's up."

"Pop?"

"That's the first thing we did," I said. "We went straight to him, and he wants Jimmy with me for the foreseeable future."

"I remember what I should do in some circumstances, but there are many places I won't know what the right thing is."

"That puts a hell of a responsibility on Zee."

"That's what family is for, Grady," I said.

He nodded.

There was a splatter of raindrops on the windshield of the old car.

"This could be good," I said. "If the roads are wet there won't be any dust."

"We can get closer in the car, that way," Grady said. "We may get lucky and have paved roads all the way."

"True," I returned. "Depends on the rain, though. You know how dusty the roads get in Destil."

Destil was the town where the raiders had set up shop. It was about half way along the main road to the suburbs of the great city to our east. The city had become Obsidian years back. Once the cities that ran along the eastern sea board were known by many names, but they grew together over the years. Now the southern half was gone and the northern half was consuming itself faster than anyone ever thought possible.

"Yep," he said. "I've been through there quite a few times on police business. It was the gateway to Obsidian. Any business we had with the city went through Destil. I only got to the city twice before the Fall. It's filled with skyscrapers and people. Damn, you wouldn't believe how many people."

"I've seen it," I said. "And you're right. So many people. We did some fighting in the lower end during JalCom II."

"That's right. You were in the Consolidation Riots."

"Those were hard times for JalCom employees. Obsidian had finished off the main offices but a lot of subsidiaries didn't want to fall in line. They started bombing civilian targets, and we had to go in."

"The vids showed some of that," he said. "It was bloody."

"Much of it couldn't be shown on the vids."

"I don't doubt that."

"I never was happier than when I got to the end of my enlistment and got to go home," I said. "I met Neave and thought it was going to be a 'Happily Ever After' story. Then Teledyne raised its ugly head. They had pretty much taken the west coast and tried to hit Obsidian before they could recover from the Consolidation. Jimmy went off to war, and the IIC decided to rain fire down on the world."

"IIC?"

"Idiots In Charge," Jimmy said from the back seat.

Grady chuckled. "That just about sums it up."

"I wanted 'Happily Ever After;' I got 'To Be Continued.'"

"If we can get the Farms protected well enough, maybe you can have it."

I looked ahead through the rain toward the east. "That monster will always plague us. We have what they need. They'll never stop trying to take it."

"That could be true," he returned. "But we can always hope."

"Here's where we get out and walk," I said as we reached the outermost dwellings of Destil.

"Want me to scout the area?" Jimmy asked.

"Sure thing, Jimmy."

He was out of the backseat and into the rain in seconds.

"Damn, that boy's fast," Grady said.

"You have no idea."

The garage door opened on the house to our right, and Jimmy motioned for us to pull the car inside. It was a good idea. No use leaving the obviously armored car on the street. The door closed behind us with Jimmy on the outside.

"May as well get geared up," I said and opened the trunk.

"Yep."

We pulled two sets of black riot gear from the trunk. Jimmy had said it would just get in the way so he'd just worn a pair of slacks and a t-shirt.

We donned the Kevlar suits and helmets. I pulled a shotgun from the trunk and put it in a holster on my back. It was a riot gun with ten shots in the pipe. My .45's were holstered on right and left hip. Grady had blacked out the Police lettering on the front and replaced it with Farmer.

"Really?"

"Seemed fitting."

I shook my head and took the other rifle from the trunk. It was a sniper rifle from the SWAT team. Our little town had a SWAT unit of one. Grady had ordered it just in case. It seemed that 'Just in case' was definitely here.

"You do know we're just doing surveillance, right?"

"Well, yeah," I answered. "If we were going to attack, I would have brought the bigger guns."

"What bigger guns?"

"You'll have to ask Pop, Lawman."

He chuckled and picked up another riot shotgun and a rifle.

We both jumped as Jimmy appeared right behind us. "Everything's clear."

As I turned around, he looked at the stencil on the front of the armor.

"I would have loved that before," he said, pointing at my chest.

"Yes, you would have."

We exited the house from the front door. The rain was steady, and I was glad for it. It would make sneaking around the town easier. As we made our way through the abandoned streets I was beginning to worry.

"Where are the people who lived here?"

"Seems like there would be some left," Grady said softly.

The stench was almost overbearing as we neared the center of the small city.

"That's de-comp," Grady said.

We neared the building that was giving off that odor. I slipped inside, Grady right behind me. The inside of the building was piled with bodies. Grady barely flipped his mask up in time to spew. I felt like I could very easily follow suit. Jimmy just looked at the pile of corpses. They'd had the muscles stripped from them. The meat.

We turned and exited as quickly as we could.

"I think that was the people who lived here," Grady said, his face ashen. "What the hell is going on here?"

"Nothing good." I was feeling a familiar rage building inside me. I'd felt this when we found the civilian casualties in the Riots. I felt it when I'd heard twelve men planning the death or worse of my family and friends. We crossed the street and kept moving in towards the city center. I remembered a square in Destil with the Obsidian Justice Center right in the middle of it.

Peeking around the corner of a building I could see the Center. It was a lot different than before with iron fortifications around the building. They were fortified three stories high and the gate was ten feet tall by about twelve wide.

"They've been busy," I said.

"Slave labor," Grady pointed toward a massive set of pens that held captives.

"Gotta be a couple hundred people in those cages."

A group of men left the fortified Center dragging two girls. They were naked and could barely move.

I snarled, and Grady grabbed my arm.

The men threw the girls into one of the bottom cages. They dragged another from the cage, and I raised the SWAT rifle.

"Oh shit," Grady muttered as I put a round through the left eye of the guy who was dragging the woman from the cage.

Grady shot another, and I motioned for him to go up inside the building to our left. "Once you reach the top, let me know, and I'll join you."

I shot the third and fourth as Grady ran the stairs. When he shot the last man in the group, I headed up the stairs, Jimmy by my side.

A speaker on the outside of the building buzzed.

"Alright, that's about enough of that! Who the hell are you, and why are you shooting my boys?"

The actions I took finally caught up with me.

"Now what, Boss?"

"Shit."

"You really gotta stop doing things like this," Grady said.

"You would've if I hadn't," I said.

"Probably," he answered.

The voice on the speaker spoke again, "I have forty armed men in here, whoever you are! We have enough slaves in here to keep us going for weeks! If you think you can get to those slaves in the pens, you're sadly mistaken!"

A shot rang out from the Center, and the woman the men had been trying to drag out toppled.

"Bastard."

"Now you either back out of here and leave us be or we'll kill all of them! If you want to try to come in here…well, come get some!"

"Would you like for me to go get some, Zee?"

I turned to look at Jimmy, who had a completely serious look on his face.

"This is what I'm made for, Zee," he said.

"Can you get that gate open?"

"Certainly."

I looked at Grady who was looking at me with a "what the hell" look.

"Alright, Jimmy," I said. "Go get some."

As I watched Jimmy jump from a two story building to the street below, I had a feeling there just might be a way to bring some justice to this Fallen World.

* * * * *

Chapter Eight

"Jesus Christ!"

I fully understood the reaction from Grady. I'd seen the aftermath of an Agent during the wars. Seeing one in action was surreal.

Jimmy was across the clearing so fast I could barely track him. Then he went up the side of that building like a monkey. They'd armored three stories. Jimmy went through a window on the fourth floor.

Like the night he showed up, the screams began. I heard shots, but not many.

"We gotta get to the gate."

"Yep," Grady answered, and we ran back down the stairs.

There was still a lot of noise from the building but no one shot us as we ran across the clearing. People in the cages were standing at the doors watching bodies begin flying out the windows. They impacted the bars hard enough to send bars and broken bodies both into the street. He was on the second floor.

The gate opened, and fleeing bandits were met with fire from two riot guns. There was a thought of mercy, but it was fleeting as I remembered the charnel house and two battered women.

Dropping the empty shotgun, I drew my .45 and shot two more before they turned to run back inside.

There were more screams.

Then one form walked out the door. His arms were soaked with blood up to the elbows. There was blood on his t-shirt. You couldn't see the blood on his black slacks.

"Probably should wear black," Jimmy said.

"Damn it, Jimmy."

"Gate's open," he said.

Grady looked inside the door. "Damn it, Jimmy."

"Let's clear the rest of the building," I said.

"It's clear," Jimmy said. "Figured it was easier to just clear it on the way down."

"Top floor?"

"That's where prisoners are kept. I killed the guards but haven't opened the doors yet."

He tapped the side of his head. "Jimmy thinks you should do that part. I'll clear the rest of the area."

I nodded.

Grady and I went through every room on our way to the top of the building. Sure enough, there were no living raiders. There were bodies, guns, knives, and holes in the side of the building where windows used to be.

"What the hell did they do to him?" Grady asked.

"No one actually knows," I said. "They used nanotech, biotech, and any other tech they could. Who knows what went into the Agents? I just know what the aftermath looks like."

We reached the last two bodies. They had been standing guard on a door with several locks. I busted the locks with the butt of the SWAT rifle and opened the door. The whole upper floor was open and there were people scattered from one end to the other. This used to be four huge courtrooms, and they'd knocked down the walls between the rooms.

"I'm glad we have Jimmy," he said. "I don't think the two of us could have done it."

"Some of these folks are going to need Doc," I said. "I need you to go take one of their cars and get to the Farm as fast as you can. We need everyone to help get all these people out of here. There has to be a hundred and fifty or more in the cages and thirty or forty up here."

"I'm on it," he said and ran back down the stairs.

The women and children huddled in the corners, watching me. Others were chained to various devices. I wished Jimmy had left some of the raiders alive so I could kill them again.

"We're here to rescue you," I said. I went to the first torture device and carefully started unhooking it from the young woman who was bleeding from a number of cuts.

"A-Are you r-r-really here to rescue us?" she stammered.

"Damn right I am."

I pointed to one of the other women. "You."

She jerked.

"Help get these ladies off the damn racks." I pointed at another. "You help her. Hell, everyone help get them down."

They were slow to start releasing the others, but, after the first one was removed from the torture rack and I didn't harm them, they all pitched in. The stronger women helped me bring the weaker down the stairs. I had thought the blood and death would bother them, but I actually saw smiles on many faces as they recognized their captors.

Jimmy met us at the bottom. He was accompanied by a bearded man who looked intently at the faces as they exited the building. He was almost panicking until he saw the young woman I was carrying. She was the one with all the cuts.

"D-Deli?"

"Daddy?" the girl in my arms asked.

"What have they done to you, Deli?"

"I'm okay now, Daddy," she said. "These men saved us all."

* * *

"They're in rough shape, Zee," Doc said. "A couple aren't going to make it."

I frowned.

"Even with the medication we found, I can't save them," he said. "Three of them have sepsis and are dying. Internal injuries are the worst thing. Even if I could do a surgery, it wouldn't help."

I leaned my head back against the headrest on the chair as he spoke. "Save the ones you can, Doc."

"I'll do my best, Zee," he said.

"I know you will, Doc," I said. "You always do."

He nodded and left the room I was using to command the operation. First, we had to get these people patched up. Then we could move them back to the Farm. How did the world get so bad in so little time? I knew humanity was always on the verge of barbarism, but less than a year, and there was cannibalism and torture, slavery and rape. How did we fall so quickly? This had once been the greatest country in the world.

What were good people to do in this Fallen World?

* * * * *

Chapter Nine

"She has a total of thirty-seven different cuts, Zee," Doc said. "I stitched them up but this girl has been through hell. She's lost a lot of blood. We need to find a donor or she's going to die."

"What's her blood type?"

"O negative."

"She's a universal donor? Good for others, not so good for her. But she may be in luck, I'm O positive," I said and rolled my shirt sleeve up. "Let's get to it."

"I hoped you would say that," he said. "It's rare, but I knew both you and Jimmy are the right blood type. Unfortunately, there's no telling what they've done to his."

"Very true." I nodded.

I always hated donating blood but this was something that needed to be done. Delilah Chaney had suffered more than any person should have. She deserved a chance to survive this.

The process didn't take very long, and Doc returned to his patient. I felt light-headed. He'd taken a good bit of blood.

"You go drink something," he said. "And eat some meat to rebuild yourself."

"Yes, sir."

"Don't be a smartass." He waved me off and returned his attention to the young woman. "What the hell were they doing to these people?"

"Just about any awful thing they could imagine," I answered. "Gonna be hard for these people to come back from what those animals did to them."

"There's truth to that," he said. "What are you going to do with them?"

"I guess I'll make them an offer."

He nodded as I rolled my sleeve back down over the small bandage.

I looked one more time at the battered girl and shook my head. This was ridiculous. How did it happen so quickly?

I walked from the room and made my way to the center of the square.

"Listen up, people!"

The people spread around the square turned to me.

"You folks have some decisions to make!" I yelled. "We're going to help any of the injured we can. By the time we treat them, you'll need to make a decision. We'll turn the town back over to you, no questions asked. But if we see the same kind of shit from you people, I swear I'll burn it to the ground with you in it."

I had their attention. "Now there is different option you can choose. If you come back with us, there will be plenty of food, and we'll see to it that there will be shelters built. This option comes with a few rules. We are farmers. There are crops to plant and harvest, and our machines are dead. If you come with us, everyone works. You'll work every day, just as we do, but you'll eat every day too. That's Rule Number One."

"Rule Number Two!" I said while pointing toward them. "This world is an unforgiving bitch and I will teach you how to stand in it instead of be stood upon. We'll teach you to fight, and we'll put weapons in your hands. And the most important thing about this is, everyone fights! Every person on our farms is trained or is in training to defend them. If you come to join us you will be expected to do no less than the rest of us."

I looked out on people who had been enslaved, watched their neighbors eaten, probably been fed those same neighbors, and lived the last four months in cages. They were hurt and some of them broken, but I could see a gleam in several sets of eyes that gave me hope. We would train them to never be victims again.

"As I said, you have about a day and a half to decide what you'll do. We'll have several vehicles coming in within the next hour or so with enough to get your bellies full. We're heavy on vegetables and light on meat but I think you'll all feel a little better after dinner."

I felt that rage inside again as I saw some of the haunted looks as I said the word meat. If I could kill the group that had been holding them in cages again, I would.

* * *

The man who had been waiting outside with Jimmy when we came out of the Justice Center was the one who came back to see me a little over an hour later.

"We can never thank you enough for what you have already done," he said. "I used to be the mayor and I failed my city. I thought we could deal with those animals. They made bargains then they took more and more from us. Finally, it became what you saw here."

He pointed back toward the Justice Center.

"I don't deserve the trust these people gave me, and I certainly don't deserve the position they have placed me in." He shrugged his shoulders then they slumped in misery. "They still look to me for leadership, and I can't give it to them. I told them what I planned to do, and they all agreed. We would join you if you'll let us, after what we've done. I told them I would tell you all of it before going back with you. You need to know what we've done."

"You survived," I said.

"But we…we ate…"

"I know." I stopped him. "I figured that the moment I saw the cages. They made you?"

"We could have refused," he said in despair. "We should have refused."

"You survived."

"At what cost?"

"Hopefully, one you can live with," I said. "Because I won't lie to you. We need people at the farms. We need growers, we need workers, and we need fighters. Most of all, we need survivors."

"We'll come with you," he said. "And burn this place to the ground on our way out."

I looked back toward Justice Center. "That might be for the best."

"What do you know of my daughter, Deli?"

"Doc's watching her closely," I said. "She improved a great deal after the transfusion."

"Transfusion?"

"She'd lost a lot of blood."

"That's why your doctor asked my blood type?"

"Yes."

"She has one that's hard to find donors," he said.

"There was one that worked."

"Can you tell me who it is so I can thank them?"

"I'd rather keep it confidential," I said. "But Doc is going to need to keep a register so he knows who to go to in the future. Right now there's no way to store blood without any electricity. All the fuel would go pretty quickly if we tried to use generators."

"Understood," he said. "If you know the donor, please thank them for me."

"I'll let Doc know."

"Thank you."

He turned to go.

"What's your name, Mayor?"

"Sampson Chaney."

"You're Sampson, and you named your daughter Delilah?"

"My wife's idea."

"She out there?" I motioned toward the door.

"She passed before all of this, thank God," he said. "She was such a sweet woman. She wouldn't have done well in this place. Not that we've done too well, ourselves."

He walked out the door and closed it behind him.

My thoughts went to Neave and her father. There is no lack of people who will struggle to adapt to life in this Fallen World.

* * * * *

Chapter Ten

"See this knife, Gee?"

Gary nodded. "Yes, sir."

"This knife will be yours." I handed the combat knife to the boy. "The fact that you have it doesn't do you any good until you can use it."

I pulled a pipe with a leather wrapped hilt from the bag at my feet.

"You'll practice with this two hours per day, every day."

"Yes, sir."

Steering him to the mannequin I had set up, I pointed to the red circle on the ribcage.

"If you stab a person in that circle, at this angle," I said, placing the point of the pipe at the angle I wanted, "It goes right into the heart."

"The carotid artery is right here." I pointed at another marked spot. "Slash across here."

His face was a little pale, but he paid close attention.

"Femoral artery," I said and pointed. "Again, slash."

We moved around the back of the mannequin.

"This is where the kidneys are," I said. "This doesn't kill them outright but no one is interested in fighting anymore after they have a blade through one of their kidneys. These are your assignment. When I test you, I expect you to be able to hit these spots from anywhere you're positioned around this target."

"Yes, sir."

"Your first test will be in five days," I said. "I want you to imagine every way you can possibly reach those spots and practice doing it. When the test is done, I'll show you some more. You're pretty good with the rifle, but some day we're going to run out of bullets. At the rate we're going, it'll be sooner than later."

"This is important, Gee. Make sure you do the work. Fighting is part knowledge and a whole lot of muscle memory. You train the body, and it'll be there when you need it."

"I will, Zee."

I nodded and left the boy making stabbing motions at the mannequin.

"I almost asked you if that was necessary," Neave said as she walked over to join me. "But I know it is."

"You need to be practicing those same skills," I said.

"I do need to," she said. "But I have some other skills I need to work on as well. Something I have to learn from momma."

"Yes?"

"I missed my period."

I was two steps further along the path before what she said registered. I came to a complete stop with what I'm sure looked like a dazed expression.

"I think I've seen everything, now." She laughed. "The ferocious Zebadiah Pratt is speechless."

And I was speechless. How could I express the feelings I had. The amazement that I may get to be a father and the horror that this world would be the one this innocent would be brought into.

I did the only thing I could think of; I swept her into my arms and held her close. There really were no words to describe what was going on inside my head.

* * *

"We have all of the supplies from Destil," Grady said as he stepped from the truck. "They were hoarding a basement full of canned goods, weapons, ammo, and even some medical supplies. This is the last of it."

"Metal?"

"Got the majority of what we could move," he said. "Might be able to drag some of the vehicles but I don't think we have the fuel for it."

"We may go back for more later," I said. "Did you burn the abattoir?"

"We did. And the Justice Center."

"Good." I looked toward the east. "That place needed to be destroyed. It'll help them to get past what happened there."

"Chaney was the last person to walk out of Destil," he said. "He lit the fires, himself."

"Good," I said. "He has a lot he needs to put behind him, and that's a good start."

"I don't know if it will ever be enough," he said. "He made deals with those bastards."

"Look at the world we grew up in," I said. "Would you ever have thought people could turn into what those raiders were?"

"I've seen some of the dark side of people," he said, "and I still wouldn't think they'd turn so fast."

"Imagine what the city is like."

"Pure hell."

"I suspect so."

"Probably makes what happened in Destil look like a walk in the park."

"We need more scouts between here and there," he said.

"Yep," I replied. "I'm heading out this evening to run the east patrol."

"You taking anyone else with you this time?"

"Ray, Kyle, and Sadie."

"Good team. Sadie is probably the best shot in the farms."

"Ray and Kyle are both good but she's in another league."

"She took to guns a lot better than most of our people."

"Played vid games most of her life. Small step to graduate to real guns. She had the hand-eye coordination pretty well handled."

"She's never shot a real person, though," he said. "Keep an eye on her. That's a whole new experience. I'm sure you remember your first."

"I'll never forget it," I said. "Never thought I would get rid of that hollow pit in my gut. Took some time."

"It should never be easy."

"When it's easy, you've already lost more of yourself than anyone should."

"You're not taking Jimmy?"

"No, he's staying with Pop for a while. Pop's worried about him."

"We all are," he said. "That boy was a handful when he was a kid. Practical joker. Now... well..."

"I know," I said. "He's Jimmy but he's not Jimmy. They really did a number on my brother. Obsidian can burn in hell for that."

"From what Sam said, they're doing just that. Their headquarters were hit by one of the strikes. He was just outside the city when the bombs dropped. The south is a wasteland. No one knows how far south it goes. You can't get near it, much less get through it to see what's on the other side. Same for the areas to our west."

"When we get ourselves in a position to do it, I had thought about going north and west to see if anything remains out west."

"You know that's a long trip without cars."

"Yes," I replied. "But that may have to remain just a thought."

"Why is that?"

"A father needs to be with his family."

It took him a moment to realize what I was saying. "Neave's pregnant?"

"Just found out."

He strode forward and embraced me. "Congratulations!"

As he stepped back, he was still grinning. "It's one of the greatest joys a man can have, to become a father."

"I worry about the world we're bringing a child into."

"All parents throughout history have worried about that."

"After seeing Destil, it's a little more than a worry."

"Then it's going to be our job to make something better out of this Fallen World."

* * * * *

Chapter Eleven

The sky looked dark to the north.

"Gonna be getting wet," I muttered as I patted Dagger's neck.

He snorted.

I smiled as I reached into the saddlebags to pull out a long poncho they had brought back from Destil. I had a long duster back at the farm that Gail Turnby was giving a treatment with bees wax. The poncho would do until the coat was finished. They'd found a lot of supplies in the basement when they'd searched the Justice Center. Why they'd hoarded things they didn't need was just another part of their mindset I couldn't stand. There were four hundred coats from several stores piled in the corner.

We had hoarded grain, corn, and beans. The abundance of those initial crops were paying off now that we had grown our population by a hundred and forty-three people. The second growth of corn was in the process of being harvested. The extra hands would make that a great deal easier, since the fuel was gone.

The first fat drop of rain hit my head just as the poncho slipped on. I was glad the weather came from the north. I was worried about anything being carried from the west. So far there had been no radiation from it but it could ruin everything if it happened.

Dagger snorted again as a fat drop splattered his ear.

"Sorry, boy. This poncho's not big enough to cover your head."

I had spread it along the back to cover most of the horse's rump.

"Maybe we can find a good tree..."

The sky lit up to the south as a red flare went straight into the sky.

"Shit." I pointed Dagger toward the emergency flare. "Go, boy!" I jammed my heels into his sides, and he launched southward.

Thunder rolled to my north and gunfire to the south.

Slipping my hand inside the poncho, I drew the .45 with my right hand and kept the left on the reins.

The gunfire was closer, and I held myself low on Dagger's back. We burst into a clearing with a rock hill in the center. I recognized the form on the hill as Sadie Billings. She was firing to the south, and I had come in on the north. Two others were behind the rocks with her, neither familiar. But both were firing to the south. I saw Sadie's pale face as I thundered past on the big black horse. Rounding the rocks, I saw a group of ten or so men trying to work their way toward the three in the middle and another guy on a horse. He shot in my direction and I heard the bullet whiz past me. This guy was good. But he didn't have the one thing I did. A crazy sixteen-hand warhorse. Dagger charged right through the men, sending several tumbling. I fired into some of the others. Dagger slammed his shoulder into the smaller horse and I dove right into the other rider.

We hit the ground with my shoulder impacting his chest. I could hear the crack as my two hundred and sixty pounds of muscle and bone crushed his chest. Rolling forward, I slung off the poncho and drew my other pistol. With both guns spitting lead and fire, I walked right into the group of men. There was a tug at my leg but I was pumped with adrenaline and barely felt it. My guns ran out, and I dropped the left to replace a mag in the right. Another shot grazed my cheek and I began shooting into the four remaining men. Two went down from my shots, and I could see one of the others drawing a bead on me. He jerked to the side as a bullet from the rocks hit him.

Another hit the last living raider.

Dagger walked up behind me and nudged me with his head.

"Yeah, I know you're a badass, buddy."

Sadie walked from the rocks with her rifle in shaky hands. She was followed by two men I hadn't met before.

"B-Boss," she stammered. Then she took a deep breath. "These men were being chased by the others. I ran into them, and they want to come join us. I think they may be very useful. This is Kal Spriggs and Trevor Gaines.

"You're wearing Obsidian fatigues," I said. The clothes were worse for wear but they were still military issue.

"Yes, sir," the shorter of the two said. "Obsidian Corps of Engineers."

"Engineer, huh?" I asked with a grin. A grin that set my cheek to burning where the bullet grazed me. "Shit."

"You need to have that looked at, sir," Spriggs said. "Trevor is a medic."

"Both are skills we need," I said. "First, why were they chasing you?"

"I hate to argue, sir, but I can tell you our story while Trevor looks at that leg and that nasty cut on your face."

"Alright, but it better be quick." I gestured over my shoulder to the north. "That'll be here soon."

"Yes, sir."

Sadie raised her hand and fired the yellow flare straight into the sky.

"Really?"

Yellow meant call for a vehicle to transport wounded.

She shrugged.

Her face was still pale after shooting someone for the first time but she was doing a good job of holding her shit together.

* * *

"You ever think the way you fight might be detrimental to your health, boy?" Pop said as he sat down in the other rocker on the front porch. "I'll not argue that it isn't effective, but you're giving me grey hair."

"It works."

"It gets you out of harvesting corn, if that's what you're talking about."

"They had Sadie pinned down, Pop," I said. "Weren't many options."

"That's the conclusion I came to after everyone gave me a report. One of the new guys said you looked like some fire-breathing demon when you blew past them. Spriggs said he would give everything he owned for that horse. Of course, his house in Colorado ain't worth much nowadays."

"True enough," I said. "Wouldn't trade that bastard for a house, anyway."

"Nope," Pop said. "Besides, that horse is half of this reputation you're building."

"Not building anything like that."

"No, you're just doing your thing, and it's building on its own." He pointed at the bandage on my thigh. "I served eight years and never took a bullet. How many times did you get shot during the war? Ten? Just kept charging in. Now you been shot three times in the last four months."

"Some folks just don't seem to like me, Pop."

He snorted. "You're a damn lead magnet. I should have sent Jimmy with you."

"He needs to have more than just killing around him, Pop. He needs to see us at peace, too."

"I know it, boy." He shook his head. "But he's worth a hundred of me or you in a fight."

"Probably more."

"What are your thoughts on the two new guys?" he asked. "I just got after action reports on what happened when you got there. Sadie said they told you where they were from."

"The guy who was riding the horse was their captain," I said.

"Deserters?" Pop's eyes narrowed.

"Not until the captain had gone completely off the rails. Their company fought their way out of the city. Then the captain set up shop on the outskirts. When he started capturing refugees as they fled the city, Spriggs and Gaines wanted no part in that. Captain put them in a cell. Two others broke them out, and they stole what supplies they could and hauled ass. Both of the others died in pitched battles with the ones the captain sent after them and Sadie ran into them on her patrol. You know the rest."

"May not be as bad as I thought, then," he said. "Got little use for deserters."

"Sounds like they were in the right on that decision. But I'll have to go scout them if we want to make sure."

"Already sent Grady out to look them over. You'd go shoot them. I just want to know what sort of men they are. I understand Spriggs is an engineer? I have something in mind that he may be able to help us with.

Right now, you just recuperate. When Grady gets back we'll talk some more about it."

"That's just mean, Pop," I said. "Dropping hints and nothing more."

"That's what you get for getting shot. You manage not to get shot next time, and I'll consider letting you in on the fun stuff."

"Asshole."

"Yep. I raised one just like me."

"Don't pick on Jimmy like that."

He laughed and stood up. He looked at my leg again and shook his head. Then he walked into the house.

I grinned at him as he walked by. If you can't take a moment to just laugh, what's the point surviving in this Fallen World?

*****

Chapter Twelve

"Looks like Spriggs and Gaines didn't lie about the crew they escaped from," Pop said. "Now it's time to talk to that engineer."

"He's trying to rig some solar cells up on the equipment shed," I said. "He seems to think he can get enough power to charge some of the batteries in the cars to give us some mobility in emergencies."

"That bodes well for what I have in mind," he said. "Let's go see the boy."

"You're still not going to tell me what's going on?"

"Try not to get shot so much, and I'll trust you with the big things."

"What's getting shot have to do with it?"

"Nothing."

"Then why is that a prerequisite?"

"Because I don't like when my boys get shot."

I sighed and followed Pop to the shed.

"Spriggs!"

Spriggs still hadn't lost that immediate reaction from serving in the military. He was around the corner and facing Pop, standing at attention.

"Sir!"

"Got a job for you if you're interested," Pop said with a grin. "And you don't have to stand at attention. This ain't the army."

"That may be true," Spriggs said. "But you're building one here, and it doesn't hurt to treat it like one." He pointed toward the east.

"With that ugly piece of Hell right over there, you need that discipline."

"You're probably right," Pop said. "Probably need an official name and everything."

"The Farmers Guard would be my first thought."

"Might be a good idea."

"What sort of job do you have in mind, sir?"

"About forty miles north of here is where the old hydro-electric plant used to be. Used to supply the area with electricity until the nuclear plants went online. I want you to go with Zee, here, and give it a look."

"Yes, sir!" I could see the excitement all over his face. "I'd love some electricity, sir."

"I'd love some electricity, too. This Stone Age bullshit is pissing me off. I'm getting too old for this shit."

"You could have told me this earlier," I said.

"I told you," he said. "Quit getting shot, and I'll tell you a couple of my secrets."

"I'm not saying anything," Spriggs said. "He got shot saving my ass, and I can't say I wish he didn't do it. They were closing in on us."

"The key," Pop said, "is to shoot them before they shoot you. Not after. Now, if you're trying to get out of harvesting corn, I guess the other way around works but there's ways to do that without all the bleeding."

"Whatever," I said. "I'm going to saddle up Dagger."

"That damn horse is as bad as you are."

I walked away with Pop still grumbling.

"He's right about the horse," Spriggs said. "I read books about warhorses and that is one of them. He's got to be descended from some of those."

"He was." I reached for the gate to the paddock. "He's a Friesian. They used to be warhorses back in medieval times. The owners used to brag about that incessantly."

"What happened to them?"

"They ran to the city for safety."

"Oh."

That was enough to figure what happened to the Clarks. I felt bad for the three kids they dragged into that hell.

Dagger saw me from across the paddock and tore across the field at a full run, kicking up his heels.

"He looks like he's happy," Spriggs said. "Or he's going to stomp us into squishy little piles. I'm not really sure which."

He stepped back a few paces.

"It's really a crap shoot at this point." I shrugged.

Dagger skidded to a stop inches from my chest. Then he pushed me backwards with his head.

"Oh, come on you damn heathen," I said and walked toward the tack shed. He kept pushing me with his head until I reached the shed where I kept his saddle.

Spriggs entered the paddock and came back with a bay in tow.

"Kennedy is a good one," I said.

"Kennedy?" he asked. "The American President?"

"Nope, named him after an author whose books I found in the library, when I was a kid. Used to love to read the old classic Sci-Fi. I named the pony over there Wandrey."

"Who rides the pony?"

"Some of the kids start on him," I said. "If they can stay on that little asshole, they can ride a horse. He's a good trainer."

"Which saddle do you want me to use?" he asked. "I haven't ridden a horse in years. Hopefully I can remember how to saddle one."

"Sometimes you have to use a knee when Kennedy puffs up," I said. "If you don't, the saddle will be loose."

"Maybe you should check it."

"I will," I said. "But you do your best. Then I'll check if there's anything wrong."

For the most part, he got it all right. He didn't knee Kennedy hard enough, and I showed him how. The horse was notorious for sucking in a large breath so the saddle wouldn't be tight. A loose saddle could dump you off in a fight and cost you your life.

"Dagger doesn't play those games." I patted the big black on the neck. "He did it a couple of times when I first rode him, but he doesn't even try any more. Kennedy tries it on everyone. Wandrey's even worse. It's one of the reasons it's so hard to stay mounted on him, but it's good training for the kids."

"We taking anyone else?"

"Pop's going to send Trevor over and Jimmy."

"I hate to even ask this, but is there something wrong with Jimmy?"

"There is," I said. "He came back to us different."

"Everyone from Destil is scared to death of him."

"He was an Agent."

"Seriously?"

"Yeah," I said, cinching the back strap on the saddle. "They really screwed him up with that imprint tech they use."

"Things make a little more sense, then," he said. "Saw one of them about a year and a half before they dropped the bombs. My unit was doing a demo job on a building and a bunch of Teledyne grunts pinned us down. We were about to drop the skyscraper on them and us both when an Agent just walked into our makeshift fortifications. She said, 'Don't worry, fellas. I'll take care of this.' Damn if she didn't just jump over our fortifications and charged right into those bastards. She put down close to eighty Teledyne troops in next to no time. It was a sight I'll never forget."

"I'm pretty sure the Agent program was the thing that made Obsidian so successful in their hostile takeovers," I said. "Soldiers were much the same on both sides. The Agents were what tipped the balance."

"I wouldn't be surprised," he said. "Most of them were out on the front lines, though, when the bombs dropped."

"There were a couple who weren't. The other one was screwed up even worse than Jimmy. From what he described, the guy has about a thousand personalities dumped into his brain from the imprinter."

"Jesus, that's awful."

"Jimmy said when he left the guy was a step up from a vegetable."

"Anytime a person starts feeling sorry for himself…" he said, shaking his head.

* * *

"We're not breaking down that door," Spriggs said.

We were looking at a solid steel-double door.

Spriggs looked up. "There should be an easier door to get through on the roof. Let me see if I can find a way up."

"I'll take care of it," Jimmy said and jumped to the second story where he caught a ledge and threw himself up another story.

"Damn it, man."

"Damn it, Jimmy, is a pretty common phrase when we're out here," I said.

"That doesn't surprise me," Trevor said.

"Hard to take your eyes off of him when he's doing things like that," I said. "Humans aren't supposed to be able to do that."

Jimmy was over the ledge eight stories up and out of sight as he crossed the roof.

"Before he lost his emotions, Jimmy would have been on Cloud Nine with what he can now do." I shook my head, sadly. "He sure loved the super heroes from the comic books."

"I was always a fan of comics," Spriggs said.

"Jimmy was the friendliest of all three brothers and kept on going through life with his belief in heroes," I said. "It hurts to see what they did to him."

"I imagine so." Spriggs nodded. "There's no chance of repairing him?"

"The imprint tech was well past my skill set," Trevor said. "But from what I know of it, there's no fixing him without an imprinter."

The huge doors groaned as Jimmy pushed them open from the inside.

"Let's get a look at this place," I said.

"Oh yes." Spriggs looked like a kid about to enter a pre-Fall candy store.

As we followed him into the facility, I looked at Trevor. "You think he can fix this place up?"

"If anyone can, Spriggs can," he said. "He was a demon with electrical equipment in the Corps. Hell, they all called him Dynamo."

I watched the guy as he checked out the power relays and wiring schematics in a manual he'd found in a desk.

Just maybe there was some hope to be found in this Fallen World.

* * * * *

Chapter Thirteen

I stopped just before rounding the corner as I heard voices.
"..ime to train, Cousin."
I was sure it was Gary's voice.
"But I need to finish with this," Neave answered.

"Horse shit," Gary said. "Zee won't tell you because he's in love with you. You're my cousin and I love you, but you'll get your ass out here and train. You've seen what came from Destil. I won't have my cousin being a victim."

"You sound just like Zee," she said.

"Then you should listen," he said. "I had to kill a man, Neave. It sucks. But if I hadn't shot that man, Zee would have been killed. What if I hadn't been there? Would you have done it? Right now, you wouldn't. Get your head out of your ass. We can't go back to the way it was unless we carve out our place in this new world with guns and knives. You helped Doc with the people from Destil. You know what happened there. They were afraid to fight, and they were slaughtered like cattle. I won't be that, and I won't let my cousin be that either."

I heard her long sigh.

"Get your practice blade and your rifle," he said. "We've got a long day ahead of us."

I backed up and turned around. I knew I was too easy on Neave, and I should have my ass kicked for not doing what Gary had just done. I slipped in the back door, needing to gather my kit for a patrol.

"Did you put Gary up to that?"

Turning, I found her right behind me.

"Up to what?" I asked.

"Never mind," she said. "Going to train."

She kissed me and grabbed her rifle from the rack. "Be careful. The last time you rode patrol, you got shot again."

"I'll try."

"Hmph."

"You be careful, too."

I followed her out the front of the house where Gary was waiting. As she walked toward him I silently mouthed the words, "Thank you."

I nodded at him and his face turned red.

I grinned as the two of them walked toward the machine shed we had cleaned out for a training hall. There were wooden dummies scattered around the building, and I could see recruits working out in the various spaces.

Smiling again, I turned and went back inside to put my pack together. The grain bars tasted like dirt but they would sustain a person. I managed to get some jerky which was a rare treat. As I walked out the door with the pack over my shoulder there was a commotion by the long shed. It was the place we had designated as a meeting area.

Pop was standing in front of two men who were pretty agitated, so I made my way over.

"If I want to kill a cow, I damn sure plan to kill it, Kendrick!"

The taller of the two men, Hollis Drager, was shaking his finger in Pop's face.

The other, Oslo Trips saw me, and his face paled. "This doesn't have anything to do with you, Zee," he said.

Hollis didn't even look at me; he continued to shake his finger at Pop. "We need meat. The cows are meat!"

"If you kill the cows this year, then the beef she carries for next year dies with her. I told you all meat would get scarce this year. We have forty-eight heifers. They should throw that many calves next year. You kill one of them and you cut the number we'll have for the future. You want protein, eat beans."

"You can't stop me from killing one of the cows, Kendrick Pratt! Who says you're the damn law?"

"Hollis Drager!" My voice rang out, and he jumped. I'm not even sure he had registered what his partner had said moments earlier.

He turned and his face went white as a sheet as he realized I was standing there. They were all afraid of me, but I couldn't understand how they weren't afraid of Pop. He could outfight anyone on the farms except Jimmy.

"This is between me and Kendrick," he said.

I pointed to the others around us. "Hollis, if you kill a cow it will take food from the plates of everyone in the compound. I'm not going to let you do that." His hands gripped his rifle with whitened knuckles. "If you do what you're thinking and raise that rifle, I'm going to kill you."

"I wasn't…"

"Yes you were. You're angry and not thinking. If you were thinking, you'd see that Pop has kept the needs of this community as his highest priority from day one. The cows will not be harmed by you or anyone else this year. If you want meat, go hunting. There are still rabbits, deer, and squirrel. Set traps for small game. The books from the library have all of the knowledge we need." I stepped forward. "And if you think you can raise that rifle fast enough, you just go right ahead. But who will take care of Genny and Frank? You have people that depend on you. Don't make me orphan those children."

Any color that had remained on his face was gone as he realized he *had* been thinking of raising the rifle. He also realized how close to death he was treading. I could see those realizations on his face and his decision to back up. His shoulders slumped.

"I'll bring it to the council," he said.

"You do that, Hollis," Pop said. "They'll tell you the same thing I have."

Hollis and Oslo walked away, grumbling to one another.

"You took a hard line with him, boy," Pop said.

"Needed to be done, Pop."

"Probably so." He nodded. "But it's not going to win you any favors."

We watched as the others began to scatter. There were quite a few fearful glances in my direction.

"I don't want them to fear me, Pop," I said. "But we need them to. It'll take an iron hand to keep them from self-destruction. Better it's me than you. They can still listen to you as a moderate voice."

"Sometimes you scare me, boy." Pop shook his head. "It's like they are going through life with blinders on, and you see it all so clearly. You're right, I need to be heard as a voice of reason. If we let down our guard, this place is going to fall."

"I'm trying my best to keep that from happening, Pop."

"I know you are," he said. "It makes things hard on you, though."

"I can handle it."

"How's your girl handling it?"

"She has problems with what I have to do sometimes, but she's stronger than she seems. She just has to adjust to this new world. Pete is just as bad on that front."

"True." He nodded. "He can't seem to wrap his head around what's going on."

"I understand it," I said. "I saw Destil, first hand, and it's hard to accept that people did that."

"It was going to happen," Pop said. "I sure didn't expect it to happen so quickly."

"From what Spriggs said, it's even worse in the city."

"Humanity has always been on the edge of barbarism," he said. "We just never knew how close to the edge they were. Right now, all we can do is try to survive in this Fallen World."

* * * * *

Chapter Fourteen

"We've got a little problem, Zee."

I turned from the hole I was digging to find Grady walking toward me.

"What's up?"

"For the last two months the chickens have been putting out close to four dozen eggs a day."

"Yeah?"

"The last three days they've been laying two dozen."

"Shit," I muttered.

"Either they're not laying or someone is stealing eggs."

"I can't help but think of the thing with Hollis and Oslo," I said.

"I don't think it's them."

"Oh, I don't either," I said. "But it could be something along those same lines. Either way, we need to put someone on the coop for the night."

"I already made a schedule. I didn't post it because, if it is someone stealing the eggs, I don't want them to see the post. We need to know who it is and nip this in the bud."

"Agreed. So who's the lucky soul who gets to stay up tonight?"

"Well, you see, that's kind of why I'm here." He grinned.

"Really?"

"Yep."

"Assbag."

"Love you too, but you're still up for the first night."

I sighed as I looked at the half dug hole where the new latrine was going to be built. It was going to be a long night.

I was pretty sore as I made my way toward the back of the horse barn. Behind the barn was the chicken lot and the coop. I looked around for a moment and turned toward the half-built wall on that end of the compound. Rocks were becoming scarce inside the compound, and we were having to go further and further out to get them. It was taking longer to build the wall than I would have liked, but it was still progressing.

Jumping onto the three-foot wall and over the other side, I eased into a copse of trees where I could still see the lot. Then I hunkered down for the night. I was certainly glad for the last of the jerky. As I waited, the sun went down.

My eyes were tired but this was important, and I knew it. We couldn't let someone do this sort of thing. No one was going hungry; they just didn't have the kind of food they were accustomed to before the fall. There was a lot of porridge, beans, and bread. There was a lack of meat and the eggs were distributed evenly among the people. There were close to two hundred people in the compound and that left one egg apiece in a week. Not much, but they were a luxury to most of us. Finding that one of them was stealing these eggs would cause violence. It seemed a small thing but everyone looked forward to the meal where they would get to have eggs. Or the days when the extra eggs were used to make cakes. Yes, a small thing, but it wouldn't take much to ignite the settlement.

The shadows deepened, and I felt my eyes get heavier. This was definitely going to be a long night. Two hours of watching the coop almost did me in. My head began to nod.

I snapped awake at the sound of rustling leaves.

The shadowy form was right there in the copse with me. He was squatted down less than five feet from me and staring toward the chicken coop. He hadn't seen me at all.

"That's far enough," I said as I grabbed the boy.

He screamed in terror. Then began wailing. "Don't kill me! Don't kill me!"

I turned him around to find a complete stranger with tears rolling down his face.

"Who the hell are you?" I asked.

He was crying, and I couldn't make out much of what he was saying. It was mostly in Spanish. I could recognize the language, although I couldn't speak it.

"Ayuadame...Dios mío." His words were muttered as I dragged him along toward the house.

There was enough noise that Grady came out the door as I approached, as well as Pop.

"Caught the egg thief?" Pop asked.

"Yep," I answered. "Only it's not one of ours after all."

I turned him toward Pop, who held a candle.

"Doesn't look like a raider-type."

"Look at him," I heard Neave say as she joined our group. "He's skin and bones. And terrified. Sit him down over here and quit shoving him for a moment."

I sighed and pointed to the chair she was talking about.

He sat down with tears still rolling down his face.

"Now calm down for a moment," she said as she pulled the other rocking chair forward. Then she eased herself down into the chair.

Something about a woman who is seven months pregnant didn't trigger his fear impulses as much as my ugly mug.

Slowly Neave began to speak in Spanish. She was slow and halting, but the boy's eyes widened.

"I speak little English," he said after a moment. "You not kill me?"

"Heavens, no," she said. "But you have to tell us who you are."

"We escape city," he said. "Mi familia. We hide from bad men."

"Your family," she said. "Are they ok?"

"We starving, Señora." He raised his hands pleadingly. "I sorry for steal huevos. I not take all. This man scare me."

She looked at me with one eyebrow raised.

"What?"

She just shook her head.

Grady snorted. "Didn't take the boy long to figure him out."

"Really? Hell, he scared the bejesus out of me. I was trying to sleep."

"Were you, now?"

"How many of you are hidden out there?" I said, changing the subject.

He gulped. "There are twenty…four. I take one huevo for each. Except last time. Took extra for mi hermana. She very weak."

"This is what's going to happen," I said. "You're going to lead me back to your family."

"No hurt them!"

"Not going to hurt them," I said. "Going to feed them and bring them back here. We will help you all."

I reached into my pack and pulled the last of my jerky from the wax pouch. His eyes widened as he saw it.

"Here, take a piece. Save the rest for your hermana. Tell me. Can your people travel? I will take food for tonight with us."

"They are weak. Only three can search for food."

"Grady, go get us some of the patrol packs. At least five. That should do a couple days for twenty folks or so."

"Gotcha, Boss."

Pop was smiling.

"What?"

"Iron hand," he said with a grin.

"Shut up." I grinned back.

Not everything has to be terrible in a Fallen World.

* * * * *

Chapter Fifteen

"I want to start a school."

I raised my head from the pillow to look at her. She was standing in front of the mirror running her hands across her swollen belly.

"Okay."

She looked back at me in surprise.

"We've got sixteen children running around the compound," I said. "They need to remember a world that isn't like this."

"I love you, Zebadiah Pratt," she said and sat back down on the edge of the bed. "And I want something before we have this child."

"I do to," I said. "Will you marry me, Neave Dalton?"

She was in my arms, and all I could hear was, "Yes, yes, yes, yes, yes...."

* * *

"You're filling the wagon with books?"

"I certainly am," I said.

Logan Withman just shook his head.

"Not just any books," I said. "We're going to hit the elementary schools and see if we can find enough text books to work with our kids."

"Barely surviving, and you're worried about a school?"

"Yep."

"I guess it beats hauling corn." He shrugged. "So, where too?"

I mounted Dagger. "The closest was Oliver Springs. I imagine we should start there."

"You're the boss," he said, climbing onto the wagon we had harnessed to a pair of horses.

"I'll ride ahead and scout the trail," I said as Jimmy jumped onto the wagon seat alongside Logan.

"Hope we don't get hit while you're out too far."

"Don't worry, you got Jimmy with the wagon."

"He doesn't even carry a gun."

I laughed.

"What?" Logan asked.

"You get hit, I'll wager they'll regret it."

"If I need a gun, I'll take one of theirs," Jimmy said.

"Really?"

"Yes," Jimmy answered.

"Don't even doubt it," Grady said as he rode past on Kennedy.

"Have to wonder what I got myself into," he muttered. "You damn farmers are crazy."

I just grinned and gave Dagger a light tap with my heels. He moved out in a light canter that would eat up distance. He could go at this pace for long periods of time. We reached the road, and I held Dagger to the side of the pavement. Pavement was rough on a horse's hoofs if they weren't wearing the right horseshoes. They used to make some that gripped the pavement but all we had was the regular metal shoes for most of the horses. Old Sammel the wagon horse had the only pair of road shoes we had found. They had a coating on them which helped with the slippage.

"Why would he call us crazy?" I said and patted the side of Dagger's neck.

The big black horse snorted.

"Yeah, you got a point." I sighed as I looked toward the east. "More rain," I muttered and pulled the poncho from my saddle bags.

I was wearing the long coat I had gotten waxed, but the poncho was still better at shedding water. It would also spread out to cover most of Dagger's back. He could stay semi dry under it.

"Alright, boy," I said. "Let's go see what they left us at Oliver Springs."

The rain started shortly before I reached the school, and the big covered entry was welcome. Dismounting, I walked to the doors. There were four entry doors, and I was surprised to find them unlocked. Propping the first door open, I returned and opened its counterpart, leaving a six-foot-wide opening for Dagger to follow me inside.

"Let's give this place a good look, buddy," I said, walking down the large hallway. There were three sets of double doors on the right and another three on the left just ahead of us.

"My guess is cafeteria and gym," I muttered.

Dagger snorted.

"You don't think so?"

He snorted again.

"Well I think it is."

Dagger's ears turned forward, and his head came up. He was looking further down the hall. My eyes narrowed, and I slipped my .45 from its holster. Holding it in close to my chest with the barrel angled downward, I moved down the hall in the direction he was looking.

"Horsey," I heard a whisper.

"Shhh."

I stopped. "Alright, now, you can come out. I'm not going to hurt you."

There was silence for a moment before two shadows moved from the darkness.

"Mister," a small voice said. "Miss DiGeret told us not to trust anyone. But she's really sick, and we need some help."

The speaker was a little girl who looked to be about ten years old.

"Is she here?"

"Yes, sir," the girl answered. "She's in our classroom."

"Take me to her, and I'll see if I can help."

"She's gonna be mad," the other kid said. He was younger than the girl.

"I don't know what else to do, Timmy."

I pointed to the boy. "You want to ride the horse?"

"Really?"

"Yeah, come on."

The boy walked up with wide eyes staring at Dagger. I turned the big horse so he could see the kid. He dropped his head and blew air into the boy's face.

"Dagger, this is Timmy." I grinned as Dagger nudged the kid with his nose. "Timmy, this is Dagger."

Timmy reached out and petted the horse's nose.

"Come here, I'll put you on his back."

He smelled like a dirty little boy, and I smiled as he perched in the big saddle.

"Hold tight to that saddle horn, kid."

"Yes, sir."

"Ok, little lady, lead me to Miss DiGeret."

She nodded and proceeded down the hall. The door we stopped near was just a single door so I left Dagger in the hall and followed the two children into the room. There were seven kids besides Timmy and the girl. A pile of blankets in the corner moved, and I was staring into bloodshot eyes.

"Oh, Regina," the pale faced woman said as she tried to sit up and failed. "What have you done?"

"You're Miss DiGeret?"

"Yes."

"My name is Zee Pratt and this little lady told me you needed some help. I'm a farmer from up near the county line. We've got a doctor there if you think you can make the journey. If not I'll get him out here."

"I can't even seem to get out of this pile of blankets, Mister Pratt."

"I've got a wagon coming that should get here in about two hours. Do you have any idea what is wrong with you?"

"Unfortunately, I do," she said. "There's nothing your doctor can do for me. It's not treatable anymore."

I nodded.

"We can get you somewhere more comfortable, at the least."

"Just take care of my children," she said. "I've heard the stories about what is going on out there. I couldn't bear to see that happen to them."

"The farmers won't let that happen to them."

"I have heard stories about some farmers." she smiled. The door pushed open, and Dagger poked his head through. "My children have stayed hidden but they've watched some of what has happened."

Several kids squealed as Dagger pushed his way through the door.

I looked over at the gelding. "What? Did you get lonely?"

He snorted.

"Horses." I shook my head. "What are you gonna do?"

The teacher chuckled.

"We'll get you back to the farm and let Doc have a look at you. He's got some of the meds we've gathered. Maybe something you can use."

"It is doubtful, Mister Pratt," she said. "But there is always hope."

Yes, there is, I thought. Even in this Fallen World.

* * * * *

Chapter Sixteen

"There's not much I can do for her, Zee," Doc said. "I have some meds that will help for a few months, but no more than that."

"Just do what you can, Doc." I gripped his shoulder. "She kept those kids alive. She's good people, and there aren't as many of those in the world as one would think."

"That's the truth." He shook his head. "I heard a saying once that people are nine meals away from barbarism."

"It's about right. Hungry people aren't people anymore. You'll see what they're capable of when the food runs out. We've been lucky enough to avoid that. You can look in some of these people's eyes and see what that toll is. What they did still haunts some of them."

"Yeah, but some of them don't seem to be phased by it."

"Yeah?"

"I've had a girl in here with some injuries. Suspicious injuries. I think she was raped, but she won't say anything. She wouldn't let me do a full examination."

"There have been a lot of those."

"Yes, but they arrived in that shape."

I stiffened and my eyes narrowed.

"Exactly," he said. "This happened here."

My eye twitched.

"I'm going to give you her name so you can keep an eye on her."

"You do that," I said. "We're not having that happen here. I'll be damned if we'll let that go."

"I agree," he said. "Her name is Gail Fontaine. She's twelve years old. Her and her father came to us about a month back as refugees. He was Obsidian Special Forces before all this and he's Farmer's Guard now."

"Yeah, I remember him. Kord, or Kort, I think."

"Kord," he said. "Some of the guys who train with him have been in here."

I nodded. "I'll keep an eye on the girl."

"Thanks, Zee."

"Anything else going on?"

"Couple of new guys," he said. "One came from the west with a bullet in his arm. The other from the east claiming to be a refugee."

"Claiming?"

"I'm not sure why I said it that way." he frowned. "Something doesn't sit right with me but who knows? He went right to work. Turnbull is starting him training with the recruits."

"I'll get with Turnbull."

"The other guy is in the Commons but his arm is patched up. He claims a machine gun turret took out two of his friends and nearly got him."

"A turret?"

"Yeah," he said. "Out in the middle of nowhere."

"I probably want to talk to him."

"I thought you might."

"Turrets run on power," I said. "If it's still up and running, there's power to it. I'd like to see where it's coming from."

"His name is Curtis."

"Ok, I'll find him."

I turned and exited the infirmary. The girl worried me. If someone was trying to do that here in the compound it would need to be stopped in a hurry. Turning the corner, I caught sight of Gary, across the central square.

"Yo, Gee!"

He turned and smiled as he saw me. "Hey, Zee!"

I motioned for him to come over and waited for him to cross the square.

"I have something I need you to do."

"Whatever you need, Zee."

"I need you to keep an eye on someone for me. Report back to me and me alone. And Gee, don't be seen."

"Yes, sir. Who do I need to watch?"

"A girl named Fontaine."

"Gail?" he asked. "What's wrong with Gail? Did she do something?"

"No, I think someone has done something to her, and I need to find out who."

I could see his face harden as I spoke the words. He was just a couple of years older than Gail.

"Someone hurt her?" he asked through grinding teeth.

"I think so, Gee." I gripped his shoulder. "I need to know the places she is afraid to go. Watch her and don't interfere. You report to me, and I will take care of things."

"Yes, sir."

* * *

"You're Pratt?"

I turned to find a tall man with his arm in a sling. He was thin from too many days hungry, but I could see he was gaining strength from the solid meals he'd received since showing up.

"You must be Curtis," I said.

"Yes, sir."

"Doc told me a little about what you ran into out there," I continued. "You care to tell me about it?"

"It was a complete surprise." He wiped his brow with the unhurt arm. "Terry was right in front of me or I would have been done for. The damn thing popped right up out of the ground and just started firing."

"Out in the middle of nowhere?"

He looked a little guilty. "We found a fence that was knocked down. We should have tried to look at the signs that were on the fence. We just thought there might be food inside. I never saw a building but we didn't make it around the hill to look before the gun started firing."

I nodded.

"It killed Terry and Fox before we could do anything. I ran and it stopped firing. It had to be set up on a sensor or something."

"Could you show me on a map where you found it?"

"If you go out there, you be careful," he said. "There wasn't any warning. It just popped up and started firing."

"We'll be careful," I said. "At the least we need to post warnings so others don't wander in and get shot."

"Yes, sir."

The door opened behind us and I turned to find Gary standing there. I could tell he was barely containing his anger.

"I'll talk to you after a while about that map, Curtis."

"I'll be waiting, sir."

Curtis exited the door, looking nervously at Gary.

"What is it, Gee?"

"You were right, sir," he said through clinched jaws. "But it wasn't anyplace she went in the last few days. The only time I saw her hesitate was when she had to go home. I followed her home today. She must have been late or something, because he met her at the door and yanked her inside. Sir, I think it's her dad."

"Shit," I muttered.

"We can't just let him do…"

"We're not," I said. "I want you to stay here and out of the way. I don't want you involved in what has to happen."

"But you'll need help, Zee."

"You've done your part, son." I squeezed his shoulder. "Now I'll do mine."

I felt the rage building up inside of me as I left the small building I was using as an office of sorts to keep up with the tallies from the crops. I saw Fontaine round the corner as I stepped out the door.

He was smiling and waiting in the makeshift street where we had built the housing.

"Saw your boy, Pratt," he said, loudly. "You got him spyin' on my girl?"

I walked toward him. "I heard some things that bother me, Fontaine."

"I don't give a damn if you're bothered, Pratt."

"I hear you've been hurting your daughter," I said. "I think you've been doing more than that. I think you're a lowlife piece of shit, Fontaine. I think you're a pedophile, and I think it's time you leave this compound."

He grinned. "We'll be gone tomorrow."

"You'll be gone tomorrow, Fontaine." I stopped in front of him, maybe twenty feet away. "You'll not be hurting that girl anymore."

"That girl is mine, Pratt. She's mine and I'll do what I want with her. You think you can say any different? I was Special Forces. You got this reputation of bein' such a badass. They ain't never even seen bad. You were just a grunt."

"Nevertheless," I said. "You'll be leaving without her."

"No, I won't," he said. "I think I'm gonna kill you, Pratt. Then I'm gonna kill that old man who thinks he can run this place. I'm gonna kill that retard brother of yours who just stares off into space. Then I'm gonna show these people how this place should be run. You're all a bunch of pussies."

I knew that he was probably right, at least in part. Maybe he could kill me but he would have rude surprise if he went after Jimmy. Right now, someone had to stand up for that twelve-year-old girl. I knew what my position on the farms was and what my job was. It was my job to be the one to stand for her. "You talk a lot for a bad ass. You want to kill me, get to it. I got shit to do."

I think he expected me to back down, or maybe beg, and it took a second for what I said to register. Then his hand shot toward the pistol on his side.

I reached for my .45. He was wicked fast but his pistol was only halfway drawn when my first bullet hit him in the hip. He was a big man and it rocked him back but he kept drawing. My second shot hit him in the stomach and the third hit his chest. He couldn't seem to raise the pistol past the position he held it, but I continued firing. I knew what I'd done in the past with bullets in me, and I intended to put enough lead in this bastard to sink him in the ground without digging a hole. He was a damn monster, and he had been living in our very midst.

My pistol was empty, and I dropped the mag to slam another in place with the pistol ready to continue, but he was done.

I looked to the left to find several shocked faces. Holis Drager was one of them, and his face had gone as white as a sheet. I think he was remembering a time when he thought about raising his rifle.

Two were the newest additions to the farms, Curtis, and I think the other was Lassiter. Curtis was shocked, but Lassiter didn't seem phased. He just watched the big man die.

Another was someone who shouldn't have had to watch what had just happened. Gail Fontaine was standing near the corner of the building that her dad had walked around. She sank to her knees, and I took a step toward her only to hear her sob in fear. Gary walked by me and knelt in front of the girl. She let him help her but all she saw in me was the one who killed her dad. No matter what he had done, he was still all she had left in this Fallen World.

* * * * *

Chapter Seventeen

"By the power vested in me by the state of…" the preacher said, "I guess that part doesn't matter anymore, does it?"

I shrugged, "Probably not."

"Then I'll say by the grace of God, I now pronounce you Husband and Wife." He grinned. "You may kiss the bride."

"Not sure about that," I said as Neave squeezed my hand. "She may bite me."

She was grinding her teeth as she shuddered with the contraction.

"I'll…bite you…if you don't…" she said between the moments of our little one trying to punch and kick its way out of her. "Definitely…your kid."

I bent down to kiss her sweat-soaked face.

"I…love you…Zee Pratt." She groaned as the next contraction hit her.

"Almost time now," Doc said.

Delilah joined him at the end of the table. "What can I do?"

"Just be ready to hold the child where I can cut the cord."

"And I love you, Neave Pratt," I whispered in her ear.

Tears sprang from her eyes and, I can't lie, I shed a few, too.

"Now it's time, Neave," Doc said. "You're gonna have to push as hard as you can when I say."

I saw her nod.

"Push, girl! Push!"

She screamed as she pushed and squeezed my hand harder.

"You can do it, Mrs. Pratt," I whispered in her ear again.

"Breathe!" Doc said. "And now again, push!"

I'd killed men, been shot more times than I like to think about, breached buildings under steady fire, and nothing made me as weak in the knees as I was at that moment.

"I see it!" Delilah squealed.

"Almost there, girl! One big push left!"

One last scream as she pushed, and I saw Doc's face go from concentration to joy.

"I've got her, Neave."

Neave was crying, and I was too.

"Her?" Neave asked.

Then it hit me what Doc had said.

Oh my God, I thought in a state of shock. I have a daughter. I have a little girl.

I'm sure I missed some of what happened next. The next thing I remembered was Deli placing a wrapped bundle of crying baby in Neave's arms. People say newborns are not pretty, but I was looking down at the most beautiful thing I had ever laid eyes on. Perhaps one of the most beautiful things in the world. When I saw her eyes, I couldn't stop the huge smile that crossed my face.

Some have said my eyes were pretty striking when seen by others. I now knew this to be true because I was looking right into those same piercing silver-grey eyes.

* * *

"He shoots like Pete," Lamb said. Terry Lamb was our shooting instructor.

"I know," I said. "He can't hit the broadside of a barn."

"You see that hesitation?"

"Yeah." I frowned. "Right before he shoots. Every time."

The guy we were talking about was the new guy, Lassiter. He finished shooting his allotment of practice shells. Maybe one out of five hit the target.

"We can't afford to use the bullets it's going to take to get him shooting straight," I said.

"I know."

"Well, I'm not letting that get me down, Lamb," I said with a huge grin. "I have a baby girl!"

"Congratulations, by the way. What did you name her?"

"Allison, after Neave's mother. Allison Marie Pratt."

He grinned. "It feels good, doesn't it?"

"It's like nothing I've ever felt before, Lamb."

"That feeling will change a man," he said. "It's the greatest feeling and the most frightening at the same time. I remember when we had Twiggy. He was my first child. It was an overwhelming sense of awe, I think, that I felt when I looked at that baby boy. It wasn't as overwhelming when Mia came along, but it was still there. It's worse now with the world as it is, but this place is the closest we could ever find to a normal life. I hate to think of my kids' chance of survival in the city."

"New folks keep telling us what it was like getting out of there. The death toll, alone, is staggering. There were millions of people living in that place. We've seen perhaps a thousand refugees that have made it out. The food is getting scarce, and they're killing each other. If not for the huge losses of lives, the food would have run out months ago."

"If there was some way we could help them..." he said, letting the partial statement just taper off.

"I know," I said. "We have good storage for the dry goods, but that place would go through our supplies in weeks. For us to help them, we would have to expand our farms tenfold, maybe more."

"We don't have the equipment to do that," he said. "Nor the manpower. Although our numbers grow each day."

"They say Spriggs has the power plant working now but they have to restring some of the power lines and cut some of the others to make it safe to flip the switches," I said. "Some of the newest equipment was electric. Once we get a steady power source, we might be able to expand the crops. We seriously got lucky with the fuel tanks being full. Got the crops harvested before we ran out. The electric equipment was down almost immediately. I for, for one, am glad we all hadn't upgraded yet."

"How are the solar cells Spriggs got working doing?" he asked.

"So far, they're running the infirmary. If he has to use some of the bigger equipment, they may not keep up."

"Too bad he couldn't run the air conditioning."

I nodded. "If all goes right, we should have full power in a couple of weeks. Air conditioning sounds wonderful. And electric heat for the upcoming winter. That's just around the corner. We should get a drop in temperature soon."

"And the wells will be working again," he said. "I can take a damn hot shower again."

"I miss my bath tub," I said. "Washing in the river is not as fun as one would think."

"If I do the math right, washing in the river was a lot more fun nine months ago."

"You do have a point." I laughed. "I'm off to the dam. Maybe Spriggs has the plant ready early. That sure would be a wonder."

"No doubt." Lamb nodded. "Make sure you kiss that little girl goodbye before you go. Never leave without doing that. I made it a point to spend time with mine before every deployment, short or long."

"That's a good habit to have, Lamb."

"A memory like that can get a person through the lonely times on the trail," he said.

I nodded and headed toward the corral to fetch Dagger. Seems like I'm the only one who rides the big black horse. Many are scared of him after the skirmishes we had gone through. To them, he was a killer after those fights. To me, a partner. Many of them looked at me the same way after the gunfight in the street. They knew of what I had done before, but this was out in front of everyone. Truth be told, they're right. I came back from the war with a skill that has no use in everyday life. It was what I was good at. Neave showed me I could be something else.

Dagger was excited to see me and tore across the pasture at a full run. We played this game every time. I stood grinning as he skidded to a halt inches from me. Then he started sniffing at various pockets. His nose stopped at one and he pushed at the vest I wore under the coat. I opened the pocket where a mag would normally rest and pulled out a carrot. We had only gotten a few to grow, and I would get yelled at by half the people in the compound if they saw it. Dagger gleefully munched on the orange vegetable. It was worth it to me to give up my ration of carrots for the horse. It was a small thing that brought forth memories of better days and many snacks for him. Much like the memory of kissing Ally's little forehead did for me.

Memories like that could fill many a lonely day in this Fallen World.

* * * * *

Chapter Eighteen

The air had a distinct chill as the sun dipped down toward the horizon. This was part of what I had been dreading. Winter was upon us and there would be plenty of cold nights ahead of us. We'd had an abnormally long summer after the bombs fell. They may have made our weather shift to something different. Who knew what sort of differences they would make? At least they had been cleaner than many of the old bombs that had been owned by the Federal Government before they were seized by the Corporations. There was radiation where they had fallen, but it was much more localized. Of course there had been a lot of damn bombs. I guess if winter was going to be shorter, who was I to complain?

The sun sank below the horizon but I could see brightness in the distance. The power was on at the dam, and you could see it for miles. I had become accustomed to the darkness of our nights and the lights looked out of place. But I could feel something that I hadn't felt in a long time as I looked toward those lights. Hope.

Dagger snorted and lowered his head to reach for something on the side of the trail. His head came up and I heard a juicy crunch after he snagged something from the ground.

"Whoa, boy," I said as I smelled apple.

He stopped as half of an apple thudded on the ground. He reached back down and grabbed it.

I dismounted and returned to the spot he'd found the apple. After searching in the darkness for a few minutes, I found another. As the moon slipped over the horizon and a soft light filled the night, I saw the apple tree.

Now that was a find and a half. I guess no one had come this way before. Pure luck and a greedy horse had found this one. I pulled a grain sack from my saddle bags and began picking up apples. By the time I had cleaned up the ground the sack was stuffed.

Tying the bag closed, I hefted the sack up onto Dagger's back.

"Looks like I'm walking the rest of the way," I said and pulled a second bag from the saddle bags. This one was smaller but it would hold another fifty pounds of apples.

"Going to be some happy people, boy," I said and patted the horse's neck.

I loaded the other bag onto his back and fed him another apple. "Alright, let's get back to the mission."

I walked away from the apple tree toward the glow in the distance. Those lights meant so much more than they would have a year or so ago. Maybe... just maybe we could get some of that back.

I was met at the gates by a sentry.

"Zee," David Kalet said with a grin.

"Kalet." I nodded. "How goes it?"

"We have power again," he said. "I'd say it goes very well."

I looked at the lighted building ahead. "I'd say it does."

Pulling an apple from my coat pocket, I threw it to the guard. "Found a bag or two of these. Well, my greedy horse found them."

"Oh, my," he said as he caught the apple. "Haven't had any apples in over a year. Used to be the most common thing in the grocery store. Almost never bought them. Funny, that."

"I've noticed the same thing," I said. "You could always find apples and bananas at the grocery store. Finding a banana tree would be something."

"It would have to be in a greenhouse or something," he said. "They grow in the tropics."

"Maybe I'll start looking for greenhouses." I grinned and led Dagger through the gate. "God I would love a banana…or an orange."

He bit into the apple. Through his happy chewing, he said, "Apples are enough."

"Yep," I said and led Dagger toward the main plant. The other side of the building looked over the drop down to the river below. The dam was close to a hundred feet tall at its highest point. The lower plant was where the electricity was channeled through the wires, or would be when the switches would be tripped.

The upper plant was where the controls for the dam's systems could be found. More than likely, it was where I would find Spriggs.

Dismounting, I pulled the first bag from the horse's back and set it inside of the door. The hum of machinery brought a smile to my face. Returning, I grabbed the smaller bag.

"Can't trust you won't eat a whole bag, Fatty."

Dagger snorted.

I pulled another apple from my pocket and fed it to him. "One more won't hurt you though."

I left the horse chewing happily on another apple and carried the sack inside with me. Again, the sound of the machinery brought a smile to my face. The temperature in the building was comfortable, and I realized how much I had missed the climate control of electricity.

I just stood there for a moment and soaked the experience in.

"Remarkable how you can get lost in something we all took for granted a year or so back," Spriggs said from behind me. I hadn't heard him approach.

That was one thing the noise interfered with. But a minor thing in the midst of a facility full of friendlies.

"Don't I know it," I said. "Just the sound of the machinery is comforting."

"Yep."

"Brought something for you and your guys," I said as I turned toward the man.

"Are those apples?"

"Dagger found a tree along the way."

"That marvelous horse," he said with a grin.

I handed the sack of fruit to him.

"Thank you," he said. "I'm pretty sure the rest will feel the same."

"I filled a couple of sacks," I said. "Going to take one back with me to the Farms."

"It will make a lot of happy people," he said. "But I think I can do one better."

"Oh yeah? Better than a sack of apples?"

"I'm going to give them air conditioning and heat again."

"That's certainly better than a sack of apples," I said. "Are you moving up the time table?"

"We got the lines finished early," he said. "Thought it would be a good idea to get the heat on again since it's starting to get cold."

"At least all that wood I chopped won't go to waste," I said. "All the new structures are built without wiring."

"Now we can start building new stuff with power tools, as well."

"Oh, that's going to be nice. I bet Archie kisses you."

"That grizzly-bear looking bastard better not."

"Just warning you. You're giving a carpenter back his power tools. No telling how he's going to react."

"As long as he doesn't kiss me, we'll be fine."

"You're about to make some happy folks, Kal. Or are you going by Dynamo? Everyone keeps calling you that."

His shoulders slumped. "I know. I've always hated that name but you don't ever get to choose your call sign. It's usually chosen for you."

"I, for one, will say you're doing amazing things out here. And they could have chosen a much worse name."

"Not sure about that."

"They could have picked some fantasy movie character...what was his name? Oh yeah, Smeagel. Little weird-looking bald guy with some issues."

"I remember that movie, one of the classics," he said. "How long have you been waiting to work that into a conversation?"

"From the day I met you." I laughed.

"Asshole."

"I don't know what you're talking about."

"Sure," he said with a grin.

I laughed. "I guess I'll start back. You already answered what I came here to find out."

"Wait till the morning," he said. "Enjoy a night with electricity. Perhaps a hot bath."

"Oh my God, a hot bath?" I replied. "Twist my arm, won't you."

"Enjoy the moments when you can do things like that, Zee," he said with a serious tone. "There are way too few of them in this Fallen World."

* * * * *

Chapter Nineteen

I stood out in the square with a huge grin on my face. It was probably a good thing that it was dark because I didn't want to give anything away about what was going to happen. Candles lit several windows around the compound with a dim, flickering light.

There was movement in the night, and I turned toward the sound. Before I could say anything, the street light Pop had installed two years before lit up, and I was looking into startled eyes.

"Lassiter?"

His face was pale.

"What are you doing out here this late?"

He looked around a second, and his shoulders slumped. "I was meeting a girl."

I laughed. "No need to feel guilty about that. I snuck out to see Neave quite a few times. Who's the lady?"

"She's a new girl," he said. "She came in with the last group of refugees."

He was staring into the light, almost mesmerized. "I never thought I'd see that again."

"Me neither," I said. "At least until I made the trip out to the plant yesterday."

I heard gleeful exclamations from various places around the compound and grinned. The house had lit up like a beacon, over past the barn. The bunk house where we used to house the guys that worked for Pop was also lit. I had gone through earlier and turned on all the switches so that the effect would be all the more drastic.

Neave came out of the house with a broad smile on her face. I went to meet her.

She looked at all the lights and back at me. "This is why you were fiddling with the switches earlier today. I wondered what you were up to. You knew this was going to happen."

The last statement was accompanied by narrowed eyes.

"Spriggs wanted to surprise…"

"You didn't tell me."

"But he…"

"Don't you blame that poor wonderful engineer."

I raised my hands. "Surprise!"

"Hmph," she said and turned around.

Her act would have fooled me if I couldn't see her reflection in the glass of the door as she went back inside. If she'd been smiling any wider, her head would have split in two.

I turned back to find Lassiter was gone. For a moment I wondered which girl he was sneaking out to see. I didn't remember any that lived out to the east of us. Most of the refugees had been expanding the settlement to the west, away from the city. Pete's farm was the only one to our east and we had moved all the civilians out of the place. It was manned by a Farmer's Guard. We would have left the place altogether except it had four silos we could still use for storage.

I shook my head and headed toward the house. People were beginning to come out under the street lights, and I already heard someone playing music. I'm not sure if I could imagine a better day than this. Then I heard a sound that proved it could get even better. The heating unit on the side of the farmhouse kicked on.

Cheers began to sound from various places around the farm, and I smiled. Then I eased back out into the darkness. Someone would have to be on patrol around the perimeter, and I would let the others enjoy their time as the lights filled the night.

I kept my eyes turned outward so that the lights wouldn't kill my night sight. Slowly, I made my way around the stone perimeter wall listening to a celebration going on inside the square. There was music playing, something I hadn't heard for a very long time. At least music that was recorded. Grady could pick at a guitar and several of the others played various instruments but it had been a long time since we had heard music like this.

A shadow moved ahead of me coming from the other direction. There was a slight jingling from the metal studs on the vest he had found as they hit the metal belt buckle.

"That you, Grady?"

"I knew these damn studs were a bad idea," he said. "They aren't that loud are they?"

"May as well carry a neon sign."

"Bite me."

I laughed.

"I'll take the patrol if you want to go join the party," he said.

"Never was much for parties," I said.

"Me neither."

"You should go see if Deli wants to dance," I said.

"I take it you noticed?"

"Yeah, you've been spending a lot of time with her."

"You'd think she wouldn't want anything to do with a fella after what she has been through. I was afraid to even ask her until she got tired of waiting and just kissed me."

I chuckled. "Then go on in."

"She's out at the dam," he said. "Doc is out there doing his check-ups on the folks out there, and she went with him. I think she wanted to use those showers."

"She's doing pretty good as a nurse for Doc, too."

"True," he said. "But I'm thinking the showers are a big part of it."

"I can't blame her there."

"So you go on in and spend time with that wife and daughter."

"Alright," I said. "Sound off if you need anything."

"You got it, Boss."

I crossed through the north gate into the farm and made my way back to the house. I had an idea and needed to make a few preparations.

Twenty minutes later, Neave came through the front door with Allie in her arms. Allie was so tired her head kept nodding. I reached out, and she handed the baby to me.

"Left you something in the back."

"Oh?"

I followed her to the back room where she saw the steam coming from the door across the bedroom.

"Oh, my," she said and crossed the room.

As she went through the door, articles of clothing began to fall.

"Oh, you beautiful, wonderful man."

Across the room was the garden tub filled with steaming hot water. Alongside was a bowl with three apples and some wild flowers.

I grinned. "Now, little lady, let's leave mommy to her bath."

"Oh my god, oh my god…" Neave muttered as she lowered herself into the hot water.

Something as simple as a hot bath can be taken for granted until there aren't any more of them. And they were few and far between in this Fallen World.

* * * * *

Chapter Twenty

I heard a power saw as I walked toward the barn. Rounding the corner, I stopped and cocked my head to the side.

"What the hell are you doing, Pop?"

He was building a platform of some sort.

"We need more horses."

"And you're building what?"

"See, you put the mare here…" he was pointing at the inside of the u-shaped platform.

"Oh, hell no," I said realizing what the platform was for.

"He's the only one that isn't a gelding."

"You're going to breed the mares to that fat lazy pony?"

"You have to use the cards you are dealt, son."

"You know what?" I raised my hands. "I'm not going to have anything to do with this one. You're on your own."

"What?"

"I'm not taking part in your whacked out plan today, Pop."

"The only other way is to do the job manually and fertilize the mares, artificially."

"I'm damn sure not doing that, either," I said. "I think Jimmy and I are going out to look at this turret Curtis told us about. Maybe put up some signs to keep folks from getting killed."

"You sure you don't want to help…"

"I'm damn sure," I answered and turned toward the paddock where Dagger was already at the gate, waiting.

I heard Pop chuckling as I walked away. I just shook my head as I saw Wandrey at the other end of the field. Some of the kids had found some hair coloring. His mane was rainbow colored and his tail was the same. I was pretty sure there used to be a cartoon that looked like that but, for the life of me, I couldn't remember what it was called.

Gary was next to the watering trough but he didn't have his customary five gallon buckets.

"Gee," I said.

"Sure is nice to have the power back on, Zee," he said. "I haven't had to carry all those buckets of water this week."

"I'd say."

"Do you know what Pop wanted me to do?"

"What?"

"He said we needed to 'milk' that damn pony. I said it was a boy, and he said it wasn't really milk we needed."

I snorted.

"That's what I said," he replied. "Now, I love you guys like my own family. But, not just no…Hell no."

"I guess that's when he started building the platform behind the barn?"

"Yeah, and I'm not helping with that either. If he'd have asked for help with that first, yeah. But, no, he wanted me to jerk…"

"You wanna go with me and Jimmy?"

He took a breath. "I saw you over there with Pop. If you're trying to get me to…"

"No," I said. "I told him hell no, too. We're going out to check on that turret that shot Curtis."

"Now, that, I'll be glad to do."

"Alright." I grinned. "Why don't you go see if Grady wants to join us? Then go jerk o…I mean catch one of the horses and saddle up."

His eyes narrowed.

I laughed. "Who knows? We might find a stallion out there somewhere and not have to witness the creation of a bunch of half-pony, half-horse abominations."

"Half breeds aren't that bad," he said. "My Uncle used to have a couple. They were really good barrel racers."

"It's not the half breed part I'm thinking about. Just look at him."

He looked across the field at the pony and started laughing. "I see your point."

He was still laughing as he rounded the corner of the barn—on the opposite side from Pop—to go find Grady.

I shook my head and turned back toward Dagger. "You would have made a damn fine dad."

He snorted.

"Yeah," I said as I unlocked the gate. "I never thought I would be one."

He pushed me toward the tack shed with his head.

"I know you don't want to witness this, either," I said. "Maybe we can get the hell out of here before he goes and tests the damn platform."

"What platform?"

I turned to find Jimmy standing behind me.

"The one Pop is building to breed the mares to the pony."

"I see. Pop asked me to come help with something but I told him you had already made plans for us to go out."

"And you're lucky I did."

"Okay," he said and jumped over the fence to go catch a horse.

Sometimes his lack of emotion wasn't as obvious, but I really noticed it in a funny situation. I missed my brother's sense of humor. Damn the corporations and their wars. Or hostile takeovers, as they used to call them.

I had Dagger saddled, and Jimmy had Kennedy out of the lot when Gary showed back up with Grady in tow.

"Thank God you sent Gary to get me," he said. "Pop has some hare-brained idea about the horses. You'll never guess what he asked me to do."

Gary and I were still laughing as we rode out of the farm.

Some things I just won't do. Even in this Fallen World.

* * * * *

Chapter Twenty-One

"This has got to be the place," Gary said. "There's what's left of the fence."

I nodded. "Curtis said they went in about a hundred feet before the turret went active."

"What, exactly, are we going to do about the thing?" Grady asked.

"I guess we should figure out where the sensor range is and put up some signs."

"I'm not going in to test it," Grady said. "How do you suppose we'll find out the range?"

Jimmy dropped from the back of Kennedy and walked up to the fence.

"I doubt even you could dodge turret fire, Jimmy."

"I'll take care of it."

He apparently found what he was searching for and bent down to pick up a log. I doubt any of us could have lifted the six feet long piece of a tree. He set his feet and with the log held straight up in front of him, strode forward three steps to hurl the log forward. I remembered a time very long ago when Jimmy and I had watched what some folks called Scottish Games. They used to call what he was doing the Caber Toss. If any of them had been Agents, they would have undoubtedly won the games. The log sailed forward.

Then the ground rose and bullets slammed into the log.

"Close to a hundred feet," Jimmy said. "Curtis was close."

"Damn it, Jimmy," I muttered.

He was looking at the firing turret with his head cocked to the side.

"What is it?"

"That isn't one of our turrets."

"What do you mean?" I asked.

"That's a Teledyne weapon."

"What the hell would a Teledyne turret be doing this far into Obsidian territory?" I asked. "I could see finding old JalCom stuff in the area, but Teledyne was strictly west coast."

"Regardless," said Grady, "It's a live turret. Do you think we could keep throwing stuff in there until it runs out of ammo?"

"As long as this place is unmanned, whatever it is."

"I think I'll just turn it off," Jimmy said and walked forward.

I looked at Grady who shrugged.

"He's just going to turn it off," Grady said.

Jimmy stopped just out of range and started looking around.

"Uh, Jimmy?"

He held his hand up and kept examining the area.

"There it is," he said. He walked to his left, staying just out of range of the sensors.

I looked at Grady who shrugged again.

"He's just going to turn it off," Grady repeated.

I sighed and watched as Jimmy stopped to kick a rock. It flipped back and a control switch rose from the ground. I could see the number pad atop the switch.

"Great," I said. "It needs a code."

Jimmy punched in a long series of numbers and the keypad lowered back into the ground where the rock flipped back over to hide it. He turned and walked toward the turret.

"Wait…!"

But the turret didn't fire.

"Holy shit, Zee," Gary said. "He did it."

"Damn it, Jimmy," I said, then muttered under my breath, "He's going to give me a damn heart attack."

We followed him inside the perimeter. I kept a wary eye on the turret.

Jimmy reached into a compartment behind the gun and did something. The turret sank into the ground.

"That should do it," he said.

"How did you do that?" Gary asked.

"The program they were uploading into my head is an assassin. He knows all of the Teledyne codes. He specializes in high priority targets, and there are master codes for anything they kept behind security."

Gary was quiet as he listened to the answer, then nodded. Surprisingly, he didn't ask anything further. Jimmy had said all that really needed saying, but the youth was usually filled with questions.

"That hill over there is probably an entrance to whatever this turret was guarding," Jimmy said.

"Let's go see what it is," I said.

"I'll take point," Jimmy said. "If there are any Teledyne forces inside, I'll be better equipped to deal with them."

"Not arguing," I said and drew my .45. "I got your six."

He nodded, and I followed my brother around the hill.

He stopped and looked at another rock for a couple of moments.

"Another keypad?"

"No," he said. "That's a trap."

He reached past the stone and pulled on a sprout of a tree. There was an audible hum and the mound split right in the middle and opened up like a dome folding down. Inside was a platform.

"There's the keypad," Jimmy said.

"You think?"

He just looked at me. I really missed my brother.

"Never mind," I muttered. "Let's see what's inside this place."

Jimmy punched in the long series of numbers again, and the platform jerked as it started sinking. It descended for a long time. We had to be down a hundred feet by the time the lift stopped. You could see the daylight from the hole above until the top closed back over the elevator.

The wall straight ahead of me opened and my mouth dropped open. The room on the other side was enormous.

"How the hell did Teledyne build something like this right under the noses of Obsidian?" Grady asked.

"This took a lot of planning," I said, stepping from the lift into the warehouse-sized cavern. "Those look like weapon containers."

"A lot of damn containers," Grady said.

"Stay here for a minute," Jimmy said and moved off into the warehouse so fast I could barely follow him with my eyes.

"Damn it, Jimmy," I muttered.

"You can say that again," Grady said. "I swear he freaks me out when he does that."

"He freaks everyone out when he does that."

"If those are rifle crates, there's enough to arm every man, woman, and child on the farms."

"And then some," I said.

I saw a shadow move and Jimmy was back from his recon. He was carrying something.

"Is that what I think it is?" Grady asked.

"That is the most awful and glorious thing I've ever seen," I said. "How many of them are there?"

"The whole back half of the cavern is filled with them."

"If Teledyne's are anything like Obsidian's, they'll suck. But they're good for decades and they'll keep you alive."

"They can't be that bad," Grady said.

"Some of them were edible," I said. "Some, not so much."

Who would think a former grunt would be this happy to see a warehouse of MREs? It could only happen in this Fallen World.

* * * * *

Chapter Twenty-Two

"Those rifles are going to be a game changer," Grady said. "We can really do some training with those."

"There's enough ammo to even train that kid, Lassiter, how to shoot," I said.

"He's pretty bad," Gary added.

"Can't hit a damn thing," Grady said. "You think we found enough ammo? I'm not sure."

I laughed.

We rounded the bend in the road that led west from the farm to see a lot of activity going on near the square.

"What the hell?" I asked under my breath and nudged Dagger's ribs to send him into a canter.

I saw Pop beside the barn. He was saddling one of the horses. What worried me was the pair of pistols on his side and the Winchester leaning against the barn.

He turned to see me, and the troubled look on his face sent me his direction instead of the square.

"What is it, Pop?"

"It's Neave, son. Pete and Neave are missing. We just found out what happened and those damn cowards are hiding their heads in the damn sand!"

There was an icy pit in my chest. "Alli?"

"She's with Deli."

"Tell me everything."

"We found Lamb at Pete's place. He was shot and next to dead. He was escorting Pete, Neave, and a couple of the students to the old farm. Some sort of field trip about food storage."

"Lamb come out of it last night and told us they were hit by raiders. He was holding them off until that damn Lassiter kid shot him in the back. They loaded up all the stored food at Pete's and took Pete, Neave, and the kids. They had a truck and headed east."

"Grady!" I yelled. "Mount the Guard!"

"Council won't let us take the Guard into the city," Pop said.

"What?!"

"I was about to head east, myself."

I could see several people in the square staring in my direction.

"They won't allow it?"

"We made the council because we aren't tyrants, son."

"I'll be going, too."

"Jimmy?"

"I'm with you," Jimmy said.

"Thanks, son."

"I'm coming," Gary said.

"Me, too," Grady added. "Damn the council."

"Get the horses fed and watered," I said. "I have to see Lamb."

I walked toward the square and Doc's infirmary. The people who were watching us from the square hurried to be elsewhere. Hollis Drager dropped his head in shame and walked away. I didn't have time for them. My mind was on the whereabouts of my wife and those children.

"Zee?" Lamb asked as I strode through the door. "Zee, I'm sorry…"

"What happened?" I asked and grasped his right hand in my left. His left arm had a drip attached with an IV.

"Took Pete and Neave and some of the kids out to Dalten Farm to show them some of the storage facilities." He shook his head in misery.

I could tell he was barely staying conscious. "Figured...four of us with guns should be enough. Raiders...hit just before we reached the farm. Neave...little Neave, shot three of the bastards. I got another three, and even Pete got one...But then that son of a whore, Lassiter shot me in the back...and clubbed Pete with his gun stock. I saw them close on Neave, and she stabbed another one before they took her."

"Jesus," I muttered.

"Oh, God, Zee...They took my babies. They got my Twiggy and Mia...I couldn't stop them..."

"This isn't your fault, Lamb," I said. "It was Lassiter that shot you?"

"That traitorous bastard...Got my babies...Can't do anything with my legs..."

"You rest," I said. "We're going after them."

"You'll find my babies?"

"I will."

"Thank..."

He lost consciousness.

"That's a tough man there, Zee," Doc said from behind me. "Dragged himself, with a spinal injury, close to a quarter mile."

I turned to Doc. "Any of the raiders live?"

"I got one of them in the next room."

I walked toward the door.

"Zee, now I can't let you..."

"What?"

His face paled as I stared at him.

"Don't say something you and I will both regret," I said. "They have my wife and her father, and they took children."

I opened the door and looked inside at the man on the bed. He was unkempt but not as dirty as most of the raiders I had seen up to this point. My eye was drawn to a tattoo on his right arm. It was of a bird. I knew that tattoo.

"He won't talk," Doc said. "We tried."

"He'll talk."

I walked into the room.

"I told your people," he muttered. "I got nothin' to say."

"You're going to tell me where they took my wife and father-in-law. You're going to tell me where they took those kids. You'll tell me the location of their base and how many men they have."

"Not gonna happen," he answered.

"I remember a time when there was a group of men and women who started a movement, using a symbol left from another era. It was a Falcon that had symbolized a team of players in what used to be known as Atlanta. They took that symbol and built a group of anarchists."

He shrugged. "What's it to ya? I still got nothin' to say."

"That movement was behind the Food Riots down in the south."

"Piss off."

"If you were familiar with that group of men, you would know what happened to them when those riots were put down."

"What the hell is your point?"

"The point is this." I leaned close to him. "My name is Zebadiah Pratt."

All the color left his face.

"And I'll skin you alive, right where you lay, if you don't talk."

"His name is Morgan Lassiter, he sent his son, Owen to infiltrate this place and learn of any weakness…"

Sometimes the carrot worked, more often than not, one needed to use the stick in this Fallen World.

* * * * *

Chapter Twenty-Three

"So this Morgan Lassiter was a Falcon?" Pop asked.

"He claims to be the one that started the Falcons, but I have my doubts on that," I said.

"Why's that?"

"All intel said the guy who started it was named Harliss Grye. I know for a fact Grye didn't leave the Falcon HQ alive."

"Do you now?"

"After the massive loss of life in the Riots, we were sent after the Falcons, Pop." I looked toward him. "I put a bullet between the eyes of Harliss Grye. We took his records and hunted down just about every name on the Falcon membership list. A few may have gotten away, but there were none in high level positions remaining. This Morgan may have been a low rank, just like Fieago, back there."

"We couldn't even get a name," he said.

"They learned to fear the name of Pratt. I was the last person most of them ever saw."

"Soldiers shouldn't have been used for assassinations," Grady said.

"We were used for whatever Obsidian needed done," I said. "But that mission was my last. I didn't re-enlist after that and came back home."

"And Fieago told you where they took our folks?"

"If we follow the main road toward the city from Destin, we'll hit the first zones at Main Street. Three blocks down Main and right on D Street. Two blocks to Lassiter."

"Named it after himself?" Pop asked.

"Seems so." I looked to our east, my left eye twitching. "We'll have to cross through three of what they call zones to reach Lassiter. May be some fighting to get through those. He says they travel in groups of twenty or more so they won't be attacked. The good thing is that most of them won't have guns. Lassiter's men do but the zones we need to cross may leave us be if we have guns in sight."

I was lost in thought for a minute as my mind strayed to Neave. I hoped she was alive. I needed her to be alive.

"She's tough, son."

It didn't take a genius to figure what I was thinking about.

"She's such an innocent…"

Pop chuckled. "That innocent girl took out three men and cut another. Son, you've taught her well. If any of them can make it through this, it'll be her. Right after you two got married, she started training with Lamb. You know how slow she was to finally accept it. But she told me, 'I'm a Pratt, now, Pop. Best I start acting like one.' Made me proud, son."

"She has to be okay, Pop," I said softly. She had to be.

We rode on in silence.

Destil was two days out on horseback.

"Looks like the fire spread," I said.

"I don't think they cared if it took the whole town," Grady said. "We set fire to the main buildings but this whole town was a reminder of what they did to survive."

Destil was a burnt out husk of a town. Almost all of the buildings had suffered fire damage. The highway was covered in blackened mud from the ashes blending with the dirt. Rain had washed the black mud across the streets in spots.

"Ugly place," Pop muttered.

"Ugly things happened here," I said.

"Yep."

"Truck," I said.

"That looks recent," Pop said as he saw the same thing I did. A box truck was parked in the middle of the road.

"Lot of tracks around it." I dismounted and drew my .45. "Hold here until I can check it out."

The tracks in the mud around the truck told a tale if you knew how to read the writing. It looked as if they had offloaded the truck into cars. The tire tracks were much smaller. But they looked strange. There were quite a few footprints in the mud, all staying within the width of the car tire tracks.

I looked over the truck but there was no one still there. Taking a deep breath, I opened the back of the box truck. The smell hit me in the face like a fist. I backed away for a moment.

Pop walked past me and peered inside.

"It's not any of ours, Son."

I'd seen more death than anyone should have to see, and it never gave me this feeling. I couldn't stand the thought of finding her dead.

"This one has a stab wound in his chest," Pop said. "Looks like the same blade that got the guy in the infirmary."

"Neave," I said with a small grin I couldn't keep from showing.

"Told you," Pop said. "She's tough."

He stepped back from the truck and shut the door. "No one is here."

I opened the fuel tank on the right side of the box truck. "I'm guessing they ran out of fuel."

"Looks like they loaded everything in cars," Grady said. "Or wagons made out of cars."

That explained the strange footprints.

"I'm guessing wagons." I said. "I was trying to figure these prints out. They're using people to pull wagons."

"Sounds right," Grady said, looking at the prints. "See how they look like they slide backwards just a bit as they step forward? Pulling something."

"I think you're right," I said. "That might be some good news."

"We're on horses," Pop said. "They're on foot, pulling loaded wagons."

I climbed back on Dagger. "We may make up those two days by traveling faster than they can."

Pop remounted Kennedy. "Then let's ride."

We set out from Destil at a bit faster clip than before. We rode past nightfall for an hour before stopping. Pop lit a fire and I took the radiation badge I kept in my pack to check the stream. This one ran from north to south and most of the radiation was far to the west. There was some destruction to the north of us, closer to the coast, and I wanted to be sure the stream was safe.

The badge didn't change color so I led Dagger to the stream for a drink. After he had drunk his fill, I pulled the feed bag from the pack and poured corn and wheat grain into the bag. Hanging it over his head, he munched happily at the feed. Then I brought Kennedy down to the stream. Pop was putting a pot on the fire and heating beans. We had the MREs but we had to stop and feed the horses, and they would need rest. Gary, Grady, and Jimmy were taking care of their mounts as I brought Pop's down to the stream.

As much as I wanted to just keep going, the horses could only do so much. I remembered traveling halfway around the world in the time we had spent just in a day traveling on horseback. More and more frustrating were the limitations in this Fallen World.

* * * * *

Chapter Twenty-Four

We saw no sign of them before we could see the silhouette of the buildings in the distance.

"We knew it was a longshot," Pop said.

"I know," I answered, pointing toward the buildings in the distance. "But chances of getting them out alive drop drastically when they get inside that."

"I never went into the city," Gary said. "Destil was as big of a town as I went to. That place looks enormous."

"It is," I said. "Used to be a lot bigger before they blew up the lower side of it."

"How much got hit?"

"Can't be certain. They definitely hit the Obsidian Corporation Headquarters. I'd say they saturated that area with bombs. There weren't many Corporate outposts in this part of the city so it seems to have gotten spared."

"After the stories we've gotten from the refugees, it would have been better if it had been destroyed."

"I tend to agree with that," I said. "But there wouldn't have been any refugees if it had. And this part of the city is close enough to us that we'd be gone too."

"Well there is that," Grady added.

"It's been hard, but I still would rather be alive," Gary said.

"Me too, Gee." I said. "When we get close, there's probably going to be some fighting. Keep that rifle ready and mind your horse.

There's no telling what's in the streets. Gotta make sure you don't run him through something that will damage his feet."

"Yes, sir."

"I want you behind us," I said. "You hear me? You're supporting fire. Same with you, Grady. Pop and I will be point. Jimmy, you be ready to do that thing you do."

"Gotcha," Grady said.

I looked at Gary, "You hear me?"

"Yes, sir."

I looked toward Jimmy, who nodded. I couldn't see any expression on his face. I really missed my brother. But this Jimmy would be invaluable where we were going.

Any small talk dropped off as we got closer to the buildings. The outer blocks were lower and more industrial in nature. Some large warehouses and quite a few buildings that looked like factories. I could see movement on the streets ahead of us. More activity than I really expected to see. There were several gunshots, and the people I had seen were running back the way they had come.

"That could be them," I said and lightly kicked my heels into Dagger's ribs.

He sped up to a slow canter. I wanted him moving faster but the roads were unsafe to run him with metal shoes. The activity had passed by the time we reached the first buildings. But there were four or five men dragging two others out of the street.

They saw us and dropped the dead men.

A loud whistle sounded and the crowd came from three different alleys.

"Shoot low, Gee." I said and palmed my .45.

What I could see coming toward us was about ten men from each direction carrying pipes, clubs, knives, chains, and any other assorted weapons a person could think of. I focused on the closest alley and fired into the crowd.

Dagger snorted, but I held him back. Then I heard the others open fire. Pop's Winchester cracked first, and then the two automatic rifles we brought back from the facility opened up.

The fight ended before it even began. These men wanted nothing to do with the weapons we carried. Running back into the alleys, they left behind twelve dead men.

"Reload," I said. "We keep going. If that gunfire was the guys holding our people, we can catch them before they get back to their headquarters."

I looked back at Gary but he was holding up fine.

"Boy's got some steel in him," Pop said quietly from beside me.

"Yeah, he does. Keep watch on him, Pop."

"I'll be doing that."

"When we catch up, I need you and that Winchester working anyone near Neave and the kids. It's got the range. We'll be working the ones in closer."

"I'll fall back with, Gee and Grady."

I nodded. "Jimmy, you're on point with me."

"Be careful, son," Pop said. "You can bet they heard that gunfire."

I nodded and nudged Dagger to move forward.

"Boy, we can't afford to lose the horses," I heard Pop talking to Gary. "Now, if we have to dismount, your job is to get the horses back out of the way."

I should have thought of that. If we got separated from the animals they'd be in someone's stew pot.

We rode forward to turn down the street to our right. Close to two blocks down, I could see them. We had covered the first block when they saw us. There were people pulling the remains of two vans and a crowd of men had joined them from the adjoining street that led to Lassiter. I turned to Pop and heard the angry buzz of a bullet pass my head to hit the ground to my left and rear.

"Sniper!" I dove from Dagger's back and pulled him toward the closest alley.

"Jimmy, take the sniper!"

He was in motion before I even finished the sentence. He slammed through the reinforced door to the building that held the sniper like it wasn't even there, and I heard screams.

Gary took Dagger's reigns and, drawing my Colt, I ran back out from the alley to take cover behind an old car.

"Here they come!" Pop yelled from the corner of the alley.

"Light 'em up!"

I raised and fired three times. Two of the leaders fell and bullets began to hit the car. Pop fired the Winchester and another fell. Another sniper from across the street fired and the bullet chipped stone above Pop's head. He raised his aim and calmly shot the man who was peering out the fifth floor window with a rifle.

The first sniper sailed out the window he had been shooting out of, and I rose from cover, firing into the running crowd. Then Jimmy followed the sniper out the window and landed on top of a car with a crash as the windows shattered.

I was walking straight for the gunmen, and they had no idea what was amongst them. Pop kept up a cover fire from the corner of the alley, and Grady made it to a spot where he could fire. When the full automatic opened up, the gunmen broke. They had pistols and a couple of rifles. Grady was shooting one of the Teledyne rifles.

I ejected the mag in my pistol and slammed the next one in. They had reversed course and were running back toward the vans, which were much closer. I could see Lassiter close to the rear van screaming at the running men. Then he saw me. He turned to say something to his men just as Pop fired. His bullet went through the spot Lassiter's head had just been as he dove to the side.

"Damn!"

Lassiter ran behind the van.

"Let's move in," I said and started walking forward. Then three kids ran out from behind the van.

Lassiter ran down the street toward their headquarters and was out of sight in moments.

Another form staggered from behind the van with two others helping to hold him up. Pete looked like he was in rough shape but I only had eyes for the form on his right. Her hair was all tangled, her clothes were ragged, and her shirt was bloody, but she was the most beautiful thing I had ever seen.

I strode toward her and saw her face light up as she saw me. Then men came around the corner from Lassiter's zone. I dived behind a car as they opened fire toward me. But I popped right back up and returned fire. More men fell.

Then the kids were behind the car.

I kept firing and drew my second Colt.

Pete fell behind the car, and I turned to find myself staring right into her blue eyes. Why was she just standing there? Something was wrong. Then the blood on her chest registered. It wasn't a stain, it was growing. She toppled forward into my arms. Dropping the pistols, I caught her and we sank down to the pavement.

"No... No..."

"Zee!" I heard Pete's voice and it seemed so far away.

My hand came from behind her and it was wet with blood.

"No..."

"I'm sorry..." she gasped.

"Zeeee!" Pete's voice was almost a wail.

As I watched the light drain from her eyes, I felt like a weight had settled on my chest, and I couldn't breathe. The part of me she had taught to be Human slid away. I had come from the wars a killer. She had taught me how to be more than that. That veneer slid away as I pulled her closer.

"They didn't deserve her." I muttered.

"Zeeee! Oh God!" Pete was trying to pull himself closer.

I held her to my chest. "Her light... her kindness..."

I eased her down to the ground with tears in my eyes.

"Zeeee! Nooooo!"

I picked up the pistols.

"They deserve me," I said through gritted teeth. There was a rage in me like nothing I had ever felt before. We never would have even pursued them if they hadn't taken Neave and the others. With them freed, we would have retreated and left them be.

"Get them to safety, Jimmy."

He nodded, and I stood again. This time I strode down the center of the street with both guns spitting fire and lead. Bullets whizzed by my head. I could feel tugs on the long coat I wore. I didn't care. When the left hand pistol was empty, I dropped it and pulled a mag for the other. They charged forward toward me and I emptied the Colt again.

They were too close for the guns so I pulled the knives from sheaths at my back and charged into their midst. Then Jimmy plowed into them from my right side and bodies began to fly out of the group. He would punch and the man would sail backwards. I saw his open hand take a man's head off.

I could hear automatic fire from Gary and Grady and more men fell. The Winchester fired, over and over. Then there were no more of them standing. I stood in the midst of the bodies with my lungs heaving from the adrenaline. I could see Lassiter, in the distance, climbing the steps to the skyscraper two blocks away.

I turned back toward the street littered with the dead or dying. Pop was helping Pete to his feet. I walked back to the spot I had dropped the .45s and retrieved them.

A man left the building to our left with his hands raised. He approached, slowly.

"Old Morgan won't let this go," he said. "You better get out of here."

"He's not going to have the luxury of letting this go," I said.

I walked up to Gary who was looking at his cousin with tears in his eyes.

"Gee," I said. "I need you and Grady to take her home. Get the kids back home and bury her proper."

"You'll be needing help," he said.

"Where I'm about to go is no place for good folks," I placed my hand on his shoulder. "Grady, you and Deli take care of my little girl."

"Zee, you can't..."

"I'm going to finish this," I said and turned back toward the skyscraper.

As I walked forward, I pulled a handful of bullets from my pocket and began feeding them into one of the empty magazines.

Pop walked to my left, feeding shells into the Winchester. Jimmy joined us and walked between us.

There would be justice, even in this Fallen World.

* * * * *

Chapter Twenty-Five

      Grady Conner watched as his friends strode down the street toward the skyscraper. Not sure if he would ever see them again, he helped Pete onto one of the horses.

Gary was staring down the street at the three men.

"We got to go, Gee."

"I know," he answered. "Will they come back?"

"I'm not sure. But he gave us a job to do."

"Yes, sir."

They carefully loaded Neave's body onto the back of Dagger.

"Hey," the man who had come from the building said. "They're going in there?"

"Yeah."

"Just who the hell are they? I've never seen anything like this."

Grady looked back at the three forms walking down the street.

"They're Farmers."

# # # # #

ABOUT THE AUTHOR

Christopher Woods has been an avid reader all of his life. Soulguard, the first in a series of books, was his debut novel in a series that currently spans five novels. He currently lives in Woodbury, TN with his wife and stepdaughter. His wife reminds him that he should always watch what he says, because he tends to fall asleep long before she does. You can contact Mr. Woods by email at soulguard0@yahoo.com.

* * * * *

Titles by Christopher Woods

Soulguard Series

Soulguard
Soullord
Bloodlord
Rash'Tor'Ri
Freedom's Prophet
Freedom's Challenge (forthcoming)

This Fallen World Series

This Fallen World
Broken City
Power Play (forthcoming)

Four Horsemen Universe

A Fistful of Credits
Legend
Luck is Not a Factor

* * * * *

Connect with Christopher Woods Online

Learn more about Christopher Woods at:

Facebook: https://www.facebook.com/ChristopherWoodsSoulguard

Amazon Author Page: https://www.amazon.com/-/e/B00PEAG6WM

Website: http://soulguard4.wixsite.com/christopherwoods

* * * * *

Connect with Seventh Seal Press

Get the **free** prelude story "**Shattered Crucible**,"

join the mailing list, and discover other titles at:

http://chriskennedypublishing.com/

Facebook: https://www.facebook.com/chriskennedypublishing.biz

* * * * *

The following is an
Excerpt from Book One of The Turning Point:

A Time to Die

Mark Wandrey

Available Now from Blood Moon Press

eBook, Paperback, and Audio Book

Excerpt from "A Time to Die:"

An hour later, Ken tried to drink some of the water and eat some of the food Erin had left for him, only to vomit it up moments afterwards. His head swam with pain and confusion, and sweat poured from his forehead despite the cool evening breeze. Suddenly he stumbled to his feet, not knowing why, completely unable to concentrate. "Wha—what?" he choked, spinning around and searching for the source of the disturbance with blurred vision.

He heard something behind him, and he spun again to find only darkness. "Damn you," he snarled and took a step in that direction, only to fall over a root in the gloom and sprawl in the dense pine needles. His mind exploded in lights, pain, and voices. Whispers and screams, thoughts and ideas he could not understand. "Stop it, stop it, stop...stop...STOP!" The last word came out as an anguished wail from the depths of his soul that echoed through the woods and down to the Rio Grande thousands of feet below. He shuddered in the brush, and the man that was Ken succumbed.

Small animals and night birds flitted around for a time, sniffing the air and trying to sense if the man had become food. But after a few minutes, it was standing again, wildly searching the darkness. It noticed the birds and scurrying creatures, and it shook its head and snarled. The snarl turned into a clipped scream, more visceral than the previous one. It turned toward a narrow goat trail that descended the cliff.

The descent would have terrified Ken and likely sent him plummeting to the rocks below. The creature that now walked in his skin, though, felt no fear and held close to the sharp rocks with single-minded, painless determination. By the time it reached the river, its hands were torn nearly to the bone in several places. It paid no mind to the blood-dripping wounds as it scanned the opposite riverbank. Moonlight illuminated the far shore where it saw a group of people, all moving slowly to the west. A little moan escaped its lips, and its teeth gnashed as it jerked forward and plowed into the water.

* * * * *

Get "A Time to Die" now at:

https://www.amazon.com/dp/B0787VQ8RJ/.

Find out more about Mark Wandrey and "A Time to Die" at:

http://chriskennedypublishing.com/imprints-authors/mark-wandrey/.

* * * * *

The following is an
Excerpt from Book One of The Darkness War:

Psi-Mechs, Inc.

Eric S. Brown

Available Now from Blood Moon Press

eBook and Paperback

Excerpt from "Psi-Mechs, Inc.:"

Ringer reached the bottom of the stairs and came straight at him. "Mr. Dubin?" Ringer asked.

Frank rose to his feet, offering his hand. "Ah, Detective Ringer, I must say it's a pleasure to finally meet you."

Ringer didn't accept his proffered hand. Instead, he stared at Frank with appraising eyes.

"I'm told you're with the Feds. If this is about the Hangman killer case…" Ringer said.

Frank quickly shook his head. "No, nothing like that, Detective. I merely need a few moments of your time."

"You picked a bad night for it, Mr. Dubin," Ringer told him. "It's a full moon out there this evening, and the crazies are coming out of the woodwork."

"Crazies?" Frank asked.

"I just locked up a guy who thinks he's a werewolf." Ringer sighed. "We get a couple of them every year."

"And is he?" Frank asked with a grin.

Ringer gave Frank a careful look as he said, "What do you mean is he? Of course not. There's no such thing as werewolves, Mr. Dubin."

"Anything's possible, Detective Ringer." Frank smirked.

"Look, I really don't have time for this." Ringer shook his head. "Either get on with what you've come to see me about, or go back to wherever you came from. I've got enough on my hands tonight without you."

"Is there somewhere a touch more private we could talk?" Frank asked.

"Yeah, sure," Ringer answered reluctantly. "This way."

Ringer led Frank into a nearby office and shut the door behind them. He walked around the room's desk and plopped into the chair there.

"Have a seat," Ringer instructed him, gesturing at the chair in front of the desk.

Frank took it. He stared across the desk at Ringer.

"Well?" Ringer urged.

"Detective Ringer, I work for an organization that has reason to believe you have the capacity to be much more than the mere street detective you are now," Frank started.

"Hold on a sec." Ringer leaned forward where he sat. "You're here to offer me a job?"

"Something like that." Frank grinned.

"I'm not interested," Ringer said gruffly and started to get up. Frank's next words knocked him off his feet, causing him to collapse back into his chair as if he'd been gut-punched.

"We know about your power, Detective Ringer."

"I have no idea what you're talking about," Ringer said, though it was clear he was lying.

"There's no reason to be ashamed of your abilities, Detective," Frank assured him, "and what the two of us are about to discuss will never leave this room."

"I think it's time you left now, Mr. Dubin," Ringer growled.

"Far from it," Frank said. "We're just getting started, Detective Ringer."

Ringer sprung from his seat and started for the office's door. "You can either show yourself out, or I can have one of the officers out there help you back to the street."

Frank left his own seat and moved to block Ringer's path. "I have a gift myself, Detective Ringer."

Shaking his head, Ringer started to shove Frank aside. Frank took him by the arm.

"My gift is that I can sense the powers of people like yourself, Detective," Frank told him. "You can't deny your power to me. I can see it in my mind, glowing like a bright, shining star in an otherwise dark void."

"You're crazy," Ringer snapped, shaking free of Frank's hold.

"You need to listen to me," Frank warned. "I know about what happened to your parents. I mean what really happened, and how you survived."

Frank's declaration stopped Ringer in his tracks.

"You don't know crap!" Ringer shouted as Frank continued to stare at him.

"Vampires are very real, Detective Ringer." Frank cocked his head to look up at Ringer as he spoke. "The organization I work for...We deal with them, and other monsters, every day."

Ringer stabbed a finger into Frank's chest. It hurt, as Ringer thumped it repeatedly against him. "I don't know who you are, Mr. Dubin, but I've had enough of your crap. Now take your crazy and get the hell out of my life. Do I make myself clear?"

The pictures on the wall of the office vibrated as Ringer raged at Frank. Frank's smile grew wider.

"You're a TK, aren't you?" Frank asked.

"I don't even know what that is!" Ringer bellowed at him.

"You can move objects with your mind, Detective Ringer. We call that TK. It's a term that denotes you have telekinetic abilities.

They're how you saved yourself from the vampire who murdered your family when you were thirteen."

Ringer said nothing. He stood, shaking with fear and rage.

"You're not alone, Detective Ringer," Frank told him. "There are many others in this world with powers like your own. As I've said, I have one myself, though it's not as powerful or as physical in nature, as your own. I urge you to have a seat, so we can talk about this a little more. I highly doubt your captain would be as understanding of your gift as I and my employer are if it should, say, become public knowledge."

"Is that a threat?" Ringer snarled.

Frank shook his head. "Certainly not. Now if you would…?" Frank gestured for Ringer to return to the chair behind the desk.

Ringer did so, though he clearly wasn't happy about it.

"There's so much to tell you, Detective Ringer; I'm afraid I don't even know where to begin," Frank said.

"Then why don't you start at the beginning, and let's get this over with," Ringer said with a frown.

"Right then." Frank chuckled. "Let's do just that."

* * * * *

Get "Psi-Mechs, Inc." now at:
https://www.amazon.com/dp/B07DKCCQJZ.

Find out more about Eric S. Brown and "The Darkness War" at:
https://chriskennedypublishing.com/imprints-authors/eric-s-brown/.

* * * * *

Made in the USA
Middletown, DE
26 November 2018